THE CREEPER

ALSO BY A.M. SHINE

The Watchers

THE CREEPER

A. M. SHINE

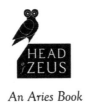

HEAD
of ZEUS

An Aries Book

First published in the UK in 2022 by Head of Zeus Ltd,
part of Bloomsbury Publishing Plc

9 7 5 3 1 2 4 6 8

A catalogue record for this book is available from the British Library.

ISBN (HB): 9781801102179
ISBN (XTPB): 9781801102186
ISBN (E): 9781801102209

Cover design: Nina Elstad

Printed and bound in Great Britain by
CPI Group (UK) Ltd, Croydon CR0 4YY

Typeset by Divaddict Publishing Solutions

Head of Zeus Ltd
First Floor East
5–8 Hardwick Street
London EC1R 4RG

WWW.HEADOFZEUS.COM

THE CREEPER

Prologue

'Emergency services. What is your location and the service you need?'

Fiona knew before hearing the operator's voice that she was beyond saving.

There was nowhere she could hide that it wouldn't find her. It was as though the stars themselves were its all-seeing eyes and the pale moon a searchlight. By day she had fled as far as she could. But no distance would ever be enough. It would always follow her, and the dread of this realisation eclipsed all else – the life she had known, her dreams for the future, and the belief that such horrors didn't exist.

They were just meant to be stories.

Fiona was only being kind. The man had been so agitated, slapping his hands over his mouth, staring stupefied at the dirt between his feet. His simplicity was more pronounced than the others and she'd approached him out of pity, to offer a smile when no one else cared so much as to look at him.

You see him three times. You see him three times. You see him three times.

The words were spoken so quickly, slicing through the air like a scythe. She'd waved a hand over his eyes but the man was spellbound by delusion, repeating that same line over and over, terrorised by the sound of his own voice.

'Who do you see three times?' she'd asked, crouching close enough to make sense of him.

He'd grabbed Fiona's shirt, holding her down as he breathed the horror all over her.

She'd been running ever since.

It didn't make sense to stay in the city, not after seeing it outside her apartment. Her parents were away until the weekend, but home still seemed the safest place to go. It was there that her dad used to sit by the bedside whenever the nightmares came. He would stroke her hair with one hand and dry her cheek with the other. The monsters knew better than to mess with him, he used to say, stifling a yawn. Warm memories such as these were all she had to thaw the terror now closing around her life.

There was only one other person who could understand what was happening but he wouldn't answer his phone. Fiona wanted to empty her lungs with a scream, to vent all that frustration in one deafening blast. She didn't know if Tom was alive or dead. But he was studying in a different university, in another county. Maybe it hadn't found him like it had found her.

She couldn't afford to see it a third time. That's what she had been told. And now, in these lonely hours, with the night pouring down on her like black soil, Fiona knew it to be true. No matter what happened, she mustn't look outside.

She'd closed every door and sealed the curtains, leaving only a darkness so haunting it felt tight to breathe. That sense of being chased never went away. Fiona hadn't slept. She couldn't remember when last she had eaten. She yanked down the kitchen blind, taking a moment to scan the surrounding fields. All was still. Only the hollow thrum of her heart broke the silence.

She scrambled up the stairs to her old bedroom, locking its door behind her and pocketing the key. Through its skylight – set high in the ceiling – the firmament above was darkening. Soon the stars would return to recommence their search. But spy as they might through the glass, they would never find her in the room's corner, where Fiona had slept as a child and watched them with a sense of wonder, not the fearful distrust that plagued her now.

If she could wait out the next few days, her parents would know what to do. Her dad would chase the monsters away. He would keep her safe like he used to. Until then, she would fear the dark wildering world outside as though night and death were one and the same. She had no other choice.

A square of moonlight shone from the skylight to the floor. Fiona was curled up on her bed, arms around legs, swaying back and forth. She couldn't calm her breathing. She could barely swallow, her mouth was so dry. She hadn't thought to bring any water. In the morning, she would grab everything she needed. This was her shelter and the storm would pass. That's why she chose this room. She could see the sky. She would know when it was safe.

Her phone was sunken into the duvet beside her feet. It still held some battery, if she needed it. But who would she call? What could she tell them that wouldn't curse their lives too? Maybe the Guards could come and take her somewhere safe until her parents returned. They could lock her up in a cell for all she cared, so long as there was someone to stand between her and the one that stalked her relentlessly.

Fiona tried to focus on *anything* else. She pictured the downstairs rooms in perfect darkness. The kitchen's cold granite countertop. Unopened letters scattered across the floor from when she had run indoors. That vague but welcoming scent that hung in the hallway, where her mum burned candles throughout the year, never expecting any visitors but keeping their wicks lit all the same.

Even if she had been followed, how could it possibly find her here? There were no lights. No sounds. Nothing to lead it to her.

She reached for the phone. Maybe Tom was still okay. He had seen it that first night too. Fiona hadn't spoken to anyone else since then. She had carried the truth like a poisoned chalice, careful not to spill a drop. She wanted to call him again, if only to hear he was okay, that she was overreacting. But what if the phone was how it found her? If speaking kept the curse alive, then silence could be the key to lifting it. There was so much she didn't understand.

Fiona's tired eyes returned to the floor. They weighed too much to look any higher. She stared at that silver tile of moonlight in the centre of the room. Her heart contracted; its pace quickened. Something was wrong. But through the depths of her exhaustion, the revelation was slow to rise.

And then, finally, she saw it – the dark shape framed within the light on the floor.

Terror snapped the air from her lips. The phone creaked as her fingers clamped around it. Somehow, fumbling blind, she called for help.

The dial tone sounded only once.

'Emergency services. What is your location and the service you need?'

Fiona's eyes lifted to the skylight, to that which blocked out the moon and the stars, and the hope of ever seeing her parents again.

I

The doorbell chimed.

Alec glanced up from his desk to the grandfather clock in the corner of the room, sighing as he did so. Eleven minutes remained until the hour. He clicked his pen and carefully aligned it beside his pocket diary where this meeting had been jotted down for nine o'clock on the dot, not a second before or after.

'That is disappointing,' Alec whispered under his breath.

The hours of the day had been mapped out like a journey. That was, after all, the whole purpose of keeping a diary. Any delays or detours, such as this, made Alec uneasy. And uneasy men made mistakes. Too much time had been invested in this transaction to falter now.

He patted down his grey shirt and straightened its collar, pinching its stays in place. It was without fault. Smooth and sharp in all the right places. Lara, Alec's housekeeper, as per his request, had ironed it with due care the prior evening. The dear girl had an alchemist's touch – like her mother before her – making golden the simplest chore.

Again, the doorbell rang. So long had it been since he received a visitor, Alec had forgotten its two-note melody and how much he disliked it. The sound lingered as if it were now trapped in the room like a filthy insect, flitting against the study's many windows and buzzing by his ear. He would make a note to have it uninstalled.

'You've arrived earlier than you were expected,' Alec muttered, frowning at the door as he tugged a cuff over his slender wrist, 'and earlier than you're welcome. You will wait.'

No punctuality. No patience. For the sake of their transaction, Alec swallowed down his umbrage like a chalky pill. One more ring of that bell, however, and he might not have been so forgiving.

The room held no mirrors, and so he stepped by a framed landscape to consult his reflection. His eyes were met with that old familiar paleness. Ghostlike in the glass. Too many years with too few fond memories to add any colour to his cheeks – grey, even in the morning light when colours blossomed in the darkest places. Nothing ever changed and yet Alec had aged regardless – in this room, in this house – as one entombed ante-mortem. His father had a lot to answer for.

When he opened the front door, Detective Eamon Barry had his broad back turned to him, facing the grounds of the estate. A plastic folder was held in one hand. The other scratched around his neck as though shame were an itch that a man could dig out with his fingernails.

'Doctor Sparling?' he asked, as though Alec hadn't met his expectations.

'Yes,' he replied, standing aside, gesturing for the man to enter. 'You're early, Detective. Did we not arrange this meeting for nine o'clock?'

'I'm sorry,' Barry stammered. 'I didn't realise.'

'Are you aware of the significance of the number nine?'

The man's eyes practically crossed at the question.

'In Pythagorean numerology,' Alec explained, 'it symbolises the end of one cycle and the beginning of another. Perhaps you can appreciate that. Perhaps not.'

Alec walked over to his desk and Barry – understanding the unspoken invitation – followed, leaving his scruples at the door like a loyal dog abandoned. Given the man's profession, he was likely searching the study for some clue as to how Alec had accrued such wealth and why, in spite of it, still appeared so profoundly miserable. A chair had been set in place for him; an antique Chippendale that now cried beneath his weight.

Barry's face was solid and simple, as though chiselled out by an unimaginative stonemason. The closest shave wouldn't lift the shadow from his skin. His dark hair was cropped short with a few silvered flecks trailing back above his ears, and he was dressed in a well-worn black coat and brogues. The man's looks epitomised the model detective in a paperback thriller. But Barry was no hero. His reasons for being in Alec's home were far from honourable.

'You must understand, Doctor,' he said, shifting uncomfortably in his chair, 'I don't usually do this. As I'm sure you are aware, these files are not openly available to the public.'

Alec slid open his desk's top drawer. There he procured the unmarked envelope, weighty and sealed, and dropped it between them like a slab of meat for a hungry dog.

'I'm more than glad to support local law enforcement,' he said, looking the man directly in the eye, ignoring the envelope's existence. 'I've no doubt that my donation will be put to good use.'

The detective sighed as he handed his folder over the desk. He took the envelope and quickly pocketed it inside his jacket, as if everyone who once respected him had lined the windows to spectate this moment of weakness. Both men forced a smile.

'What's your interest in this case?' the detective asked, rubbing his hands together, trying to clean them of a stain only he could see.

Following the succinctness that had defined their past exchanges, Alec assumed Barry to be the quiet sort – a man muzzled by defeat. He sat back, coolly as he could, and lowered his clenched fists out of the detective's sight. Alec was not in the habit of taking questions.

'It's just a hobby of mine,' he replied, careful not to glower too intently. 'Are you familiar with it? This particular case, I mean.'

'I didn't work that one.'

'Oh, but I didn't ask if you worked it. I asked if you were familiar with it.'

Judging by Barry's hesitation, the man was unsure if his compliance in conversation was part of the deal. Alec's eyes bored into him as though they could extract the answer regardless.

'The case concerns a missing student,' he began. 'Her name was Fiona Quinn.'

'And what do you know about Ms Quinn?' Alec asked, leaning forward.

'Good student, hard-working. She was always good at keeping in touch with friends and family. But in the days leading up to her disappearance she dropped off the radar. It seems that she got herself involved in something she shouldn't have. Her parents were abroad at the time. They thought she was doing college work, but they didn't know any more than that. Nobody did.'

'And do you know what she was studying in university?' Alec asked.

'Archaeology,' Barry replied. 'She was in her final year.'

'And have you linked any similar cases to this one?'

That last question was enough to press Barry's back into his chair; it squeaked like a trampled field mouse. He had obviously been a detective for long enough to know when something wasn't right.

'Should I be concerned, Doctor?' he asked. 'Your interest in this case seems a little more than *just a hobby*.'

'Detective, I assure you that my interest is strictly above board. I like to imagine that I may be of assistance in someday solving one of these "cold cases", as they call them. It's tragic. It truly is. Whatever must—'

The grandfather clock tolled, startling Barry forward in his chair.

Alec rested both elbows on the desk and laced his fingers together, staring at his guest as the nine bells sounded aloud. Only when the silence returned did he pick up where he had left off, reciting the lines he had planned that morning like a part-time player.

'As I was saying, whatever must Ms Quinn's poor parents be going through? It's too short a time to heal such a wound, I'm sure you can agree?'

Alec emptied the folder's contents onto the desk, spreading them out before him like jigsaw pieces. There were pages bound by paper clips, some loose photographs, and an audio disc with the case number scribbled on it in black pen. He picked this up and held it as if to advertise its importance.

'And who was the detective on this case?' he asked, leafing through the pages.

Barry probably guessed that Alec already knew the answer, and that was quite permissible. It would benefit both parties if the detective proved himself not to be a stupid man. There was, however, no way he could have understood Alec's reasons for testing his knowledge on the matter.

'That would have been Will Collins,' he replied.

'And he is...' Alec said, looking to Barry to close the sentence.

'He's dead. He died not long after that case.'

'I see,' Alec said, indifferent, placing the pages down carefully, pleased with his investment. 'Is *this* the only copy?' he asked, tapping his index finger on the disc.

'We only make one,' Barry replied, looking more and more like a schoolboy sitting in the principal's office.

'Have you listened to it?'

'No, I haven't. Like I said, Doctor, it wasn't my case. I have other investigations that demand my time.'

'But you know what's on it?'

'It's a recording of Fiona Quinn's phone call to the emergency services,' the detective replied. 'It's the last known trace of her before her disappearance.'

'And you have never been curious as to what she said?' Alec asked.

'No, Doctor, I haven't.'

After a moment's thought, Alec attempted another smile and rose to his feet. Barry eased out of his chair, visibly relieved that the whole sorry transaction was over. Alec crossed his study and opened the door. Daylight washed across the floor, reaching like a tide as far as the Persian carpet; its pattern faded and worn like an epitaph, every wash of light leaving it a little less than before.

'You understand the delicacy of this matter?' Barry said, having stepped out.

'Of course, Detective,' Alec replied. 'No one shall hear of this. I'm quite adept at keeping secrets, I assure you. I'll be in touch when I need you again.'

Barry's eyes widened as these parting words were spoken. It was as though he had just realised, in that moment, the gravity of his actions and the shackles they had cast. So dire was the man's gambling debt that he had seen only his financial reward, not its ramifications. He wouldn't tell another soul so long as his livelihood and reputation were at stake. Of this fact Alec was certain as he drew the door closed and turned its key, leaving the detective to drag his fresh chains behind him.

For months he had pursued some means to acquire the file and, more specifically, the only recording in existence of Ms Quinn's phone call. This was the last loose end – that thread dangling from an otherwise flawless tapestry, now cut.

Alec took his time, teasing himself as he fed the disc into the system. He returned to his desk and there he opened his diary. A red scar was drawn through Detective Barry's name. It had been a most productive morning. But as much as a celebratory brandy would do well to toast his success, Alec was not his father.

He reclined in his chair and closed his eyes, and only then did the man press play, with the sunlight glazing his grey skin, alone as he always was until Lara's arrival at the stroke of midday.

'Emergency services. What is your location and the service you need?'

'There's something outside,' came the reply – whispered, terrified.

'Miss, please try to stay calm and tell me your location.'

'It's at the window. It's smiling at me.'

2

Morning was night to Ben's eyes. Darker even without the stars.

Two years had passed since he sat behind the wheel of a car, and more than once his numb fingers fumbled with the gearstick. Not that he was overly keen to shift above second. The frost glittering in the headlights was cause enough to take it slow. There were few others on the road at that hour. Owl-eyed delivery drivers and factory workers on the wrong side of a twelve-hour shift. Ben offered due sympathy and respect to both.

Cold mornings were the worst. They chilled more than the bones. They iced over the soul and all its unspoken optimism. He was already doubting if it was all worth it. This was the big break he had been waiting for and the morning was trying to sour it for him. It didn't matter. There was no turning back now. Contracts had been signed. The equipment was bought. And he had already told his parents. They deserved more than the usual disappointment.

Chloe was where she said she would be, bundled up in

her parka jacket, waiting at the bus stop outside her estate. The streetlights were losing their colour like rotting oranges. She waved as he pulled the car up beside her. There wasn't another person that Ben could see beneath the wakening sky, just rows of lightless homes, their curtains closed, and the dead sound of a town before the dawn. So quiet, even the birds were still rehearsing uncertain verses.

Ben couldn't afford to botch this job. But he tried not to think about it. Whatever worries travelled with them that day, they could keep their opinions to themselves. And if they didn't, he'd turn on the radio full blast and drown them out. This was what he wanted. This was the kind of assignment he was actually good at. But even still, looking forward, the horizon was fogged with a cold uncertainty.

'It'll be fine,' he whispered, clicking off his seatbelt, trying to convince himself that not every scene in his life played out like a Shakespearean fucking tragedy.

Ice cracked and fell like flaky paint when he opened the door to help Chloe with her rucksack. Everything was sharp and brittle, and sticky to the touch. The bag was almost as big as she was. It just about fit inside the boot beside his own after all their straps were tucked in place like limp arms.

Good mornings were exchanged – the ironic, deadpan sort that suggested the contrary.

Ben's phone was slotted into its crooked stand above the radio. He tapped it once to check the time. Daybreak wasn't far away. But given how quiet the roads were, they might even make it to the motorway before then.

'Who's the kid?' Chloe asked, holding her hands over the fan heater.

She'd seen his phone screen and the photograph that Jess had sent him the week before. Ben had shifted the icons around so that her smile beamed in its centre. Both eyes were scrunched up tight, giving his heart a little jump.

'Aoife,' he replied, smiling until it switched to black. 'She's mine.'

'Cute,' was all Chloe said.

She wasn't chatty like the day before and of that Ben was glad. Even the flowers knew to keep their petals closed until dawn. Besides, there would be time to talk later. The journey was long and the drive was the easiest part of it.

Ben had been queuing at a coffee shop, two days earlier, when his phone pinged with an email. The building was no bigger than his bathroom, its air moist from the milk steamer. A mirror on the left wall was eternally fogged up. Reflections were shapeless shadows led like blind mice to the churn of the freshly ground. A bronze bag of coffee beans and a fake plant had shared a shelf to Ben's right. There had once been a *Live, Laugh, Love* sign between them but someone had the common sense to remove it. This wasn't the time or place. Maybe there were those out there, somewhere, who had a love life and liked to laugh about it. But wherever they were, looking back through the queue, they weren't buying coffee that morning.

It was another routine Monday whose dreary skies fitted the mood. Streets were stained black with rain and blocked on both sides with delivery vans, all indicators flashing. The working-class machine had groaned to life, spluttering out bodies. Shopfronts were half-lit but not yet open, glowing like vending machines in the gloom. A few cold, managerial fingers blundered with their keys while their minions watched on, already wishing away the next eight hours of their lives. Others were walking at a pace somewhere between a walk and a jog, like soldiers assembling for a war they didn't really believe in.

Ben had three minutes to spare before he would be late for work again. But his manager wouldn't call him on it. She never did, and he respected that about her if nothing else. Hers was a more nuanced approach to chastisement: a long look at the clock or some arbitrary reminder about his upcoming performance review. Sometimes she would just smile sadly at his coffee.

Ben took out his phone, copying the line of yawners leading back to the door; those powered-down bodies on a factory line waiting to have their batteries reinstalled. It was far too early to attempt anything as bold as eye contact, never mind conversation. Theirs was a silent, sombre solidarity. The man ahead of him – built like a fridge, with dandruff sprinkled on his shoulders like icing sugar on a cake – ordered three cappuccinos. *Of course, it had to be cappuccinos.* Any hope of making it to the shoe shop on time disappeared in another blast of steam.

Ben opened the email for the sake of deleting it. He had time to kill and a weary manager to disappoint. That was after all what his email account had become since finishing up in college – an unentertaining deletion app. And he played it every morning, Monday to Friday, usually around the time that he was expected to clock in to work.

'Doctor Alec Sparling,' he read. 'Never heard of you, buddy.'

The subject line stated simply: *Project Proposal for Mr French.* This wasn't like the usual junk mail. It was a letter, one addressed only to him – to the titular *Mr French*. And so, he read on.

I am currently funding a private project. You come highly recommended by Professor Joseph Cunningham.

It is my wish to meet you in person to discuss taking this collaboration further. The details regarding both the time and venue are attached below. Please notify me before the close of day if it is your wish to attend.

The details were scant at best – some of the broadest strokes that Ben had ever read – but projects paid money. He was probably one of fifty candidates for the role. There was always a never-ending stream of graduates and not enough jobs – like passengers on a sinking ship with too few lifeboats. But given his current situation he would happily go all in on fifty-to-one.

Ben had already served a year's sentence in full-time retail and the whole dour cycle was starting to repeat itself. He could suffer through part-time; at least he had had his studies to prod his mind occasionally. But this was different. The majority who worked in the shop were kids, fresh out of school or first years in university, undeveloped in mind and manners. They all dressed the same and shared some mongrel dialect that Ben blamed the internet for – words that infected local colloquialisms like a parasite. These bastards were the carriers.

The job was hardly engaging enough to occupy thirty-five hours of Ben's week. Even he zoned out whenever he described the benefits of their patented *memory foam* insoles, reciting his lines like an ageing stage actor locked in a role for too many seasons.

Sparling's email requested that Ben attend a lecture hall on his old campus at twelve o'clock the following afternoon. What was another day missed from work? He had called in sick the week before, having woken up with eyes still stinging from two bottles of cheap wine, the flavoursome equivalent of balsamic vinegar. If the stars aligned, they might even fire him this time. Jettisoning his half-hearted contribution could only have been good for business. He replied there and then.

'See you tomorrow, Sparling,' he muttered. 'Maybe you can save me from this shit.'

His thesis had been surprisingly well received. Not that Ben doubted his own ability. He had never failed an exam in his life and couldn't quite understand the *adults* in third-level education who had sat through year after year of schooling and still couldn't get their shit together; those who had to focus when writing their name. The interviews just gleaned more interest than he had expected. Truth was that it hadn't been especially difficult. Instead of trawling through scholarly articles and chasing up sources like a bona fide historian, Ben just had to press record and ask a few questions.

With the master's under his belt, some commissions paid well. Lecturing alone could bag him sixty euros an hour. But jobs of that pay grade were usually fastened to the cobwebs of some decrepit academic who had become one with the university's furniture.

Ben, on the other hand, survived week to week. There was never enough money and never the means to make any more. He walked somewhere between poorness and abject poverty, in a gutter that seemed to deepen as time rolled on. Even when he sent Jess all he could afford – having subsisted on a diet of thin sandwiches for a week – still she had scoffed at it. He literally only had the loose change in his pocket left. But that was nothing new. If Ben's bank account was a bird feeder, he ate the nutty shards on the ground.

Embarrassment kept him from telling her the truth. The bills weren't being met. His rent had been overdue for two months. Losing his home was inevitable unless his luck had a quick change of heart. There were only so many times he could ignore his landlord's calls until he came knocking at the door. And it was highly likely that the lad had a key to let himself in.

Maybe this was the break Ben needed. He could finally answer with his head held high when asked, '*Where are you working these days?*' He hated that question and he always hated his answer. Not even thirty yet and the world was starting to grind him down. But Ben knew the reason why. He had become a mindless, money-making cog. And even the money wasn't enough to make ends meet.

Two hours had passed since he and Chloe abandoned the car. The afternoon sun wept through clouds pulled apart like cotton wool in the breeze. The trek was proving worse than Ben expected. Much worse. Hidden beneath the grasses was a knobbly causeway of soil and stone. Sometimes he sank and sometimes he tripped, and every time his rucksack pounced on his shoulders like a bear.

'How much farther is it?' he called out, using his scarf to dab his brow like an out-of-shape boxer who'd just gone twelve rounds.

'A little bit more, Benny Boy,' Chloe called back to him, shading her phone from the sun. 'We're past the halfway mark, I think.'

'Benny Boy?' he groaned, trudging towards her. 'Please don't make that a thing.'

The press of his boots on the earth was like an insect crawling on skin. The forces of nature sought any means to swipe him away. Maybe it meant to crush him outright like a flea, leaving just a red smear in the mud. The camping gear on his back was doing that anyway – scratching the discs of his spine like flint for a fire. It had occurred to him to simply collapse in whatever godforsaken field he stood in, to accept defeat on his own terms. The grasses could mummify his bones in coils of green and Chloe could even sprinkle some wildflowers over him to mark the occasion.

Her cheeks weren't even flushed. Every hair on her pixie head was picture-perfect. Ben had to run a hand over his sandpapered scalp to keep the sweat from seeping down his forehead. He felt like fresh fruit squeezed into oblivion.

'Do you want to take a break?' she asked, chuckling away to herself as though this wasn't the single most torturous experience of their lives.

Ben wouldn't have classed himself as low-shelf material. But in that moment, with his body coiled up like a rusty spring and gurning through a fresh sheen of sweat, Chloe stood leagues ahead, watching him with a smile that was hard to look away from.

'Just give me a moment,' he gasped. 'I'll be fine.'

Ben had what his mother called a *kind face*. But then, mothers have an even kinder way with words. He never quite understood what she meant by it. His eyebrows were forever a tad bushy. But the eyes made up for that. Each one was a polished conker like his father's; an heirloom gladly inherited. When his retreating hairline became too obvious, he had shaved it back. That family trait hadn't been so eagerly received. His smile was the key to his interviews, or so he used to gloat after a few pints, when his woes and misfortunes were, for a while, forgotten. *Lock eyes and always smile.*

'Here,' Chloe said, handing him a torpedo-shaped flask, 'drink some water before you pass out on me.'

'Cheers,' he wheezed, his lungs working hard to keep him up, like two paper bags pressing against his chest, primed to pop at any second.

'You're a wreck,' she said, lifting her red-framed sunglasses to look him up and down. 'Ye city lads don't know easy money when you have it.'

'Easy?' He laughed. 'We should have asked for more off the bastard.'

Doctor Alec Sparling was a man of some wealth. Not that Ben would have guessed that when he first saw him. When he'd pushed in the door, the doctor had been stood at the lectern, alone under the hall's mellow spotlight. The room's emptiness made it seem larger than it was. Every surface was flat and polished – plastic impersonating wood. No litter. No smell that he could place. He imagined a hundred ghosts all turning in their seats to look at him.

'Mr French,' Sparling said, gesturing towards the front row. 'Please, take a seat and we'll begin once Ms Coogan arrives.'

Ben did as he was told. The heavy hand of uncertainty was brushed away before it could hold him back.

Sparling was possibly in his sixties, with a grey complexion more commonly identified with illness. If ever the man had seen the sun, he had watched it from the shade. The bags under his eyes carried a lifetime of restless nights. His small lips were perpetually pursed as if from a tartness on the tongue, and his eyes were a dull blue. Thin, black reading glasses perched on his nose; functional, unfashionable. The man's salt and pepper hair was combed back and had receded slightly. There was no ring on any finger. He was perhaps a man too enamoured by knowledge to seek companionship elsewhere. His attire was predictably academic. Black slacks and grey shirt, both meticulously ironed.

Ben prided himself on his first impressions, but even he wasn't quite sure what to make of the man. Each individual part of Sparling was colourless and forgettable. And yet, there *was* something remarkable there. He resembled less a man, and more the shadow of one.

He kept glancing nervously to the door as he typed at his laptop. The projector had thrown a blue rectangle onto the wall like an unconvincing sky. The colour had probably been chosen for that reason. It wasn't natural. It never could be.

Ben had worn his denim jacket over a white Oxford, noticeably grubby around the collar but the cleanest shirt he could find at such notice. He had, at least, shaved his head and tidied his light beard the night before, so he was mildly presentable. He considered doing up the shirt's top button. But that would only advertise his unease. It was no better than putting on a tie mid-interview. He pictured the blazer hanging in his wardrobe and couldn't recall the last time he had worn it, like a suit of armour gathering dust since his surrender to full-time retail.

'She should be here by now,' Sparling said impatiently, pulling back his cuff to check the time. His watch's face and strap were also black. The man clearly had an aversion to colour.

Ms Coogan might have been some hotshot history lecturer. Perhaps this drab Sparling character was a kind of lackey? The Igor to her Frankenstein; hired more for his aesthetic than any actual aptitude for the job.

Ben's thesis was on the lectern. It looked thinner than he remembered, like an old lover that had fallen on hard times. The crimson binding had seemed so plush when he first held it. He recalled its softness and the weight of its words, and those months of work once so consequential, now seemingly so pointless. The graduation scroll was still tucked in its envelope – *Benjamin French, Master of History*. It was about as useful as an expired coupon. For now, all he had to show for five years of work was *that* book in front of him.

A conclusive tap came from Sparling's keyboard. The man looked to Ben and smiled his little lips like worms. It was a mechanical action, so devoid of any thought or feeling that it made the skin on Ben's neck crawl.

The projection now displayed the man's laptop screen. Its desktop was chaotic. The cursor flittered like a fly above its many documents, never landing long enough to open one. There were moments when it seemed to shiver. Ben couldn't tell if it was excitement or nerves, and the doctor's stolid expression didn't offer any hints. It reminded him of a rubber Halloween mask. The eyes alone could move.

'Do you know Ms Coogan?' he asked. 'I thought that maybe you two had crossed paths. History and archaeology are bedfellows after all, aren't they?'

'No,' Ben replied, clearing his throat, 'I don't believe that I have, Doctor Sparling.'

'Please, call me Alec. No need for all this Doctor Sparling carry-on.'

Rich words coming from the man yet to refer to Ms Coogan by her given name. But Captain Pedantic had let slip that archaeology was her field. This didn't bode well for Ben's notions of being headhunted by human resources. On the plus side, his odds had shortened to two-to-one. He just wished he knew what shiny prize awaited him at the finish line.

Chloe's pace had eased, if only for Ben's sake. Up ahead, great lumps of stone rose through the weeds like distant dolphins. Trees were few, cold and naked; miserable husks so skinny it was as though the cruel earth had denied them even a bead of moisture. They stood around awkwardly in every direction, like party guests that didn't belong, offering some sense of the miles journeyed and of those yet to come.

'So,' Chloe said, glancing over to him, 'do you think you'll find anything interesting? Stories, I mean. Our boy, Sparling, seemed a little too excited by it all.'

'I hope so,' he replied, breathing easier now. 'We'll have to see when we get there. People like to put their own spin on things and if this place is as backward as he thinks, then there's no knowing what they still believe in or what superstitions survive.'

'When did he say the church was deconsecrated?' she asked, stomping on some deadwood with her oxblood Doc Martens.

'Around the end of the nineteenth century, I think.'

'Well,' Chloe said with a smirk, 'whatever they believe in, they sure as shit don't believe in God.'

The best storytellers worked the shadows when they spoke. And the night was never so dark than when they let that silence linger, inviting all ears to lean in that bit closer. Theirs was a craft honed through generations and Ben took it as a privilege to have experienced it first-hand. Some spoke only by the light of a single candle or by a carefully chosen window where the trees outside rustled like a nervous audience.

The older ones genuinely believed what they were telling him. He respected their lives, their memories, the vivid colours they retained. But in a way, he felt sorry for them. Myths and folk tales were make-believe; stories to be told but not taken to heart. And yet for these people they were real. They had spent their lives believing in fairies and monsters. Such beliefs didn't bring happiness. They were passed like a flaming torch with too short a handle, scalding impressionable fingers, imprinting old scars on youthful minds.

The younger generations didn't get it. That's why Ben insisted on interviewing the oldest: the grandparents, the great-grandparents, even some distant uncles who didn't quite fit in at the family table. They trusted him to keep their stories safe. That had been the whole point of his thesis – to preserve what would otherwise have been lost.

The bulk of these stories were never written down and could fade out of existence in a few short decades. Details would be forgotten or changed. Interest in them would dwindle until the kids were throwing their eyes to the heavens whenever grandad mentioned the olden days. And then that was that. The superstition would die and so too would its monsters.

There was one interviewee, not old *per se*, he was probably in his sixties. Mickeen was his name. He was constantly cracking jokes and slapping Ben on the back as if to make sure their punchlines physically landed. He had a thick navy jumper, hair like an Eighties' perm, and one of those Irish beards that captured every shade of autumn. He'd leant forward in his chair, inviting Ben a little closer with a twitch of his finger. His wife had been interviewed before him. She had spoken mostly of the banshee. Nothing Ben hadn't heard before.

'Do *you* think it's all true?' Mickeen asked, smirking as if awaiting some hilarious response.

'It doesn't matter if I do or not,' Ben replied. 'I'm just here to collect the stories.'

'You don't.' Mickeen laughed, slapping his thigh. 'I knew you didn't. Sure, why would you? It's all just a bit of fun, isn't it?'

'You should have heard your wife talk earlier. She certainly seems to believe in it.'

The banshee tradition was common as rain across the island. Though the stories were often rewrought between counties, she was always an omen of death, her eerie cries foretelling a death in the community. For the most part she was a woman dressed all in black, with long white hair that she could often be seen combing, or so the stories went. Details varied depending on who was telling them. There were examples where some hapless sod had found a comb on his walk home only to have the banshee follow him, hammering on his door with horrifying force, practically shaking the thatch from the roof. It was usually returned by means of iron tongs, which oddly enough were either broken or melted from the banshee's touch. The Irish were certainly inventive; Ben couldn't deny his people that.

'Aye.' Mickeen grinned. 'My wife has seen and heard enough. The grandkids, too, whenever they're visiting.'

'And you?' Ben asked. 'You haven't *seen* or *heard* anything?'

'I'll tell you a secret,' Mickeen offered, winking down at the recorder, 'between you and me.'

Ben agreed. The reels were stopped.

'It was all me. My wife hasn't seen anything. But I told her that *I* had and she believed every word. Her family is like that. There were a few nights that I crept out and howled my head off, just so she could hear. The young ones were staying over and now they think it's all real.' His whole body jittered with excitement. 'I even left an old comb out on the road for them to find. And sure they brought it into my wife and she almost had a conniption.'

'Why would you do that?' Ben asked him.

'It's only a bit of fun,' Mickeen replied, sniggering to himself. 'There's no harm in it.'

No harm? Because of this eejit's antics, his grandchildren were going to grow up terrified. No wonder these traditions had lasted so long. The world was full of pranksters of Mickeen's ilk. There will always be those out there who just want to fuck with people.

'What about your side of things?' Ben asked Chloe. 'If Sparling's right, you're the first archaeologist to ever set foot in this place?'

'I'll believe it when I see it,' she replied. 'I'm more than happy to take our dear doctor's money, but we're not going to find anything out of the ordinary. Trust me, I've had my arse in the air, digging around in the dirt for a few years now. There are no more mysteries on this island. And there's no chance that we're the first ones to ever come this way.'

Sparling's projection had presented Ben with a map scanned in at a slightly crooked angle. His closeted OCD screamed internally. The font betrayed its antiquity but it wasn't dated. Though probably white once upon a time, the paper had yellowed, especially in its centre. Ben examined it with his head atilt, feigning some appreciation. He hadn't a clue what he was supposed to be looking at.

It was a rural section with few dwellings. None of them looked any larger than a garden shed. The land was divvied out by mismatched boundaries. Big fields, small fields. *Who cares?* Ben perceived the symbols for a cemetery and a church, or possibly some other ecclesiastical building. Even a child could identify them. Other than that, it could have been an aerial view of anywhere in the country. Cartography was an archaeologist's tool. Ben didn't care for ruins and relics. The height of a hill and the length of a lake were somebody else's business.

'Am I in the right place?' a voice asked from the back of the room.

A young woman was standing at the top of the stairs, holding the door open with her foot, ready to retreat at any second. Her hair was bleached white and chopped short. Spikes of pearly floss jutted out from every angle as though she had just fallen out of bed. Her face was petite, its eyes bright and soulful. And she was about as tall as Ben had been back in secondary school before the customary growth spurt. She might have been in her early twenties – a few years younger than Ben – and she wore a black string top and pale skinny jeans. Her olive parka hung open and had a collar like a lion's mane.

'I suppose that depends,' Sparling said, his pasty cheeks pinched into the smallest smile, 'are you Ms Coogan?'

'Yes, sir,' she replied, returning his smile with one ten times its size. 'At your service.'

'Please, come and sit by Mr French,' he said, again pointing to the front row, 'and I'll explain why I've invited you both here today.'

'Mr French?' she repeated, obviously amused by the stiffness of it all.

'Ben,' he said, introducing himself, unable to contain his smile as she skipped down the steps. 'I don't think anyone except Doctor Sparling, I mean Alec, has ever called me Mr French before.'

'Chloe,' she said, sidling towards him between the desks and fold-down seats, 'or Ms Coogan, if you prefer? I'm not too particular about it. Is it just the three of us or are we expecting more company?' she asked, looking to Sparling.

'No, this is everyone,' he replied, standing tall, striking that familiar lecturer's stance. 'I need only the two of you.'

Chloe slid into the seat beside Ben and slipped the jacket from her shoulders. The October sun had awoken the freckles on her cheeks like a light sprinkling of brown sugar. The woman's eyes were satin grey, moonlight over mist. Her nose was delicate, with a tiny point. Ben stole a lingering glance at her profile and the shape of her lips. They seemed to rest in a half-smile, like a subtle first defence against the world – the refusal to take it too seriously. She laid her bare arms on the desk. Beads adorned both wrists, and her right ring finger wore a small emerald stone.

'Now then,' Sparling began, removing his glasses, 'the university has kindly given me this room so that we may meet today. You see, I am backing a project that interests me a great deal. And you, Mr French and Ms Coogan,' he said, nodding at them individually, 'I believe are the perfect candidates. And I have done my research,' he added with that odd smile of his.

Ben and Chloe turned their heads in unison, each respecting the other's confusion. She seemed particularly entertained by it all, giggling as though Sparling just landed some top-notch stand-up. Since his graduation, Ben hadn't been the *perfect candidate* for any job. His history master's had yet to open any doors that didn't lead to a retail shop floor. And those doors could be soldered shut for all he cared.

'Ms Coogan,' the doctor continued, 'I've heard wonderful reports of your work. There is even talk of expanding your research into a PhD next year. Your study on the archaeology of indigenous communities in the nineteenth century is coming along quite nicely, yes?'

'Yeah,' she casually replied, sitting back, 'it's coming together.'

'And Mr French,' he said, placing a palm flat on his thesis, 'you've done sterling work here. Interviewing is no easy feat. You obviously have a knack for it. Very promising,' he said, almost to himself, 'very promising indeed. And now, before we go any further, I'll need you to sign these.' Here he produced two pages, presenting one in each hand.

'And what are they?' Chloe asked bluntly, cocking an eyebrow.

'Non-disclosure agreements,' Sparling replied as if it should have come as no surprise. 'It is my wish that your findings be kept between us for the time being, until I've had opportunity to study them.'

Ben needed a job. He needed money. This sounded like an internship – experience that would bolster his supposed employability but leave the lint in his pocket undisturbed. Judging by the pout of Chloe's lips, her reservations had also been raised.

'Are we getting paid for this?' Ben asked, frowning at the man.

'Yes, of course, Mr French. How much would you like?'

Ben's throat felt dry. *How much would you like?* No words came to mind and certainly no fee. He heard Chloe tittering to herself beside him. Did she think the man was joking? Sparling didn't strike Ben as the type to indulge in a sense of humour. Not with a smile like that.

'Tell you what, Mr French,' he said after a moment of no response. 'Sign this, and after I explain the project's various ins and outs we can discuss payment. How does that appeal to you? Time is precious and I'd rather not waste any.'

He dispensed the pages without waiting for an answer, taking care not to meet either of them in the eye. The pronounced crease in Sparling's pants was more striking than the man's social skills. Ben took his contract with clammy fingers. Its typeface was small. Its words were many. The paper was as fat as card. Ben's name was printed throughout the text in bold. It looked amiss, as if *Benjamin French* had no right in having his name inked on such a document. There was always a first time for everything. A pen was placed between them; the expensive *Parker* kind that always smeared under his left hand.

How much would you like? Ben couldn't believe his luck.

'I'll give you a moment to read through the details,' Sparling said, returning behind his lectern. 'May I just say as you seem especially apprehensive, Mr French, that this project will be of great interest to you both, regarding your chosen specialisations, that is. Regardless of any financial reward that you will stand to receive, the furthering of knowledge is our ultimate goal here. You should, perhaps, see this as a springboard to new and better opportunities.'

Chloe signed without hesitation. She slid the page forward and slouched back in her seat, having not read a word of it. Ben looked to her in quiet disbelief as she handed him the pen, still sleek from her touch.

'Come on, Mr French,' she said with a wink. '*What have you got to lose?*'

Those words echoed through Ben's head as his foot plunged into yet another pit. True of any foe underestimated, the journey had the upper hand, skilfully stabbing him whenever and wherever it pleased, entertaining the many insects keen to set up shop in his ears. Both thumbs were tucked under the rucksack's straps to ease some of its weight off his shoulders. But it just caused the pain to travel elsewhere. His lower back seemed the most popular destination.

Chloe's legs were a welcome distraction for now, and that's where Ben's eyes fell. She was forever a few steps ahead like a carrot dangling on a string. Her jeans looked as if they had been spray-painted on. He could see her calf muscles tightening.

'What age is your kid?' she called back, stopping for a moment to look at him.

'Aoife's three,' he replied, lifting his head hastily to meet her eyes.

'Do you see much of her?'

'Not enough. Her mum, Jess, moved back to Donegal, so I only get to see her maybe once a month.'

'How long were you guys together for?' she asked.

'One whole night.'

Chloe blocked his way like a bouncer in a nightclub, hand extended but not quite touching.

'It was a *long* night.' Ben grinned.

Her eyes narrowed on him and he regretted his glibness immediately.

'Did you get her pregnant and then run off?' she asked, and Ben knew they weren't moving until she had his answer.

'No, of course not. Why would you think that? I see Aoife every chance I get. It was just...' *choose your words* '...a surprise. That's all.'

'A fucking *surprise*,' Chloe snapped before walking away. 'Honestly, you men are the worst.'

Ben had phoned his parents the night before. One day, he promised himself, he would justify their faith in him. This project of Sparling's was a step in the right direction and his dad – always with his glass half full – believed it was the beginning of something wonderful; chapter one in a new book of Ben's life after the old one lost its plot entirely. They had covered his tuition fees and supported him all the way. He wished that he could have told them more. But his mum would have been in touch with the whole family, the neighbours, and then denied having ever done so. Every shitty thing he did was celebrated like a medical breakthrough. Hopefully, when he saw them again, he would have some good news to trade for all they had done for him. Ben knew that was all they wanted.

'Wonderful,' Sparling had said when they'd both handed back their agreements, fixing his glasses to his nose as he checked for their signatures. 'Now we can get down to business.'

'This better be good,' Chloe whispered, leaning into Ben's ear, the warmth of her breath caressing his neck like silk.

Sparling examined the non-disclosure agreements one last time before setting them down. He glanced cautiously around the hall, his eyes resting for a second on both doors at the back, and only then did he speak.

'This ordnance survey map is from the 1830s,' he said, drawing their attention to the projection behind him. 'It's the first of its kind to record a village by the name of Tír Mallacht. Trust me, you haven't heard of it. You can see here a cluster of cottages. Each one small, in most cases no more than a single room. Their layout and proximity are nothing unusual. To the east you can mark the location of a church and graveyard – the only features worthy of note from the cartographer's point of view at least. Mapmakers back then had few tools at their disposal, so we shall forgive the possibility of any shortcomings on their part. As you both know, such cloistered communities were commonplace in the nineteenth century. There is nothing in this map bordering on oddity or anomaly.'

With a jab of his keyboard the map was replaced by an aerial view of the same area. It was a modern photograph. The parched yellow paper had been bland as desert sand, but now all details were defined in full colour. Its angle and range from the earth had been altered to mimic the original map, so the photograph was still skewed to Ben's eyes.

'Now then,' Sparling continued, 'here again we see the same village. This image was captured only a few months ago. Almost two hundred years have passed and practically nothing has changed. *Two hundred years*,' he repeated. 'A number of new homes have been built. But that is, of course, to be expected. Free from disease and hardship, families inevitably grow. All original buildings are still intact, Ms Coogan. Even the outhouses and stables are as they were.'

Ben noticed Chloe shifting in her seat. It would have seemed that Sparling had caught Ms Coogan's attention. Some people were more easily excited by outhouses than others.

'This aerial photograph and the original map have another common trait,' the doctor added. 'There is one key element missing from both. Can either of you identify what that might be?'

Ben sat forward to scan the details. Was this a test? Sparling had recruited him because of his knack for charming stories out of the elderly. He had a map of Ireland in his thesis but that was no more than filler – a means to fatten up the page count; tricks of the trade for any budding academic. His was a layman's eye when it came to cartography. Still, he frowned at the map as though suddenly enlightened by a hundred fantastic theories as to what Sparling wanted from him.

'There's no road,' Chloe said simply.

'Precisely, Ms Coogan,' Sparling replied. 'Tír Mallacht was a curiously insular community, even by Irish standards, and still is to this day. Accessible only by foot, it is in essence a time capsule. One unaffected by the world around it.'

'You mean to tell me,' Chloe said, 'that the same families have lived in that little village for nearly two hundred years?'

The door atop the stairs was heard to slightly open, like an airlock, and close back into its frame. Ben turned in his seat at the sound of it but there was no one there. It could have been a draught. Or some caretaker who hadn't realised the hall was occupied until they heard Chloe's voice. Either way, Sparling's body stiffened. He stared at the door, waiting longer than seemed necessary.

'That is correct, Ms Coogan,' he eventually replied.

'So, their gene pool is…'

'Most limited.'

'But why have they never left?' she asked.

'A fine question, Ms Coogan, and one that I would very much like answered.'

There was no hint of doubt in the doctor's voice. Ben knew honesty when he heard it. Sparling could have said *two plus two is four* and looked less convinced. But his case didn't check out. Ben knew that there were sources on everything. Even the shortest, simplest life left some trace behind it, and this was a full village. Ireland was too small an island for what the man was proposing.

'There must be some mention of the village out there,' Ben said. 'What about the church and census records?'

'The church was abandoned in the late nineteenth century,' Sparling replied. 'If there were any records, they are lost. And as for the census, those employed to visit each household were shunned and left empty-handed. No records, no names. The people of Tír Mallacht wanted nothing to do with them. Eventually, it would seem, the village was simply omitted.'

'Sure, they're all one big family,' Chloe giggled. 'They

could have just taken a head count and called them the Tír Mallachts.'

'Yes, indeed, Ms Coogan,' Sparling said, dead-faced.

'What about its history?' Ben asked. 'Do we know anything about the place bar the fact that it's been forgotten for two centuries?'

Sparling gazed back at the projection with strange adoration. One would swear that he had discovered Atlantis.

'No, Mr French,' he replied. 'No historical or archaeological record of Tír Mallacht survives, if ever any did exist.'

'And I take it that we're going to fix that,' Chloe said.

'Precisely, Ms Coogan.'

'And when do you want us to go there?' Ben asked.

'There's no time like the present, Mr French. I would like you both to travel to Tír Mallacht tomorrow. Your expenses shall, of course, be taken care of.' Here Sparling held up a fat envelope for them both to see. 'Given its secluded location, you will only be able to drive so far. I've already prepared a route that will take you as close as possible. You'll have to walk it the rest of the way. I suggest you rent a car if neither of you already have access to one, and I suspect that you will need a tent or other camping equipment to stay overnight or however long it may take to conduct your respective surveys.'

'I can drive us,' Ben said, turning excitedly to Chloe who couldn't have appeared more relaxed.

'Neither of you have any children, do you?' Sparling asked.

Chloe laughed it off, but the question had caught Ben off-guard.

How much would you like? There was no knowing how much they stood to make. And he desperately needed a cash injection, if only for his daughter's sake.

'No,' Ben replied. 'I don't have any kids.'

He felt sick just saying it.

The doctor looked to Ben and then to Chloe, almost nervously. And though his lips imitated a smile, the eyes remained glazed and mirthless. 'If you would kindly return your attention to the wall, you will see another map. I have highlighted the network of paths and laneways that run through the village.'

These were defined by red lines, trickling like blood between a dozen or so cottages coloured in yellow blocks. They broke into longer veins that touched the surrounding fields. There was no order to any of it. The lay of the land and its seasonal yielding were the roots of its design. Ben gleaned some comfort from Sparling's diligence. But he wondered if the doctor ever stopped to appreciate *who* had made the path they were to follow. So focused was he on their course, his agenda seemed to bypass what awaited them at their destination.

'You will enter here,' he continued, 'from the north. This small woodland should lead you directly into the village.'

'How would you like us to approach them?' Ben asked. 'We don't know how they're going to react to us.'

'You're the one who's going to make best friends with them,' Chloe put in with a smile.

'With an open mind, Mr French,' the doctor replied, as though he hadn't heard her. 'Be patient and attentive, and sensitive to their circumstances. This is the reason why I chose you. I'm told you have a way with people.'

Ben and Chloe worked their way through Sparling's *small woodland* – kicking through the sticky stems that grew from all sides – trying to follow what once might have been a pathway, so tight that a slender fox would strain to break it. It was the only way through that Ben could see. Not that he could see a whole lot. Nervous birds rustled the sparse leaves above, most likely terrified of the chaotic giants breaking through their hometown, flattening anything that stood in their way.

Sparling's map had shown them the sun-kissed treetops and their stubby shadows, but it had kept the murky seabed of vine and thorn beneath the surface.

Chloe was frowning at her phone. Whatever she was trying to do, it wasn't working, and the swipes soon turned to stabs.

'There's no coverage,' she sighed. 'I suppose the Tír Mallachts aren't exactly renowned for their social media presence. There'll be no tagging on this trip.'

'But the GPS still works, doesn't it?'

'Yeah, don't you worry. We're not completely lost. I inputted all the information from Sparling's gazillion maps. We're nearly there. Less than a…'

Clang!

A bell tolled in the tallest tree, scattering all wings to the sky, deafeningly loud amidst the lifeless, veined leaves of autumn. The shock of it came like a volley of gunfire, nearly knocking Ben off his feet.

'What the holy shit!' Chloe shrieked, holding her hands to her ears.

He moved up behind her to see what had happened.

The tripwire was a length of fishing line tied across the forest's only path, right at its treeline, where the promise of fresh air invited clumsy feet to run. It was set high and tensed against Chloe's waist; unavoidable unless you knew to expect it.

It was an alarm. And they had blundered right into it.

'Sparling never said anything about traps!' she shouted over the ringing.

'I think there's a lot that the doctor hasn't told us,' Ben replied, a few steps behind her, his eyes directing her to look up.

There were more. Bells hung across the woodland's edge, amongst the brittle nests on the uppermost branches, as far as the eye could see. The trap was set too high to alert for animals. Ben guessed this but kept his mouth shut.

'Well, that's probably the creepiest thing I've ever seen,' Chloe said, carefully lifting the line, but still the bells jangled like wind chimes in a gale.

'Bells aren't so bad, you know!' he called from behind her. 'Herdsmen used to tie them around the necks of their flock. The belief was that the sound of them could chase away evil spirits.'

'Could they chase them away a little quieter?' she yelled back.

'I hear you,' Ben said, crouching low, crimping his aching knees as he ducked his rucksack under the wire. 'It's safe to say that they're expecting us.'

Ben saw Chloe flutter her shoulders as if chilled water had just trickled down her neck. The sudden noise had startled her, scared her even. And that was perfectly understandable. Ben was shaken, too. Only she hadn't seen him jolt back like he had just jammed his fingers into an electrical socket.

'They haven't left their village in two hundred years.' Chloe smiled, almost convincingly. 'There's no chance in hell that they're expecting *us*. We're practically from the future.'

Sparling closed the lid of the laptop and took his papers in hand. He tapped them on the lectern, and then slid the stack into his satchel.

'One last point, Mr French,' he said. 'When you're conducting your interviews, there's one particular superstition that you might mention, for curiosity's sake, to see if it still exists.'

'And what superstition is that?' Ben asked confidently.

'The creeper,' Sparling replied. 'I do believe it's known as the creeper.'

'I've never heard of it.'

'No,' the doctor said, taking his satchel in hand. 'I don't suppose that many people have.'

3

The woodland broke onto a path hemmed in by rickety walls no taller than Ben's waist. Purpling ivy twined through them, holding their parts together like sickly fingers. He had a vague idea of where they were, as a sailor lost at sea can hazard a guess as to what ocean he's in.

There was no birdsong. No noise that wasn't their making. There hadn't been a sound since the bells.

Every new mile had felt like a repeat of the last. Even the trees looked alike, as though they had drawn up their roots and run ahead to fill in the blank spaces. But the earth here was worn and even, and the wilder thorns had been slashed back. People came this way.

Chloe's red sunglasses were propped on her forehead. She was squinting down at her phone. Those big boots scuffed across the clay, kicking up a powdered mist around her ankles. From here on out, Ben was determined to keep an imaginary tether to her side, like a jaded dog out for a stroll with its master.

'Are we close?' he asked.

His mental wellbeing – now more so than the physical – hung on Chloe's answer.

Her eyes narrowed towards the horizon. 'We're here,' she announced. 'Look!'

Plumes of smoke curled through the distant sky, as though giants slumped across its hidden pastures, puffing cigar smoke into the air.

Where there were fires being stoked, there were villagers in need of interviewing.

'Finally,' Ben said, unable to contain his smile.

'I know,' she gasped, letting her tongue hang out. 'Not much farther now, Benny Boy.'

They continued along the path, forsaking Chloe's GPS in lieu of good old-fashioned chimney smoke. He'd been her passenger since they left the car, tailing her legs on autopilot, but his eyes finally opened as they passed a loose grove of aspen. Golden light sliced between their branches, making all those leaves shimmer like paper coins. The undergrowth had thinned. But the slender aspens stood strong, their roots entwined as might lovers' fingers under a candlelit table.

The throes of cross-country travel had obviously darkened Ben's take on the world. He had seen only the trials, not Mother Nature's triumphs. But now she was no longer laid out on her deathbed, lips too parched to speak, her once luscious hair wilting like dead weeds. She was youthful and alive, her honeyed hair captured in every spear of light.

'This isn't so bad now, is it?' he said, wincing slightly as he straightened back his shoulders.

'Since we hopped that gate, you haven't peeled your eyes off your boots.'

'That was different.' Ben chuckled. 'I'm all the about the destination.'

'There are literally thousands of inspirational quotes about the journey being the important part.'

'Pay no heed to them, Ms Coogan,' he replied. 'They're all bollocks.'

Chloe suddenly tugged on his sleeve. 'Jesus,' she whispered, 'where'd she come from?'

At the end of the laneway there was a child.

She was barefoot. Her dress shapeless and cut from discoloured fabric. Its stitching was crude; reminiscent of Frankenstein's monster with its mismatched skin tones sewn together. Her head was a tousled mess of brown hair. She was stood perfectly still but slightly atilt, as though one leg were shorter than the other. Her face had an odd little nub for a nose and was daubed all over with muddy fingerprints.

Ben took a tenuous step forward, hands held up in mock surrender. The child wasn't exactly a wild animal but her hard stare was eerily reminiscent of a cagey tomcat.

'Hello,' he said, waving both palms like a mime.

She just stared at him, unblinking, as though her eyes were lidless.

'What's your name?' Ben asked.

The girl's lips stretched into a lurid grin but the eyes remained dark. She didn't seem at all surprised to see them. Perhaps the tripwire was to thank for that.

'My name is Ben,' he said, his voice velvet soft, 'and this pretty lady is called Chloe.'

'Pretty lady?' Chloe whispered.

'Shush your gums,' he replied, still focused on the child as though any sudden movement might chase her into the trees. 'What's your name?'

The smile was set on her face, with cheeks like lumps of hardened pottery clay. Ben waited for some response to show that she understood. But she just held his gaze, her head hanging slightly downward as though it stored secrets too heavy to hold up.

'What's your name, kid?' Chloe asked, far louder than Ben's measured whisper.

The child turned and bolted, her bare feet taking her down the lane and around the corner, disappearing behind a hedge twice her height.

'Nicely done, Ms Coogan,' Ben said.

'Hey, in my defence she *did* scare me first.'

'Come on.' He chuckled, patting her on the shoulder. 'Let's see where she went.'

They walked on, more cautiously now, suspecting that their presence had been advertised on some ivy-clad billboard. The walls on either side had grown in height, and a cool shade reached out from the wilder privets. When they rounded the corner, Ben had half-expected for the girl to be waiting for them like an apparition always just out of reach, but she was nowhere to be seen.

'You'd better keep that out of sight while we're here,' Ben said, winking down at Chloe's phone.

'Oh, do you reckon?' she replied sarcastically. 'I doubt we'll need phones to make an impression on this crowd.'

Without coverage there was no way to call for help should they need it. A few unexpected causes for concern had joined their party, but they wouldn't slow them down. Ben was more than capable of doing that on his own.

'Do you reckon the car is safe?' he asked.

'You're a bit of worrier, aren't you?' Chloe replied, nudging into him. 'The car's the least of your problems now. You've an entire village to charm with that smile of yours.'

'What do you mean?'

'Oh, come on,' she replied. 'You could woo an Amazonian tribe with those teeth.'

'Your smile is twice the size of mine.'

'Yeah, but I only use mine for good. City boys like you are only after one thing.'

That was probably true once upon a time. But how would the rental company react if they knew that their shiny asset was half-sunken in a ditch? Ben hadn't had much of a choice. The road had come to a dead end, as though whoever was building it realised the pointlessness of it all. It was easier to hang a gate and call it the end.

'Don't worry about the car,' she said reassuringly. 'Everything's going to be fine.'

The bells still tolled over his thoughts but offered nothing in the way of song or sense. Their sound was more uneasy feeling than memory. He had brought with him more questions than he needed, but the tripwire added another to the tally. *Why go to the trouble of rigging an alarm system if no one ever came this way?* Hopefully the answer would come by word and not the sharp end of some farming tool.

The path ahead dipped out of sight, curving down alongside a vast open field cut into the hillside. Its soil had been freshly tilled and at its far end – like lead soldiers on a tabletop – Ben saw the distant shapes of a dozen or so men. They were standing around in a loose circle. A few of them leaned on tools. Others were squatted on the ground with tiny clouds billowing from their pipes.

'Check it out,' Chloe said, resting forward on the wall, 'the Tír Mallachts in all their glory.'

A warm, sorrel light washed over the earth. Cocoa in the shade of its ploughed channels and bright as orange peel atop its taller ridges. The friable soil was already hardening in a crust of cold. Breaking into view was the child, a good twenty feet below them, running towards the men, bobbing from side to side like a boat on stormy water.

'Well would you look who it is,' Chloe quipped.

The sight of her reminded Ben of Aoife's first steps. Not that he had been around to witness them in person. What kind of half-decent father had the time for that? Jess had sent him a video while he was in work; part-time then, and still in college. Thirty seconds of unbridled, blink-and-you'll-miss-it drama. He must have watched it twenty times on repeat. Ben had shared the clip with his mum, popped on his name badge, and went back out to the shop floor. He'd still had three hours left on his shift. All the while his little girl was walking, every step leaving him behind.

'Come on,' Chloe said. 'I'm pretty sure we can catch her. The kid's got energy, I'll give her that. But she lacks a certain finesse.'

'Sure, her legs are too different lengths,' Ben said as he peered down the hill. 'I'm surprised she can even walk.'

He'd seen cliffs less steep. But if the girl could make it down, then surely they stood half a chance. Chloe held on to his sleeve. He, in turn, gripped a fistful of her furry hood. And together they worked their way down, inch by near vertical inch until Ben had to tug her back. Ever the liability, he hadn't the strength left to dig his heels into the loose clay.

'Christ,' he gasped as a fresh pain seized his calves, 'my legs are going to go.' He arched his knees, trying to realign his balance. 'Do you want go on ahead in case I drag you down with me?'

'Fucking city boys.' She smiled, shaking her head. 'You've come too far to fall now. Just hold on to me.'

Avalanches of grit broke around him as he scratched his way downward. 'You're like a little anchor with those boots,' he said, now clutching on to her with both hands.

'Is that how you charm the ladies, Benny Boy? By calling them fucking anchors?' Chloe replied as level ground peeled into sight. 'There,' she said, pointing towards a narrow hollow in the wall, framed by coils of thorns. 'I reckon that's where she crept through.'

Chloe was right. The whole wall was a mass of leaf and stone. But where the midges misted the shadows and those twiggy arms reached a little shorter, there was an opening, like a secret passage in a Gothic manor that only ghostly children could travel through.

Ben recalled the blood vessels on Sparling's map. The path, if they stayed with it, would lead them into the crux of the village. Or there was option number two – follow the kid.

'What do you want to do?' Chloe asked, prompting his decision.

Ben peered through the archway of vine, back stooped, peeling apart its glossy leaves with careful fingers. Another sharp bank led into the field. There was no way to see into the open without first climbing down. No easy feat considering their backpacks and the thorny barbs that spiralled through the shrubbery like steel wire.

The child would have reached the men by now. One might have even caught sight of them before they turned down the hill. Either way, their presence was known. He was certain of that if nothing else.

'I say we follow her,' he said. 'They already know we're here.'

'Yeah, I suppose you're right. We did ring a big bell, didn't we?'

'That was all you. Come on.' He smiled. 'I'll go down first in case you blunder into another trap.'

'Hey!' she protested. 'That's no way to talk to your anchor.'

Sparling's enthusiasm, however deluded, had awoken in Ben a nervous energy. These wouldn't be like past interviews, praised by academics who already knew the answers to every question. Nobody knew what secrets the Tír Mallachts had hidden away.

He crept towards the edge of the embankment, where the tunnel dropped into the leafy unknown. Briars scratched and swished against his rucksack as he squeezed his way down. He blinked away the clay that crumbled as dust in his fingers. One branch even raked across his head like a long fingernail. Eventually, traumatised and blind, he fell into the open, narrowly missing his head on a low-hanging branch.

'How is it?' Chloe's voice asked from above.

'It's grand,' he called up. 'Come on down.'

There was nothing to be gained by telling her the truth.

He looked towards the far end of the field, where the men had convened over tools and pipe smoke. But where there had been many, there was now only one. The child stood crookedly to his side like a devious familiar. They seemed to be waiting for them.

Ben could hear Chloe shrieking to herself as she bumbled down the bank.

'Are you okay?' he shouted back.

'I'm just fucking fine, thanks.'

The man by the child's side was stood so stiffly, as though every muscle in his body were tensed like a cat charging up to pounce. There was no telling if this implied hostility or not. He was too distant to discern his expression, but Ben knew that he was staring him down across the upturned soil. Welcome or not, it was too late to go back now.

Chloe landed in gracelessly beside him, spitting, and brushing dirt from her hood. She fell still when her eyes lifted to the horizon.

'Where'd they all go?' she asked.

'Let's find out.'

Ben forced his legs back into action. The soil drifts were loose like desert sand, crumbling with the lightest touch as the man and child stood motionless, watching their approach. There was no sign of the others. Even their farming tools had been taken by the rapture. Maybe the heavens had land in need of harvesting.

The man was tall and wiry as though a sculptor had picked his creation apart, leaving only the skeletal frame. Such was the stoop to his shoulders that from a distance he appeared to have no neck, just this baggage that built up beside his ears. His clothes were all brown or black, their fabric indistinguishable from the dirt. He wore breeches the colour of oak, with high boots. His shirt was loose, open around the chest; a patchwork of muddy hues, repaired so many times that there was no isolating its original elements.

As novel as the man's old-timey appearance seemed to them. What must he have been thinking? Chloe's red sunglasses were probably enough to justify burning her at the nearest stake.

'Don't scare away the kid again,' Ben whispered to her. 'No interviews. No happy doctor. No financial reward.'

'Oh, don't you worry, Mr French. I'm not saying a word.'

Ben caught the first tang of sweat; a warm, nauseating scent that surrounded the man like strong cologne. His skin was as leather. Burnished from the elements and cracked with heavy lines that travelled like a road map from his forehead down to his knobbly chin. The man's jaw was skewed slightly to one side. His nose was swollen and drooped down to his upper lip like a bulb of garlic. A handsome man he was not.

Ten feet now stood between them. Close enough. The child looked at Ben with the same vacant expression. Her irises were eclipsed by an unwholesome darkness, as if they belonged to one much older.

'Hello again,' he said, crouching down to her level. 'Sorry if we startled you.'

Chloe had stopped a step or two behind him, reinstating his role as chief diplomat.

The girl's cheeks slowly contorted into that impish smile of earlier, but neither she nor the man said anything. There was never any question about the indigenous speaking the same tongue. Sparling wouldn't have omitted information as pertinent as that, would he?

'My name is Benjamin,' he began, 'and this—'

'What do you want here?' the man interjected, his consonants hard as a punch.

Gruff as he was, at least he spoke English.

'I'm an historian, and Chloe here is an archaeologist. We've been sent here to conduct a survey. I was hoping that I might be able to do a few interviews and Chloe is—'

'Who sent you?' he said, cutting Ben short again.

'A university sent us,' he lied, hoping that it would make their presence seem more official.

It carried more clout than saying *someone I met on Tuesday.*

'We don't get many visitors here,' the man said.

'Obviously,' Chloe whispered under her breath.

Ben had expected to dazzle and confound these people with the factory cut of his denim jacket. But the man couldn't have been less impressed. Tír Mallacht's ambassador had yet to unclench his lumpy knuckles and the kid still ogled him like some mongrel under a table. Maybe they were genuinely unnerved by their arrival and their nerves had translated into this. Whatever *this* was.

'If you bring us into the village and introduce me to some people,' Ben said, bracing his smile against whatever response awaited him, 'we'll be gone before you know it, and you'll never hear from us again. But we can't leave until then.'

The man chewed his gums in thought for a long moment. He glanced down at the child as though seeking her counsel, and then nodded his head.

'Run along now,' he said to her. 'Tell your mother we've visitors.'

The girl's bare feet broke into a run, squishing across the mounds of earth. Ben could hear her panting fade behind them as he waited for his answer.

'You'll leave tomorrow,' the man said as an order, not a request. 'Though it'd be for the best if you walked now. We live away from the world here and we have our reasons. Whatever it is you hope to find, trust me when I tell you that you don't want it. Do you understand me?'

If he had seen the five-figure sum on Ben's contract, the lad wouldn't have sounded so certain. And *living away from the world* was putting it mildly. They hadn't just walked their bones to near fracture to turn back now.

No more letting people down. Only this time it was his daughter, his parents, and the odd monochrome creature that was Doctor Alec Sparling.

'I understand,' Ben replied, fixing his eyes on the man in a show of determination.

'No,' he said with a sigh, 'you don't. Nobody ever understands until it's done. If you knew what you'd just walked into, you'd already be on your way.'

'Like I said, we can leave as soon as I talk to a few people. We don't want to be any trouble.'

With a plaintive groan the man looked to the sky and scratched around his chin with long, filth-edged nails. Their very presence seemed to irritate him like a rash. Dirt peeled from his skin and parted as shavings in the air.

His beady eyes considered Chloe with a look of unfiltered disapproval. It was enough to raise a few platinum hackles.

'Are you going to take us or not?' she asked him. 'I'm sure we can find our way there without your stimulating company.'

Ben kept his smile intact. *Be nice. Please, be nice.* They needed this grump on their side until they reached the village. The man hocked up something foul from the back of his throat, swallowed it, and then proceeded to walk away.

'Come on so,' he said, without looking back. 'Follow me, if you must.'

Ben turned to Chloe, expecting her face to mirror his own concern, but instead she was barely containing her laughter. She wasn't the one who had to sit down and talk to these people.

He had to mentally reorganise his expectations. Their arrival had gone off like a dud firework. Where was the sizzle and excitement? Sparling's theories were lifting like a fog, revealing just another village; the same simple minds reciting the same simple stories.

4

'We really appreciate it,' Ben called after the man.

Not surprisingly, no response came.

'I don't think he likes you,' Chloe whispered with a smirk.

He had the gangliest strides Ben had ever seen. Nothing about him was in proportion. And so hunched was his back that only the tip of his head was on show.

The man led them through a breach in the wall, onto a narrow dirt track. They skirted alongside the field, walking single file back in the direction where Ben guessed the village to be. The trail was tight and tinted overall with shade, and it wasn't long before the sun's cool absence was felt.

Eventually the lofty briars to his right fell away, revealing a dismal, lightless hollow with a slab of stone in its pit. Days had passed without any rainfall, and yet pools of moisture oozed through its soil like a leaky septic tank. Everything – from the lowest root worming through the black to the highest branch straining to steal some light – glistered with a sickly dampness, like sweat drawn from diseased skin.

'Jesus,' Chloe whispered, 'this place is grim, isn't it?'

'Check that out,' Ben replied, leaning back to her and pointing ahead. 'Can you imagine living there?'

A cottage stood atop a low knoll, set apart from the trees that had drawn their branches away from it, as though the sorry thing was infectious. The black soil – raised like a sore – had been smoothed by the elements and bore no tracks, be they from man or beast.

Fire had scorched this building. No more than a single room and surely too small to have once sheltered a family. To imagine such a death was to succumb to its spell.

Planks of wood, discoloured from decay, barricaded its doorframe shut. And it was capped with timber boards upon which stones had been laid like a pauper's burial. A sense of tragedy haunted the air around this tomb, sealed on all sides and abandoned.

'What happened there?' Chloe asked, shouting over Ben's shoulder towards their guide.

He didn't answer back. Maybe Ben had imagined it, but he thought the man's pace had quickened.

There was something unnaturally cold about that cottage. A memory, maybe; a tragedy that pined for peace but instead lingered eternally in the one spot it yearned to escape. Ben never understood why hell was sold as a fiery place. Death and sadness were always cold.

They soon reached those familiar laneways. Pink wildflowers speckled the drab shrubs that fenced them in. And these became more prominent as the man led them through a series of softly winding turns.

'You ready for this?' Chloe asked.

'Does it matter at this stage?' Ben replied, smiling back at her.

The lane widened at the next bend and there they saw the first two cottages not left to ruin; set on either side, facing each other. These were the coloured blocks on Sparling's map, dropped around the village like yellow Lego bricks. The reality was somewhat less vibrant.

Both were built of bare stone, packed tight, with their cracks filled in with dirt. By the windows, a piece of wood had been worked into the stone like a miniature door. The roofs were thatched thick with straw; their once golden blonde now dulled to a dirty brown. Edges were unevenly chopped, with cobwebs and other filth clotted under their awnings.

Ben had envisioned doors painted in bright primaries, and window boxes spilling over with garlands of fresh herbs. Instead, the cottages' every aspect was faded and dispiriting. Someone may have, in the past, taken pride in washing their walls or trimming back the thatch, or maybe they had nurtured seeds and watched them blossom, inviting colour and life where now neither were welcome, estranged for so long that even their memories were as black and white.

'What do you think?' he whispered back to Chloe.

'I can't believe they still live like this,' she replied, moving up closer to him.

'*Two hundred years*,' Ben said in his best Sparling impression, to which she giggled and pushed him away.

His nostrils caught a scent in the air, pungent and moist; cabbage or some similarly foul vegetable boiled into a watery soup. Luckily they'd brought their own food for the trip. He tried to peek inside one of the cottages as they passed but there was no light within; not a single ember to break the black. There could have been someone standing right there, lurking a step back from the threshold – like a trapdoor spider, always waiting, always hungry – and Ben would have been none the wiser.

'Just up here now,' the man said, pointing ahead towards another corner, where the sun spilled across the pathway.

They were approaching the cluster of homes set around a clearing, like a marketplace or square. It was the only one of its kind in the village.

Sparling's aerial map had shown them the cracks of white clay that ran through the green, and distinguished the bad fields from the good, where deep-rooted stone kept them aside from the harvest. But the land meant nothing without the people.

Ben's aches and the bruises that marbled his skin from his shoulders to his calves were relieved by that old excitement. He had visited more villages than he could recall, like a travelling magpie searching for shiny trinkets. But this one promised a unique experience. He expected to happen upon a hive of activity, of sound and colour, and personality – a window into the chores and amusements of a time gone by.

'Okay,' Ben whispered in Chloe's ear, 'I'll do the introductions and then...'

They both stopped mid step.

'Jesus,' Chloe said, her hand grabbing on to Ben's jacket.

Everyone was standing outside their homes – men, women, children – waiting for them like corpses nailed into the ground, imitating the living. Their faces were deathly still. Eyes as opaque marbles; lightless and veiled with shadow. Ben counted thirty of them. Maybe more.

Impoverishment, ill health, and oddity; their collective impression was startling. Unwashed bodies were clad in the simplest rags. Only a few of the men wore shoes. The children, including the boys, wore dresses similar in rough cut and colour to the girl from earlier. They shared the same filth and gormlessness. Women held tattered shawls to their shoulders. Some wore them as hoods, with their beady eyes peering out from the shadows like jewels in muddy water. The men were dressed as the one who had brought them there, and their bodies were as his, contorted from labour or defect of birth.

Two of the older women looked to be blind. They were nestled between the others, their cloudy eyes turned skyward, listening for some sound to soften their curiosity.

Disease and injury must have thrived in such an environment. No medicines to cure. No knowledge to nurse even the simplest affliction. This wasn't living. This was survival, and even that couldn't have come easy.

Every countenance carried some feature awry or ever so slightly askew. Though not overly conspicuous in some cases, such peculiarities were ever present. The distance between the eyes perhaps, or a wrinkled dome of a forehead that swamped the face below. There was tiredness and there was sadness, and there was also distrust amidst the ugliness.

Ben felt like a trespasser caught standing where he shouldn't, uninvited and unwelcome. He and Chloe stood apart from the crowd, bewildered by the many dead eyes and their silent, lurking expectations.

His limbs froze up. All sleight of tongue was tied. Ben had no clue as to what he should do or say, and so he just stood there.

The man from the field had shifted through the crowd, whispering like the devil in their ears. When his words had been spread amongst them, he returned to Ben.

'How many do you need to talk to?' he asked.

'As many as possible,' he replied, his voice sapped of confidence.

'*As many as possible,*' the man imitated thoughtfully, looking at those around him. 'You have until dark.'

'That doesn't give me much time.'

'Then you had better get a move on, hadn't you?'

Ben didn't know where to begin. His mind was a damp match, its sulphur striking dead every time he tried to think. Even the clock was working against him.

'Is there somewhere he can start doing his interviews?' Chloe asked the man. 'In someone's house, maybe? If you're only giving us a few hours, then you'd want to fucking organise something fast.'

Oh, God. Ben couldn't believe this was happening. This was not how he wanted to approach this.

'You won't be setting foot in anyone's house,' the man replied, indifferent to Chloe's shift in tone, 'and you won't be talking to any of the children. If you need somewhere, you can take the stable out the back.' Here he gestured vaguely over his shoulder. 'It's sheltered, and I'm sure someone can find you some chairs, if needs be.'

Chloe glowered at the man as though resisting the urge to swing at him. She looked at the other villagers, huddled anxiously together and then back to Ben, her lamb lost amongst the wolves. She ignored the man with no neck and turned her attention instead to anyone else who would listen.

'Okay,' she said, letting that smile flood across her cheeks. 'My friend here just wants to talk to a few of you, to listen to your stories. That doesn't sound so bad now, does it? He won't be any trouble. *Tell them,*' she whispered, grabbing his arm and pulling him forward.

'That's right,' he said. 'Everyone has a story to tell and I just want to hear yours.'

A few long seconds of silence followed.

'Would anyone like to…?' Ben's voice faded out.

Did anyone understand what he was saying?

A woman stepped out from the crowd.

Dark hollows showed around her eyes, further accentuating the nasal bone that dwarfed the sum of her features. Her skin was tan and dappled overall with freckles. Ben would have guessed her to be in her forties, but it was impossible to tell. She held herself as one much older, with a spine so arched that it would probably split if ever straightened.

Her gnarled toes clawed into the ground as she bowed her head with the strangest and most unexpected air of courtesy. She had, or so it seemed, understood.

'Would it be okay if I spoke to some people?' Ben asked her. 'We can leave first thing in the morning.'

He figured that a little time was better than no time at all.

'You can,' she replied with a voice that was surprisingly soft. 'No children though,' she added as if Ben might have forgotten. 'I can't have you talking to the young ones.'

'Of course,' he replied.

'And only until dark?'

'If that's what you want,' Ben agreed.

He tried to ignore those watching him from all sides. Some edged closer, unsteady from either unease or excitement. One drew his face so close to Ben's that he could feel and hear his clogged nostrils, like a beast breathing by his cheek. He didn't acknowledge him. He didn't flinch. Ben played that smile like a violinist on a sinking ship.

'Okay.' The woman nodded, looking at those who had yet to utter a word. 'Let's meet who you'll be talking to.'

Ben had no say in the matter. And he was in no position to complain, even though there were a few faces that he'd rather not share a stable with for any length of time.

'Nora,' the woman announced pointing to another who could have easily passed for her sister, 'you'll let this young man listen to you.'

Ben extended a hand that she didn't accept. 'It's a pleasure to meet you, Nora, it really is. I'm sure you've as many questions for me as I do for you.'

His pleasantries passed over her like a cloud, shading where he had hoped to bring light.

'Aye,' she replied, looking over his shoulder, 'you'll want to be talking about what exactly?'

'Oh, don't worry, I'm not going to ask—'

'Get the children away,' she shouted, shaking her hand at someone further up the clearing. 'Mary,' Nora said irritably, turning to the woman doing the introductions, 'would you ever keep an eye on the young ones. You know the way it is.'

'That's quite all right,' Ben stammered. 'I'm happy to sit with just the adults.'

'Happy, will you be? We'll see how happy you are once you're gone from here.'

A name was uttered and its bearer would nod in response. This was Mary's way.

The villagers were shy and openly lost as to how they should behave in the company of strangers. And yet, in the early overtures of friendship they were not opposed to the idea of sitting with Ben, though most didn't seem to understand what was being asked of them.

The man from earlier had loitered around when he was introducing himself, watching everyone that he spoke to as if taking a mental note. Life might have been a whole lot easier had Chloe knocked him out. He was that one wasp on a sunny day that wouldn't fuck off.

'Is Nu not supposed to be away from here?' a voice asked.

'No,' Mary replied, 'I trust her more than most.'

Voices were volleyed back and forth, and Ben – lost in the crossfire – tried not to flinch too noticeably. No single element of that experience wasn't besieging his senses. Even after their circle fragmented, the odour of their bodies remained. His stomach was twisted enough by nerves without swallowing back that air.

An old woman – toothless, with hollow gums that sucked in the folds of her face – stood by the open panel of her home, watching Ben like some devilish effigy. It was as though she lacked a skull to define the shape of her head. The eyes were as slits, buried beneath a sagging brow, all shadows and filth. She belonged in a fairy tale. The witch in the woods, hungry for young bones. He couldn't tell if she was locked in or if she was set there like a guard dog to keep intruders out. Both seemed plausible.

'You okay there, love?' Ben whispered, staring back at her.

He raised a hand slowly, thumb up, hoping for her mouth to crack like dried dirt into a smile. It didn't. Maybe she hadn't understood the gesture.

A sudden cry came from within her cottage, grief-stricken and so pained as to make Ben stagger backwards. He couldn't tell if it was human or animal. Somehow, it could have been either. The woman disappeared into the darkness immediately, drawing the door shut behind her.

Still, Ben listened, but there was only the disjointed din from the villagers behind him.

He tried to act as though he hadn't heard anything, not wanting to discard his smile when he needed it most. But that voice wasn't so easily forgotten, lingering amidst his thoughts like the smoke from a snuffed-out candle. It had almost sounded like a plea for help.

Chloe was busy chatting to two thirty-something men who had been invited into their fold. One of them squeezed his cap like a wet sponge. He had the ungainly manner of a child dragged from his bedroom to meet the visitors. Chloe had turned the charm up to ten, brandishing that smile of hers like a headlight on full beam. Her distemper was strictly reserved for one man – the wasp. He watched them both from afar like a school headmaster who had singled out the troublemakers.

'Do you like them?' Chloe said, popping the sunglasses off her head. 'My mam got them for me. Here, try them on.'

The man took a step back, shrinking as though his bones had turned to powder.

'Suit yourself,' she replied, perching them back on her nose. 'But can you honestly tell me these aren't the epitome of *cool*?'

The poor man retreated even farther, unsure if *cool* was something he wanted to be. A creamy drool leaked through the corner of his mouth. Eyes were lifeless prosthetics as he lifted an arm and pointed over Chloe's shoulder. There was nothing remarkable there that she could see. Chloe waited for the man to explain himself but he seemed incapable of the simplest speech.

'What's over there?' she asked. 'Isn't that where your church is?'

'Carol,' he said, directing his finger towards Chloe's sunglasses.

'Who's Carol?'

'Come now,' Nora butted in, pinching him by the neck. 'You know that Carol won't be talking to these people, don't you?'

The man was guided away, as though he had embarrassed the whole village and was being sent to bed early without his supper.

'Steady on, Nora,' Chloe whispered. 'The poor lad was trying his best.'

Whoever *Carol* was, she wasn't going to feature heavily in this project. Not so long as Nora had her way.

The village resembled an abandoned building site. Buckets, farming tools, and sodden clumps of wood and other debris had gathered in its centre, piled together like some avant-garde art installation.

There was scarce space between the cottages to even sidle between them. Tangled clots of briars filled in the gaps. No effort had been made to make this plot of mud any less miserable. Their homes were perhaps too poky to fit anything other than their bodies, and so their possessions were thrown by their doors like rubbish waiting to be collected. The whole scene was enough to darken one's spirit. To live there must have been to know no light at all. Even the sun could only do so much without colour or laughter.

The girl from the field had sided with the other children.

There was no telling which child belonged to which parent or what the blood bonds were between them, though it was safe to assume that everyone was related in some way. It was difficult to identify even the children's genders as they were all dressed the same. They lay on the ground, picking at stones, basking lazily in the low sun like opium addicts. They all looked so similar, but only one of them had those dark eyes. Such was the sternness of her pudgy little face that it made her smile of earlier seem like a false memory.

Their isolation had taken its irreparable damage on these people, undermining more than the physical. Some of them watched Ben with glassy eyes, their mouths hanging agape, like puppets abandoned by their masters.

'Are you good to get started?' Chloe asked. 'We don't have much time left before nightfall and I've got a survey to run.'

'You're going off by yourself?' Ben asked.

'Well, if muggins over there wants us gone tomorrow, I've no choice, do I?'

Ben frowned at the prospect of Chloe being on her own. There were too many unknown elements and an underlying sense of uncertainty that hadn't fallen silent since the tripwire tolled in their arrival.

'Don't worry,' she said assuredly. 'I'll be fine. I know exactly where I'm going and I'll be back before it gets dark. The church isn't far and—' here she leaned into his ear '—I want to check out that cottage we saw.'

'Just be careful,' he said.

'Ms Coogan,' she replied, with her chin held high, 'is perfectly able to take care of herself. Go get your stories and I'll go do the important stuff.'

★ ★ ★

The stable, as promised, was sheltered. Someone had recently carpeted its earth with shards of bark, soft to the step, with a rotted moistness that Ben could taste. Two open frames admitted sufficient daylight. Nets of ivy draped over their plinths and clawed their hooks through a ceiling of branches bound in wire and misty web. In lieu of a door there was a wooden board that Ben had to shift out of place to get in and out. Its base had been a mass of woodlice. Some fleeing for their lives, others upturned with their myriad legs squirming at nothing.

'Okay,' Ben said to himself, taking the recorder from his rucksack, running a finger across its chunky buttons like a knight polishing his steel, 'here we go.'

History demanded a respect for certain antiquities, and so Ben recorded his interviews on cassette. Unlike the newfangled digital recorders, his plastic block had a history of its own and had come through it with no shortage of nicks and scratches. It was strange to think that something so dated – this relic from the Nineties with its battery lid taped in place – had to be kept hidden in case it spooked his interviewees.

'Testing, testing,' Ben spoke into his recorder, and then rewound it back.

Testing, testing.

'Interview one,' he said, with one eye on the stable door to make sure no one was coming. 'Interviewee's name is Mary. Surnames don't seem to factor into their identities. It's highly possible that the close-knit nature of their community has unified them into a single clan, free from any divisive labels. Mary was the first woman to engage with us upon our arrival to the village.'

Click.

If Sparling had ever doubted Ben's professionalism, a few more lines like that would quickly convince him otherwise.

'Okay, Benny Boy,' he said to himself, steadying his nerves, 'time to get to work.'

5

'Now, Mary,' Ben began, smiling as though they were old friends sitting down between a pot of tea. 'Thanks for volunteering to go first. I honestly don't know what I would do without you.'

The woman nodded. Her fingers fidgeted as if trying to loosen an invisible knot.

Ben's jacket was propped on the ground between them. His recorder was tucked discreetly under its collar like a spy behind enemy lines. Mary sat across from him, within the square of sunlight that lit up the stable, making her freckles glow like embers. The board had been pulled across the door, if only to keep the wasp out.

'I'm going to ask you a few questions, okay?' Ben said softly to put her at ease. 'I'd like to hear about your life and any stories that you would consider *a part* of your village. And you don't have to answer anything that you don't feel comfortable with. Hopefully, you might even enjoy yourself.'

Again she bowed her head. *This might be easier than*

expected. Outside the stable, all was quiet, like a sky at rest before a storm. Tír Mallacht was such a joyless place. Even the children – those whose sparks should burn the brightest – seemed to speak only in whispers.

'Have you lived here all of your life?' Ben asked.

'I have.'

He waited for more. It didn't come. Mary smiled at him, content that she had answered his question correctly. *Top marks, Mary.*

'And tell me,' he continued, unfazed, 'what was it like growing up here?'

She thought long and hard. Twice her lips parted soundlessly before she spoke. 'When we're young we don't know very much, I think. We do what our parents ask of us. It's always been important to do as you're told, especially when you're a child. And then, when you're older you understand it more. You appreciate why you do it.'

'It's all part of growing up, isn't it?' Ben said, not quite understanding her answer.

'Yes, I suppose it is.'

'The summers here must be lovely?' he asked. 'Other parts of the country can be so loud. You know, so busy all the time what with all the cars and people.'

She just blinked at him. If Mary knew what a car was, she had no strong feelings towards them. It was a test. Ben wanted to disturb the waters slightly to see if anything moved. He had to know if they were as preserved as Sparling thought them to be.

'Have *you* ever left this village, Mary?'

'No,' she replied, shaking her head, eyes shifting to the open frame. 'We don't leave here. My children will spend their lives in Tír Mallacht, as I have done and as did my parents before me.'

'And why don't you leave? There's nothing stopping you, is there?'

'We have everything we need here in the village,' she said, feigning a weak smile no more convincing than the tone of her voice. 'Everyone is safe so long as we stay here, and that's what matters.'

'Safe?' Ben asked, puzzled. 'Everyone is safe from what, Mary?'

The woman looked everywhere except at Ben. Lips pressed together so tight that they disappeared entirely. Her fingers tugged harder on that imaginary knot. It was a bafflingly childish reaction, as if by averting her eyes, Ben – and the question – would cease to exist.

'Where'd your friend go?' she asked, quite obviously changing the subject.

'I think she was going to look at your church,' he replied, 'or whatever's left of it.'

'She shouldn't go there,' Mary whispered.

'And why's that?'

Again, silence. Ben had perhaps naively expected Mary to talk at length with the slightest push. She had understood the questions. She deliberated over her answers. And still she had given him nothing. Whatever information the woman had hidden away, she stored it in a closed book, its binding sealed with a padlock.

'Were there any stories that you were told when you were growing up?' he asked, leaning forward. 'Any stories that you still tell the children?'

'What kind of stories?' she asked innocently.

'Oh, I don't know. I noticed that all the boys here wear dresses. In many parts of the country this was to fool the fairy folk. The changelings preferred to steal away the boys, you see.'

'I wouldn't know anything about that.'

'You don't believe in fairies?' he probed.

'No.'

'Are you religious?'

'No,' she replied again. 'The church hasn't been used for prayer since before I was born.'

'Do you know what happened here that made the people lose their faith?'

'No.'

'Something must have happened, Mary. The church wouldn't simply abandon its parishioners without a reason.'

'You ask too many questions,' she snapped, her agitation breaking out in beads of sweat. 'You shouldn't have come here. There are some things that you shouldn't know. Nobody should.'

'What kind of *things* do you mean?'

'We live here because we have to,' she replied, clearly frustrated by Ben's line of questioning. 'We have no choice. Everyone is safer that way. I don't think I want to do this anymore. Can we stop now? I'd like to stop.'

So much for his *way with people*, as Sparling had put it. Ben should have known better than to upset her. He had thrown too many closed-ended questions at the woman and she had taken them like a biblical stoning.

'I'm sorry, Mary,' he said, and he genuinely meant it.

An awkward, clenched energy fell between them. Ben had made this mistake in the past; a lesson learned back in his academic heyday but one since forgotten. The woman had locked down her defences.

'What can you tell me about the bells?'

'I don't know anything about any bells,' she replied, her fists now balled up tight.

'You didn't hear them ring earlier?' he pressed.

'No, I didn't.'

'Is someone preventing you from leaving?' he asked. 'You can tell me, Mary. Maybe I can help you.'

She rose to her feet. 'I'd like to stop now.'

'Can I just ask you a—'

'No,' she interjected, turning to walk away.

Ben was worried he had offended the woman. He stepped over to the stable door and drew aside the board to let her out. Mary had been his star player. He had had such high hopes for her. But she wasn't off the field yet. There was that one question that Sparling had asked him to throw into the mix. Even if Ben returned to him with a report full of blank pages, he could say that he had at least answered that.

'Thanks for your time, Mary,' he said.

'You're welcome,' she replied, but her face betrayed how she really felt.

It was now or never. What was it that Sparling had called it, *the creeper*?

'One last thing, before you leave, Mary,' he asked, 'have you ever heard of...'

'Stop,' she shouted into his face, sending him toppling back against the doorframe. 'You have to stop this. No more questions.'

And with that the woman was gone, leaving Ben to wipe her spittle from his eyes. He was out of practice, embarrassingly so, like a musician who had bounded up on stage and forgotten how to hold his guitar. He had chased away the one person who had actually shown him some hospitality, and he hadn't recorded a single worthwhile answer.

The villagers' dress and lifestyle fitted the mould that Sparling had cast for them. But it was ludicrous to imagine that not one of these people had ever ventured beyond so small and socially limiting a village. Even the best-behaved dog could be lured outside its master's gate by natural curiosity.

Ben pictured Sparling's face frozen in an expression of abject disappointment. It was as he remembered, only that staged little smile of his was dragged down on either side like a sad clown. The truth would come soon enough, and the doctor would pay his fee whether this was his Atlantis or not.

When Ben returned out to the open, he couldn't see Mary anywhere. The villagers who dallied around the common – those who had reluctantly agreed to being interviewed – were whispering amongst themselves like prisoners planning a jailbreak. They had obviously watched Mary storm out of the stable, looking none too pleased. Luckily, the wasp wasn't around. He was mean enough without giving him a reason.

'Okay,' Ben whispered, slapping his cheeks, trying to focus on the task at hand. 'Let's try that again.'

He counted nine in all – five women and four men – orbiting the same worn circle of clay.

'Now then,' Ben loudly announced, 'who'd like to go next?'

They huddled in closer to one another, protecting the weakest amongst them, whichever one that was. Such was their herd mentality that they all behaved the same and looked equally as feeble. Mary's abrupt departure had obviously taken its effect on them.

Ben didn't have time for this. He barged into their circle like a comet, obstructing one of the women, sending the others splintering away. She stretched her shawl tight around her skull, staring down at his boots, hoping perhaps that some miraculous means of escape would sprout by his feet. He hated bullying his way into their lives. But if they would only talk to him, they would see that he meant them no harm.

'Would *you* like to go next?' Ben asked, stooping low to peer under her hood.

He was surprised to discover that she was probably younger than Chloe. Her eyes were striking; glossy copper laced with reams of golden thread that snared the sunlight. The woman's youth presented him with a possible advantage. A community's elders generally safeguarded their oral history, but maybe what Ben needed now was a little innocence and hopefully a little more honesty.

'Please,' he whispered, to which she bowed twitchily, her hands tugging her hood even lower as she stole those first steps towards the stable.

Ben propped the board in place, scattering the last remaining woodlice; those too at home in the stable's doorway to ever consider moving elsewhere. The woman stood by the chairs, peering around as though the building was somehow strange to her, like a fledgling fresh from the nest seeing the world for the first time.

He invited her to take a seat. She accepted with another timid flurry of nods.

'You can take off your hood, if you like?' Ben said to her,

gesturing to it with a wave of his hand, trying to keep it casual and friendly. He was determined not to repeat that woeful opening act with Mary in the leading role.

She slipped the shawl back onto her shoulders, scattering Ben's mental notes like a sudden gust of wind. The cloth that she held so eagerly had concealed the woman's disfigurement. Her chin and mouth, and the eyes and nose, were without fault, in that they appeared unaffected by the common blood shared between the others. But her skull shrank back above the eyes as though her forehead had never fully formed. Behind her cheeks it caved inward. No ears had grown, but she could obviously still hear. Her head was hairless save for a few lank wisps already faded to grey. Despite her obvious trepidation, the woman's lips attempted a smile; one that wilted before it could ever fully bloom.

'Now,' Ben began, keeping his surprise in check, not wanting to upset her, 'before we begin, can you please tell me your name?' His words barely kept their balance on his tongue.

Her gaze seemed to pass right through him. 'Nu,' she answered, as though the memory of it just came to her.

'Nu?' Ben replied, hastily reassembling his composure like the seasoned interviewer he once thought himself to be. 'Is that short for Nuala by any chance?'

The girl shook her head and stared down towards where the recorder was hidden out of sight. She edged her feet away from it. There was no way she could have known it was there.

'I'm going to ask you a few questions, Nu. Is that okay?'

'Yes,' she replied wistfully, those fiery eyes still burning a hole in Ben's jacket. 'That's okay.'

'Is it true that nobody in your village ever leaves?'

'Who's nobody?'

It was with that response Ben realised that maybe youth and innocence weren't the answers to his problems.

'I mean, sorry, let me rephrase that. Do any of the villagers, *like you*, ever leave Tír Mallacht?'

'*Like me*? No.'

'And why is that?' Ben asked, silently pleading for an answer.

'Why would *I* leave?' she responded. 'I don't look right. I would never be chosen.'

Ben had hoped that, given her society, her appearance would have exerted less influence over her happiness in life. But the poor woman had obviously been made more than aware of it by those who populated her tiny, curious world.

Ben felt horrible for having asked her to remove the hood. He counted himself lucky that Aoife had been born without any complications. Jess and her family might have pinned his absenteeism on that reason alone, as though he had ordered a child and didn't like the look of her when she arrived. It wouldn't have diminished his love for her. Ben was better than that, or so he liked to believe.

'I'm sorry,' he said, resolving to steer the conversation elsewhere. 'We can talk about something else.'

'Okay.'

'Is there anything you would *like* to talk about?'

That familiar hush retuned to the stable. *Keep it going, Benny Boy.*

'Were there any stories that you were told when you were a child?'

Nu shook her head and peered up at the ceiling as though the whole interview process wasn't holding her interest.

'Is there anything that you're afraid of, Nu?' he asked, playing a wildcard question to lure back her attention.

'What are *you* afraid of?' she parried.

Ben mused over the question for a moment. 'I don't think I'm afraid of anything, Nu.'

'That must be nice.'

'I suppose it is,' he agreed.

'You should leave here.'

'Why do you think I should leave?' Ben asked, surprised by the sudden solemnness of her voice.

She considered him sadly and shook her head again, deciding against saying whatever just crossed her mind; an idea crushed just as it was hatching. What wasn't she telling him? If he could extend a bridge of friendship between them, then maybe she would let the truth pass over it.

'I like your cloak,' he said. 'Did you make that yourself?'

Nu tilted her head down to examine what she was wearing, revealing to Ben her misshapen skull of frayed hair. The shawl's umber wool was coarsely knitted, with gaping holes from its shoulders to her waist, where a tattered skirt hung down past the knee. Her bare legs were bruised, and no part of her was clean.

'I like it too,' she replied, now staring at him. 'I don't like wearing black.'

Ben couldn't imagine Nu varying from the brown palette that coloured the villagers' garments overall like a dirty rain. The whole place was funereal enough without introducing black into their wardrobes.

'I'm not a fan myself,' he replied, deciding it was time to

mine a little deeper. 'Maybe you can tell me what you know about the creeper? Is that a name you've heard spoken here before?'

Nu suddenly stood to her feet and mashed them into the bark. 'It's been nice talking to you.'

She didn't seem upset. It was as though some inaudible whistle had concluded their conversation, drawing her elsewhere.

'Wouldn't you like to talk a little longer?' he asked, unable to hide his disappointment at her sudden dismissal.

'No.'

Nu was already walking away, leaving Ben to admit to his second successive defeat in record time. *Whatever you thought you had, Benny Boy, you've lost it.* Had she answered any of his questions? He had been so flustered by her appearance that he couldn't string his memories together. Ben followed her to the door, where she secured her shawl back around her head and left without another word.

He leaned against the wall, watching his interviewees resume their defensive positions, eyeing him like an executioner standing beside a basket of fresh heads. Two to be precise, with a contract for more.

The hours that followed were some of the most frustrating and perplexing of Ben's life. His thesis supervisor had once championed him for his interview techniques. But if the man could see him now, he certainly wouldn't be so keen to recommend him for any more projects. Ben felt like a fading pop star clinging to an old hit.

Tír Mallacht was precisely the kind of community whose

stories survived through the oral tradition. There was an unschooled understanding of the written word, but none who Ben spoke to could decipher very much beyond their own name. Any appreciation of the past and their own identities therefore relied on speaking about them, and yet they were each so tight-lipped. They were either ignorant of their history or else they simply didn't want to share it with someone whose blood wasn't home-brewed in the village.

Every answer was so terse and guarded. Often they would mutter no more than a *yes* or a *no*, and those bold enough to elaborate did so with rehearsed caution, choosing their words carefully and ultimately telling Ben nothing. No one could clarify why the church had been deconsecrated. According to Sparling's many maps it was the only building of note in the area. Surely somebody would have preserved the facts of the matter.

One woman – a few years Mary's senior, with skin like cracked eggshell – was so hindering as to deny knowing that Tír Mallacht even had a church.

'Are you being serious?' Ben had said to her, giving up on the interview in that moment. 'You've never, in all of your life, seen the church? It's not far. I can take you, if you want?'

He didn't get much out of her after that.

They gave him morsels and all these morsels were the same – unappetising, bland, and nothing like the knowledge that Sparling was so hungry for. It was possible that they had sat down together and practised how to speak without saying anything. Maybe this was why Mary had interfered. She hadn't helped Ben in the slightest. Instead she had chosen the best thespians in the village and all of them were hardened method actors, never breaking character for a second.

The creeper proved to be a conversational kill switch. And so Ben learned to play that card close to his chest until it was all he had left. Some interviewees upped and walked away at the mention of it. Others stared him down in a way that was just odd. It was in the widening of the eyes or in the slightest quiver of the lips, like a facial tic they weren't aware of and thus didn't know to conceal.

In those moments – with the creeper's name fresh in the air – it was as though another had stepped within those four walls; the mere shadow of a presence, but one dark enough to cut every conversation short.

As fittingly *creepy* as these reactions were for Ben's report, his frustration had evolved into something far uglier – despair. For all he knew, Sparling had other big-money projects planned for the future. It was doubtful that Ben would qualify as one of his *perfect candidates* after this shitshow.

Whenever he left the stable, Ben never once saw the wasp. As much as he loathed the sight of him, his absence was more than a little disconcerting. Chloe was out there alone. What if he had followed her? Ben tried to suppress his worries but at times they felt like the strongest part of him. Their voices overpowering the meek cries of reason and rationality. She was more than able to take care of herself. She had told him as much.

The last man he spoke to was especially anxious. He was constantly peering outside, speaking obsessively about the daylight. He seemed to be the youngest of the bunch. Ben had enquired after his age but the man wasn't entirely sure; he was confident only of the fact that he was no longer a child. *No arguing with that.* He was tall as the wasp but built like an Eighties action figure. *He-Man* sprang to Ben's mind.

Every toy in that line shared the same ripped torso mould, as though *Castle Grayskull* was a multi-storey gym. Men of his strength were never given a day's leave; not when there was land to be turned. He had a chin like a knobbly potato, and a kind glimmer to his eyes that had caught Ben by surprise. His head was a mass of black curls that he was constantly scratching at as he spoke.

'I love the summer,' he said earnestly. 'There's more daylight. We're coming into the winter soon and that'll be tough. You'll see now, the sun won't be long disappearing. It makes for too short a day to get any work done.'

There were only so many yawns that Ben could stifle. He was surprised the recorder's reels hadn't knotted themselves into oblivion out of sheer boredom. *The furthering of knowledge is our ultimate goal here.* And this villager just confirmed that there is more daylight in summer than there is in winter.

'The night isn't so bad,' Ben replied, if only for the sake of saying something.

'Not much to be doing inside,' the man said, 'except wait for the dawn, I suppose, and keep the little ones entertained.'

'Are there no animals or livestock around that need looking after?' Ben asked. 'I didn't see any on the walk here.'

'Oh, you wouldn't. They're kept a fair distance from the village. And sure, you'd hear the sheep with the bells around their necks if they wandered too close.'

'The sheep wear bells?' Ben echoed. 'And what's the reason for that?'

'It's so the blind can find them,' the man replied.

'I'm sorry, what? Did you say the blind?'

'Aye, that's right. The blind tend to the animals at night.'

'Okay,' Ben said, jolting forward as if someone just pinched him, 'and tell me why do—'

Ding-a-ling-a-ling-a-ling!

The sudden blast of noise nearly knocked him off his stool. *Another goddamn bell.*

Its ring was rapid and constant, like a town crier calling for everyone's attention.

The interviewee bolted up from his chair as though the bell had summoned him home for dinner. Judging by his eagerness, it must have been a whole lot tastier than boiled cabbage. The man could probably lift an iron cauldron and drink it back like a mug of soup. He threw aside Ben's makeshift door as if it were made of flimsy cardboard, not bothering to close it behind him.

'Thanks for that,' Ben called out, wiping the weariness from his eyes. 'Good talk.'

Beyond the drapes of hanging ivy, the sinking sun bled through a light scattering of lavender cloud. It must have been approaching six o'clock.

When Ben returned outside, he saw the man responsible for the racket, pacing around in a circle, constantly twisting his head towards the sun. Any villagers that had scarpered during Ben's interviews were returning. They dragged their feet like mindless bodies enslaved by the bell's hollow toll.

Then he heard the slamming of wood on stone. Ben hadn't noticed until then, but every cottage had those window hatches, like the two they had passed on their approach to the village. Their creak and knock echoed from all sides. Meanwhile, men and women were dashing back and forth, sharing baskets of food and weighty jugs of water.

'What's going on, Benny Boy?'

Chloe had just rounded the corner into the village.

The sun cast her long silhouette across the path as another shutter was heard to lock in place. Ben jogged over to meet her halfway. The sight of her brought a smile to his face that he'd forgotten the feel of.

'What's everyone doing?' she asked.

'They're locking down their homes,' he replied.

'They're doing what now?'

'I think it must be the night. They don't want to stay outside after dark.'

'Why?' she asked. 'What happens when the sun goes down?'

They looked back towards the nest of cottages where the last few men were exchanging words.

'I guess we'll find out soon enough,' Ben replied.

The villagers had sold themselves as the most unimaginative people he had ever sat with and yet clearly there was so much they hadn't told him. There were rules and traditions here that he had never encountered.

'Hello!' a voice said, causing them to flinch forward in surprise.

The child from earlier had crept up behind them.

'Jesus, kid,' Chloe said, 'you have got to stop doing that.'

She skipped in front of them, dancing to a song only she could hear. Her eyes retained that mischievous glint, all the darker now that the sun had sunk behind the hedgerow. Unlike the others, the girl didn't seem troubled by their impending curfew.

Ben glanced back towards the village. Talking to the

children had been strictly forbidden and he expected the wasp to come running at any moment.

'He's coming,' the child said with that devilish smile of hers.

'And who's that?' Ben asked, peering over his shoulder.

'I'm not allowed to talk about him. That's how he finds you.'

'Is that so?' Chloe said, grinning back at her, playing along with the game. 'And what's his name?'

The child spun around in a pirouette, enjoying the attention, holding the skirt of her dress as she pranced around on grubby toes.

'We don't know,' she whispered. 'Nobody knows what he used to be called.'

Ben couldn't believe his luck. After all those staid interviews, this child was giving him something he could use.

'Three times you see him,' she said. 'The first night he's far, far away. And then the next night he's closer. So close that you can see him, and he can see you. And then, on the third night his big ugly face is at your window. The fourth night is your last one, because then *uh-oh*.'

'*Uh-oh*.' Chloe laughed. 'What does *uh-oh* mean?'

'That's when the creeper kills you.'

The wasp came dashing towards them, his spindly limbs carrying him like a spider. He barged right through Ben and Chloe and grabbed the child in his arms. His face turned to them. Gone was the frown and the disdain that defined it. The man looked afraid.

'What did she say to you?' he shouted.

'Nothing,' Ben replied, worried that they were in all kinds

of trouble. 'She came up to *us*. We were just standing here, minding our own business.'

'What did you tell them?' he asked the girl, on his knees, holding her head in his hands.

'She didn't tell us anything,' Chloe said. 'Relax, she was just dancing for us.'

The man stared at her, searching for some proof of the lie, but Chloe gave nothing away. He took the child up in his arms and started back towards the cottages.

The sky over Tír Mallacht was darkening.

'I don't want to see you again,' he called back to them. 'You should never have come here.'

6

Ben and Chloe stood side by side, arms kissing in the cold. Nobody so much as looked at them. The night was the villagers' sole concern.

Families were cocooning indoors, slamming hatches and squeaking bolts. Like any procedure it was fast, efficient, more muscle memory than conscious thought. Everybody knew their role and words were few amongst them, whispered in confidence, like fugitives so long on the run that the chase was all they knew.

'It's a bit early for bedtime, isn't it?' Ben whispered, secretly fidgeting with a clasp on Chloe's backpack; nervous fingers always find a way to keep busy.

Try as he might to keep it light, the whole scene was eerie enough to keep them from drifting apart. It was maddening to think that not a single one of his interviewees thought to mention *this*. Ben now realised he might have been asking the wrong questions.

Adults went about tossing vegetables and anything unwanted from their doorways. Their combined waste soon ringed the common, left to decay under the moonlight or else fatten the belly of those animals that only awaken to see the stars. Nobody had offered anything in the way of food or shelter. Maybe they were both in short supply, much like their kindness.

Ben had thought the Tír Mallachts to be a dysfunctional people, secretive for seclusion's sake. But now he suspected that something more insidious was at play. Superstitious shackles bound them to this sorry existence.

No child was seen to complain. There were no tearful pleas for a later bedtime. Ben thought of Aoife and how she would haggle like a hostage negotiator, always trying to free a few more minutes. Sad as it was, there were weeks when a little extra time before bed was all he could afford to give her.

But that's why he was here. This project of Sparling's would change everything.

The last door slammed.

A calmness fell over the village like a black sheet of silk. Faint, razor lines of light framed some of its doorways. But otherwise the darkness there was unbroken; the air crystal and clean. Within the cottages' stone walls there were no voices or music. Long was the night and they would spend it waiting for the dawn.

Tír Mallacht seemed more sinister in the silence. Ben could feel the hairs rising one by one, on his neck, his scalp, and across both arms as he drew them in tighter. No matter where they pitched their tent, it would never be far enough from the sight of all those moonlit tombs. He imagined shelves lining their walls; adults and children stacked atop one another, dead until the sunrise breathed fresh life into their bodies.

Chloe slipped the rucksack from her shoulders and

rummaged through its front pocket. The hood of her jacket flopped over as she crouched down, hiding her head in a mass of fur. A hand extended to Ben, holding one of the slender Maglite torches they had bought courtesy of Sparling's envelope. He twisted it on and a pillar of light extended through the dark. Ben waved his hand over it, half-hoping to feel some warmth. The night was only going to get colder.

No matter what the hours ahead held in store, the darkness and the distance colluded to trap them in Tír Mallacht until morning. Ben shone his light around the meagre world within its reach. There was nothing else.

It was one night, that's all. He was glad now that the wasp wanted them gone so soon.

'I found us somewhere to camp,' Chloe said as her torch lit up beside him. 'It's not far but it's far enough from that crowd.' She turned her light towards the village. 'We just have to go back the way we came, and then east for a bit, in the direction of the church.'

'If we leave before dawn, we can avoid meeting anyone,' Ben added.

'I was thinking the same. Hopefully the dark will keep them locked up until we're halfway back to the car. Miserable old fuckers, weren't they?'

'You should try talking to them.'

Stars glinted like eyes in the sky's black shawl. Brittle stones scraped beneath their feet, echoing across the emptiness, and though Ben listened for the step of another, theirs were the only clumsy feet in Tír Mallacht that night.

'How did the interviews go?' Chloe asked.

Straight in with *that* question.

Ben knew he had failed to hold up his part of the contract. But he tried not to blame himself. Even a hard-boiled interrogator wouldn't have wrung any information out of Mary's line-up. They held their secrets like a family grudge, speaking only to waste what precious little time remained until sundown.

'Not so great,' Ben replied, teeth chattering. 'I'm guessing the kid warned them we were coming. I don't understand what they're hiding. I only wish I knew more about this creeper thing that Sparling asked for. I've never heard of it.'

'Our friend gave you everything you need. What was it again? *Three times you see him*,' she said, impersonating the child's voice, holding the torch up to her face. '*The first night he's far, far away. And then the next night he's closer.*'

'Don't forget about the *uh-oh*,' he said.

'Oh, the *uh-oh* is the best part.'

Ben's flat laugh sounded as phoney as it felt. No amount of joking could hide the fact that his interviews had been an absolute disaster.

They reached the point where they had followed the child, where the archway into the field was now sealed with darkness. Ben rubbed his scalp, remembering the feel of *that* branch. Losing his hair was like losing a helmet. Everything seemed to leave a scratch or a dent on him.

If only they had kept on the path. They might have reached the villagers before they had time to prep their welcoming party. What if the bells had beckoned them to their dressing rooms to get in costume, deforming their faces with putty and frantically leafing through their lines?

As they climbed that steep, curving hill, the moon broke

into sight like a circle cut into black velvet, revealing the white within. Ben was too preoccupied to appreciate it. His mind was rolling out a never-ending list of questions that he could have asked differently.

'Listen,' Chloe snapped, throwing her hand in front of him.

Ben startled back on the spot. He crossed his torchlight over hers. The darkness closed in on them from either side. Twice the beam wasn't twice as bright.

'What is it?' he asked.

'How am I supposed to know?' she replied irritably.

'Is that a person?'

Whoever it was, they were standing perfectly still in the centre of the pathway.

'It's a woman,' Chloe said. 'Look at her shawl. What do you reckon she's doing out in the dark? Do you think the others have forgotten about her?'

Ben edged a little closer. 'No, look at her eyes.'

Chloe slapped a hand to her mouth. The scream must been right there, on her lips, but she'd caught it. He couldn't blame her. Even Ben's nerves had crawled up his spine with the quick, heavy steps of a beetle.

His knuckles cracked in the silence as they tightened around the torch. He cast its light across the woman's face. Her blindness glistened like frost. She didn't react. She couldn't have.

'Are you okay?' he asked, to which her head twitched to face him.

She approached them slowly – like an artist's sketch forming in the torchlight, ageing with each step as the ravages of time came into focus. The eyes were a horror to behold, drawn to them without sight, and yet looking nowhere else.

'What's wrong with her?' Chloe asked.

The woman cackled at the question, causing them both to wince as the constancy of her advance drew her ever closer.

'The blind take care of the animals,' Ben whispered, so low that the old woman couldn't possibly have heard him.

'The blind?' she tittered gummily. 'Don't pity me for my eyes, boy.' The woman inhaled through her nostrils with rapturous glee. 'There's nowhere that he won't find you. The night isn't yours anymore.'

Even their torches seemed to falter as those words were spoken.

Ben and Chloe parted to let the woman pass between them. She dragged her feet through the dirt, shuffling with the shortest steps as she dissolved into the night. They stared towards the ebbing sound of her laughter, waiting for the silence – and some elusive sense of safety – to return.

'Come on,' Chloe said, shivering, 'the field isn't far.'

'Are we not going to talk about *that*?' Ben asked, stepping in front of her.

'No chance. I need to forget *that* happened if I'm ever to sleep again.'

Ben couldn't stand still. He was pacing back and forth between the walls on either side, like a bird bouncing against its cage. 'This place is messed up.'

Chloe just nodded.

'But hey,' he said, realising how uneasy she had become, 'it's not all bad.'

'How so?' she asked, eyebrows furrowing.

'Oh, come on.' He chuckled. 'Blind shepherds? Don't think for a second that this isn't going in the report.'

'You're obsessed with this fucking report.'

Ben spread out his arms. 'It's why we're in this shithole, isn't it?'

'Come on,' she said angrily, 'I'm hungry and tired, and you're making me cranky.'

He held up his hands in surrender. 'My apologies, Ms Coogan.'

Chloe picked up the pace. Ben's calves ached as he tried to keep by her side. She had obviously dropped her brave front somewhere along the path. It was kinder to keep her distracted than draw attention.

'Did you find that church you were after?' he asked, breathless already.

Chloe likely guessed what he was doing and followed his lead.

'I sure did,' she replied. 'It's in good nick, even though its roof is missing and the old brambles could do with a bit of a trimming. But I've been in worse. There's some weird shit there that I think might interest our boy Sparling.'

'What kind of weird shit?'

'Oh, does Mr Historian have a sudden interest in archaeology now?' she replied, nudging into him as they walked.

'I do when *weird shit* is involved.'

'Well, all of the religious iconography has been desecrated,' she said. 'There were carvings of angels on its walls and someone's taken the time to chip all their faces off. And by the altar I found the arse of a stone cross. It must have been a serious size back in its day, I'd say. That's also been destroyed.'

'Jesus,' Ben said, rubbing his cold palms together.

'I'm sure if he was there, then he got hacked into pieces too.'

'So they tore the building apart and then abandoned it?' he asked.

'Oh, they didn't abandon it. Someone still goes there.'

'That's not what I was told. The villagers don't even like to talk about the church. Actually, they don't really like to talk about anything. Not to me anyway.'

Chloe aimed her torch over the wall. They hadn't strayed too far from where they first set foot on the path that afternoon, or so Ben thought. He tried to picture the map in his head to fathom their whereabouts, but the dark was too disorientating. It hemmed them in on all sides like a tunnel in the catacombs.

'I think this is it,' Chloe announced.

Ben lugged his feet over to the wall. 'Can't we just camp anywhere?'

'Check it out,' she said, on her tiptoes, reaching an arm around his neck. '*This* is where we're camping!'

The grass in the field had been trimmed like a haphazard haircut, leaving taller tufts here and there. Maybe that's why Chloe chose it. Most of the grasses in Tír Mallacht grew nearly as tall as her. It was a poky tract compared to what they'd seen that day, no more than a quarter acre. A grove of trees – skeletal in the torchlight – loomed in its corner. Other than that, it was surrounded by larger fields that stretched long past the reach of their torches.

'It's beautiful,' he said wryly.

'Shut up.' She giggled. 'Let's get ourselves organised so we can finally eat some food. I'm starving.'

Chloe assumed the responsibility of pitching their tent and didn't delay in rolling out its parts on the grass. She was one of the odd souls who seemed to genuinely enjoy it, like those precocious kids back in school with their heads buried in a puzzle book, as if life weren't challenging enough. The packaging boasted of the tent's *ease of assembly*. But Ben had his doubts. It was the most expensive one in the shop and Chloe wouldn't settle for anything less.

'That's the one,' she had said the second she laid eyes on it.

Ben had only known her for a few hours, but he guessed that her life's path was littered with snap decisions.

'I've spent too many nights camping at digs,' she had told him. 'I'm done sleeping in polyester coffins. We're getting the fancy one, okay? No arguments.'

Ben was given the job of collecting deadwood for their fire. Not the most demanding of missions, but this might be the first thing he did right all day.

'Okay, you bastards,' Chloe said, standing over the umpteen poles and folded bits of nylon strewn around her, 'it's time to build us a home. Give me some space, Benny Boy. I'm about to work magic unlike anything you've ever seen.'

This was exactly what she seemed to need – a familiar task to busy her mind.

'It's all yours,' he replied, chuckling as he walked away.

Ben had been a finger tap away from deleting Sparling's email that day in the coffee shop. This was a whole lot more interesting than what he had grown used to – work, sleep, repeat, with sporadic intervals of existential crisis just to make sure that the sleep part never came easy.

As an only child, his parents had groomed him for success, backing Ben one hundred per cent like the only horse on the racetrack. He was brainwashed by propaganda portraying him as some moneyed historian, travelling the world for the *History Channel*; a detective of the past, solving age-old riddles and discovering lost treasures. It was heading that way for a while. Then that horse they had gambled all their savings on started crashing through hurdles and veering into the railings.

A branch snapped under Ben's foot. He guided his torch skyward where skinny tree arms stretched overhead. Their fingers fanned apart just enough to let a glimmer of moonlight wink through. It was years since he had been in the countryside at night-time. He'd forgotten the quietness and that heightened sensitivity – the sound of the softest breeze and the crunch of leaves underfoot, curled up like balls of tinfoil.

He gathered whatever sticks he could find into a mound. Ben could hear Chloe talking to herself across the stillness of the field. She was either reading the instructions aloud or conjuring a spell. The latter made more sense judging from the way she was waving her arms around. Within the light of her torch, the tent's frame was quickly taking shape.

'That should do it,' Ben whispered, dashing any dirt from his fingers.

He was standing stock-still – shining the light onto his pile, judging if he had enough – when he heard a branch crack behind him.

He froze.

Something was there, behind the trees. Ben listened, limbs set as they were.

Seconds passed. He looked over to Chloe, to the tent nearly erected.

Branches don't just snap from the cold.

Was it the blind woman from earlier? But the animals were

supposed to be on the other side of the village; not the mark of a great shepherd to wander off from her flock.

It could have been anything. A fox, a badger, even a fat mouse that had missed a step. Still, Ben listened, and still the night yielded not another sound.

'Benny Boy, what are you doing over there?' Chloe called out. 'I'll have this thing ready by the time you pick up a few sticks.'

It was nothing. He wouldn't tell her. She'd only worry.

'Sorry,' he replied, scooping the wood up in his arms, 'I'm all done here.'

The kindling cracked and split. Its flames bravely fended off the cold from their nest of stones. Ben and Chloe sat close enough to wave their fingers over it, as though it were a sleepless child craving constant attention. Oily shadows rippled around them, never settling on the crisp grass; rigid from the promise of a frost that was felt but not yet seen.

Chloe had laid down a scarf between them, patterned in mustards and navy blues with tassels on all four sides. On it they set their bread, tins of tuna, and a packet of sliced cheese. As their sojourn was to be but a single night, they now had more than they needed. The quantity as opposed to the quality was what mattered to the cold and famished.

Aoife would probably be asleep by now, divided from Ben by more than mere distance. He often wondered if she knew how much he thought about her and how he regretted all that he had already missed – those first moments that happened only once.

With Sparling's money he could finally make some changes. He could stop being so selfish all the time.

'What are you thinking about?' Chloe asked.

'Nothing really,' he lied, zoning back. 'Just this place and how strange it is. I didn't expect it to be so *quiet*, you know?'

'There's not much night life around these parts.' She chuckled. 'I'll give you that.'

'Did you get to check out that cottage we saw?'

'Yeah, but I couldn't get into it. Whoever boarded it up wanted it left alone. Oh, and lest I forget, there were some markings on its walls.' She reached over to her backpack and pulled out a sketchbook. 'Feast your eyes on those.'

They were symbols, or so Ben assumed them to be. He saw only shapes and dots like one of Aoife's finger paintings. Their meaning and significance, if they held any, was lost on him. Chloe watched his reaction and smiled.

'Same,' she said. 'I've no idea what they're about either. But hey, it gives us something to put in Sparling's report. I'll look into them when we get back to the city. Who knows, maybe they do mean something. It could be some secret code that explains why everyone here is odd as shit.'

'Would you not just take photographs?' Ben asked as he handed back the sketchbook.

'Oh, I did. I've my phone turned off to save the battery. I can't exactly trust you to guide us home tomorrow, can I? But I always like to draw what I find. It's more old-school, like you and your gammy tape recorder.'

'Hey,' he replied woundedly, 'that's a collector's item.'

Ben hunched forward, scooped the tuna onto his bread slice and carefully arranged the cheese atop it like fresh linen.

He held it before the fire, goading his stomach into growling. The first bite was enough to roll the eyes back into his skull. It was devoured in seconds and his hands began assembling another.

Chloe nodded her approval. 'Do you reckon you and...' Here she hesitated. 'What was her name, Tess?'

'Jessica,' he corrected her. 'She doesn't work on a ranch.'

'Do you reckon ye can work it out?'

Ben chewed thoughtfully over the question, 'There's really nothing *to* work out,' he replied, smiling sadly with a mouthful. 'We've absolutely nothing in common, except for Aoife.'

'Was there ever any talk of, you know, an abortion?' Chloe asked.

'No,' he replied, swallowing hard to keep the tuna from jumping up his throat.

If Ben had had his way, Aoife would never have been born. It made him queasy now to imagine his life had Jess listened to him; how pointless it could have been.

'What about you,' Ben asked, 'any *partner* on the scene?'

'No time. Besides, *partners* only slow me down.'

He let his eyes rest and angled in towards the fire, inviting its flames to fan his cheeks. Ben tried to ignore the cold and the dark, and any thoughts of that blind woman shambling silently towards them.

'Why archaeology?' he asked, sparking up any conversation to chase the phantoms away.

Chloe held up a finger that said *one moment, please* and nodded her head in synch with every chew. She must have taken an almighty bite just as he had spoken.

'My mam,' she replied, still working the food around her

mouth. 'She wasn't an archaeologist but she loved anything that was old. When I was a kid, she used to take me to antique fairs and we'd spend hours rooting through all the trinkets and treasures. It sounds dull, I know, but she used to make up all these crazy stories about whatever we found.'

A softness swelled on Chloe's face that Ben hadn't noticed before. Fond memories have a habit of awakening the light, even on the darkest of nights.

'What kind of stories?' he asked.

'Mad shit altogether.' She chuckled. 'There wasn't a knife or pistol that didn't belong to some pirate or cold-blooded highwayman. I loved it. And then, when it came to university, I thought maybe I could get some stories to tell her for a change. You know, to keep our tradition of bullshitting alive for another generation.'

'Was your dad into all that stuff as well?'

'Jesus, I couldn't tell you. He made a runner shortly after I was born. Fuck knows where he went. Probably Australia or somewhere. It was just me and my mam.'

Ben instantly regretted touching on *that* topic, though Chloe didn't seem all that bothered by it. Her dad was never there and so the man might as well have not existed.

'So you're going to be the next Lara Croft,' Ben said with mock earnestness.

'Eh?'

'She's probably the world's most famous archaeologist after Indiana Jones. I just assumed you'd modelled your life on a video game.'

'That's a pretty bold assumption.' She smiled. 'I doubt Lara Croft ever had to scratch through ten feet of mud with a trowel for weeks on end. But who knows, maybe if I get this

PhD the university will buy me a massive pair of fake tits so I can look the part.'

Ben choked a little, mid-swallow, on a crust of bread.

'Don't make them too big,' he said. 'I hear it's not good for your back.'

'As if that's ever bothered *you men* before,' she replied, tearing off some bread and throwing it at him. 'I reckon I'm too small to be lugging around a big pair of boobs anyway. I'll just get some booty shorts and a skimpy tank top, and stuff my bra with a few socks or something.'

Ben enjoyed the imagery more than he let on. As one prone to maddening bouts of worry and self-induced despair, Chloe's nonchalance had an almost calming effect on him. If only he'd had her around when Jess told him she was pregnant. Ben didn't sleep for a month after that bomb dropped. It still gave him nightmares occasionally.

He broke up some branches and propped them across the flames. His breath fogged heavy through the air now. Ben could feel the damp earth seeping into his jeans, chilling his skin like meat behind a butcher's counter. The day's clemency had been a rare stroke of luck but there was no escaping the cold once night had fallen.

'Do you remember when we were introducing ourselves back in the village?' he asked.

'Yeah,' she replied. 'What about it?'

'Did you hear something? I mean, like someone crying out?'

'Not that I can remember. A fair few of them were wailing around the place.'

Ben took a deep breath and frowned into the firepit. 'It was in one of the cottages. There was an old biddy guarding the door so I couldn't take a look. I just thought it sounded odd, that's all.'

'Maybe they're sick,' Chloe said. 'I didn't see a pharmacy anywhere so I'm guessing they're shy a few paracetamol. I wouldn't worry about it. They don't need our help here, trust me. This crowd is beyond saving.'

'I suppose,' he agreed. 'It's probably none of our business.'

Whenever Chloe's eyes looked elsewhere, Ben found himself glancing to where he had heard that crack, where the field was full of darkness and only the trees' highest branches reached above it, snapping at scraps of moonlight. He would listen more than look. There *had* been something there. A strong step had split that branch.

'I wonder how Sparling's going to react when he hears that we're leaving after one night,' he said, poking around some glowing ash with a twig.

'Sure listen, we'll achieve nothing by staying here for another day. They won't talk to you. They won't let me examine their homes. And I've already surveyed whatever I can, which wasn't a lot if I'm being honest. This place doesn't have much going for it. Sparling probably won't like the report we write up for him but it's still a report and we're still getting paid. And you did get something on that creeper thing he asked you for. That'll probably put a weird little smile on his face.'

They sat for a while, eyelids flagging, watching the campfire slowly dwindle. An inky blackness flooded in around them.

'Come on,' Chloe said, stretching her stiff legs, 'let's get some sleep. I'm wrecked and you look as though you're about to fall into the fire.'

'Best idea I've heard all day.'

Sparling's envelope had been packed with fifties to the tune of two thousand euro. Frugal spending wasn't an option that Chloe was willing to entertain. Ben had kept his unease hidden – some veiled attempt at appearing laid-back. Nothing could have been further from the truth. He was a poor man buying premium camping gear with someone else's money. But now, squeezing the silky softness of his sleeping bag as he rolled it out, he regretted nothing. It was comfier than his bed at home.

Chloe threw her torch down between their beds, splaying shadows across the tent's blue walls. It was dome-shaped like an igloo and could probably fit four or five people, so there was more than enough space for their rucksacks. Chloe could stand at a slight crouch, which made her appear even shorter than she was.

'It's fucking freezing,' Ben said, on his knees, frantically rubbing his hands together.

'Don't worry,' Chloe said, dragging down the door's zip and sealing them in, 'you'll be fine once you slide into your bed. It's the thermal, quilted kind. If anything, you'll probably be too warm and start complaining again.'

She squashed down onto her sleeping bag to unlace those huge boots. Ben couldn't imagine her wearing anything else. Tiredness had obviously switched off his imagination for the night. His body's internal lights were dimming one by one. She had to pull one boot off with both hands, freeing her tiny, socked foot. Being a seasoned shoe salesman – not by choice – he knew a size three when he saw one. Any smaller and she would have to buy from the children's section. Ben hadn't realised he was staring until she had already peeled a leg of her skinny jeans down to her ankle.

He turned his back so abruptly as to make her cackle with laughter.

'Ah, Benny Boy, what's wrong?' she said. 'Don't you like my sexy legs?'

'Shit, sorry,' he replied, suddenly aware of his cheeks burning in the cold. 'Jesus.' He laughed, holding his tired head in his hands. 'I need to sleep.'

He listened to the swish of Chloe's body sliding into her sleeping bag and then he knew it was safe to turn his head. She was lying on her side, head resting on her hand, grinning at him.

'Pervert,' she whispered before falling back in a fit of giggling.

Ben's sore muscles seemed to sing with every stretch. He was glad to have answered nature's call before lying down. His feet went limp, and their limpness quickly crept through his entire body. Breathing slowed – now steady as a black tide sweeping the shore. Thoughts were fast to fade into some senseless fantasy. But before the plug was pulled on his consciousness, he imagined that blind woman from earlier, standing in the dark, screaming at him. In the opacity of those eyes, her pity was never so transparent.

She was telling him to run. But all Ben could do was sleep.

7

'Wake up!'

Ben was suspended in a lightless ocean. He could hear a voice – faint and distant, but it was getting louder. His shoulders were being shaken. Exhaustion, like a weight, held him down. He tugged at its chain, tensing its links, but it was rooted in the seabed of his subconscious; so deep in dream that its scape was still his reality.

It was Aoife. It had to be. She had awoken during the night.

'It's okay,' he whispered, reaching out to hold her, 'it's just a bad dream.'

'Wake the fuck up,' snapped the voice, definitely not his daughter's.

Ben jolted up, eyes blinking, seeing nothing. The black void of the tent seemed to press against him as he reached for the hands gripping his shoulders. They weren't Aoife's. Small as they were, they weren't small enough, and yet such was the darkness that he held them regardless.

'What's going on?' he asked.

'There's someone outside!'

Chloe's hands were still on him. He could hear and feel her every panicked breath. She lifted off and her fingers chafed frantically around them, searching for a torch. Before he could brace his eyes, the tent exploded in white light. Blind again.

'What did you hear?' Ben asked, shielding his face.

Chloe was knelt on the floor of the tent, holding the torch in both hands as if she were gearing up to swing it. Her legs were bare; she was wearing just a tank top and underwear. The girl was spooked. Ben was mindful enough to focus on her eyes when eventually he could see again.

'Footsteps,' she replied, barely a whisper, 'outside.'

'How close were they?'

'I don't know,' she replied. 'Too close. What does it matter how close they were? There's someone out there. They must have followed us?'

'Could it have been an animal, like a badger or something?'

Chloe shifted over on her knees towards the door of the tent. Her fingers pinched its zip like the pin of a hand grenade. She glared back at him, biting her lip.

'What are you doing?' Ben asked, slipping out of his sleeping bag.

'I'm going to shine a light on this fucking badger of yours.'

'Wait,' he said as he patted around, searching for his own torch.

He shuffled up beside her and together they listened before committing. There wasn't a sound other than their knees balancing on the tent's nylon floor. Ben gripped his torch like a baton. Their eyes locked. They nodded their heads. *Ready. One, two...*

On three, Chloe hitched up the zip and cast her light

outside. Ben had no clue as to the time, but their fire was long dead. A light enamel of frost glistened on its stones. They tracked Chloe's torchlight. It flashed around the field, taking in its walls, its corners, and every blade of crisp grass in between. There was no sign that anyone had approached their tent. Amidst the stillness, their breathing fell into a slow and steady synch.

'I don't see anyone,' Ben whispered.

The cold air was glazing over their mouths and clinging fast to any bare skin. Still the torch swept from side to side, revealing nothing and no one. Chloe pushed up onto her feet.

'What are you doing now?' Ben asked, talking directly to her naked legs.

'I'm looking outside,' she replied, her knees clattering together in the cold. 'If someone's out there we won't see them if we're peering out the door, will we?'

She stepped out and walked across the grass on the tips of her toes. Ben was equally underdressed but if he stayed behind to drag his jeans on, he would never hear the end of it. *Man up, Benny Boy.* Chloe was already standing by the stones that had cradled their campfire, spinning her light around in every direction.

Ben brought his torch's beam upon the copse of trees. They rose out of the night like scrawny giants. That was where he had heard something crack. He regretted not telling Chloe now. Ben watched and listened, as before. There was no movement that he could sense, not even the nervous foraging of some nocturnal animal. If there was something in the bushes, his torchlight should have startled it into revealing itself.

This is insane, he mouthed, but no words escaped his lips.

Ben suffered through the cold. Keeping the torch steady was impossible.

'No one's going to be out on a night like this,' he shouted over to Chloe.

Her cylindrical light was stabbing the darkness around the field's perimeter.

'I definitely heard someone,' she replied.

Twigs and frigid grass crunched beneath Ben's feet as he jogged over to her.

'Come back inside the tent,' he said. 'It's too cold.'

Chloe was panning her torch over the wall.

'Just let me check one last time. I know what I heard, and it wasn't some fucking badger.'

'Jesus, what have you got against badgers?'

They followed the shaft of Chloe's light as it scanned slowly across the distance. So vast were the surrounding fields that they couldn't see their far walls. The beam just petered away into nothingness. They pressed their bodies into each other to steady their shaking. *One last time,* Ben kept chiming in his head. Even his internal voice chittered from the cold.

The light skimmed over the sparkling ground. That's all there was to see, the same unbroken sight fading into the distant dark. No trees. No hedgerow. There was only frost-tipped grass, and then the torchlight passed over *something*; a shape too far away to make sense of in that second. Chloe grabbed on to Ben's arm.

'There,' she shrieked, 'did you see that?'

There *was* somebody out there.

The torchlight strained to reach him.

He stood inert and unaffected by the bitter cold that

caused Ben's limbs to dither in spasms. The distance between them and the faltering light obscured any detail beyond his shape. His body looked incredibly tall, but it was impossible to truly tell as there were no features in the vicinity to use as reference. His long arms arched out slightly and were set rigid by his sides with their fingers spread apart; visible only because they were so long and pale.

He was clad in black, under a tight-fitting cloak or coat that pronounced his skeletally thin limbs. In the dim, wavering light his whole frame looked somehow misshapen; wrong for reasons the eye couldn't define at that distance. The man's head was hairless like a fleshless skull. No features were discernible. But he was watching them. Ben knew that much without having to see his eyes.

'What does he want?' Chloe whispered, one hand still clutching on to Ben.

The cold was too painful to bear. Her fingers were practically frozen to the torch, its light fluttering uncontrollably. And still the man in the field remained as a statue set deep into the earth, unmoving, his intent towards them unknown.

Ben tried to focus his screwed-up eyes – to extract some detail so that he might identify him from earlier. But in that waning light, he hardly looked human at all; more like some hideous insect that had crawled up from the cold earth. And that silhouette alone was chilling to face down, no matter the distance.

'What are you doing out there?' Ben shouted. 'What do you want?'

The man's menacing shape remained unchanged, and the icy silence was a solid sheet between them. No cracks, no weaknesses, no sound.

If he had hidden or even come running at them, his reasons for being there would now be known. But to just stand there, watching them. It was more unnerving than any action.

'We can't stay out here,' Ben said, putting his arm around Chloe's shoulders. 'We'll freeze to death.'

She was shaking like an injured hummingbird. He led her to their tent. Her tired body tried to edge back towards the stranger, too weakened now to hold the torchlight towards him but desperate nonetheless to see him gone.

'Come on,' he whispered, helping her inside.

Ben zipped the tent closed behind them and brought Chloe over to her sleeping bag. The shock – of the freezing temperatures and the fright combined – had shut her down. Snap seizures of cold tortured their bodies, but Chloe's were especially severe. She was too thin, too light, to be standing outside and so exposed. He forgot his own pain, wrapping all that he could find around her as she slid her pale, almost translucent legs into the bag. She still hadn't spoken. He had known the girl for only two days and Ben already knew that wasn't a good sign. Cold as it was, it wasn't the elements that had knocked her back. It was the man. The one who had watched them from the darkness of the far field and that Ben knew in his soul was watching them still.

Chloe's body folded into a foetal position. Why hadn't they thrown their jackets on? It's not as though the cold had hit them as some surprise.

If the villagers meant them harm, then their tent wasn't going to survive a siege. But why? They had promised to leave in the morning. The rules had been set and they'd followed each and every one of them.

'Chloe,' he whispered, 'it's okay. I'll go and see what he wants.'

She didn't reply. He rubbed what might have been her arm, listening to the nylon whish back and forth, too rapt by anger to even realise his hand was moving; a steadying action, more for his sake than hers.

Ben was sick of it. The charade never stopped. Every close-minded village guarded its stories like scripture. Ghosts, devils, phantoms, and fairies – muddied words cleaned and whetted as weapons for the young and the credulous. And trembling by Ben's side, Chloe – their latest victim. Never mind the fright they had given her, luring a woman out into the night to spy on her was crime enough.

Ben reached for her parka; the warmest thing on hand. He sank both arms into its short sleeves and drew the hood over his head. There was no feeling other than the pain that throbbed hardest in his toes.

He zipped the tent's door open. The night was, at once, a presence – an oppressor and a killer. There was no peace in its dead air. No splendour to its stars. It was as though an army ringed their campsite in darkness, tiptoeing in terrifying silence, swallowing them from all sides.

The torchlight was blinding; Ben's eyes too weary to adjust. Muscles burned as he lifted himself onto the grass. The farthest reaches of space couldn't be as cold nor as dark as that tiny tract of land in that moment. He padded towards where they had seen the man. Ben's light shivered like a white sheet in a hurricane. If the villagers had found them, then they now watched on with an impossible stillness.

Ben's lungs were a bellows exploding fog with every wheeze. Even with Chloe's parka, the cold was as relentless as a thousand lashes. He stepped closer to the far field. His light reached like a ghostly arm across its white grass, waving from side to side, swiping through the darkness, but there was no one there. The field was empty.

8

Alec snapped the book closed. He held it in thought, brushing his palm over its binding, listening to the passage of time – the measured beat of the grandfather clock, its weights and pendulum a model of routine and tradition. His eyes had moved from word to word, and pages had turned, but the man's thoughts were elsewhere. He laid the book on his lap and looked to the logs, never so alive than as they were now in death, ablaze and blackening. Coal burned better, of course, and it fathered more heat. But it was by far too quiet and Alec liked to hear the wood crack.

His high-backed chair was set at a comfortable range from the hearth, with its cabriole feet sunken deep into the rug. Undisturbed since it first found its footing. Over the years its burgundy leather had dulled, especially across the arms where Alec's hands were prone to fidget.

The study was the largest room in the house, and the one where Alec spent most of his days and all his nights. As the leather of his chair had shaped itself around him, he had moulded himself around the world as best he could. He understood its parameters, their reasons, and ramifications. In much the same way that a house cat comes to realise why it's called a house cat and why it will never be like the other felines outside its window. Different lives, different rules. From his solitary perspective, Alec's life could, in private, masquerade as normal. He gleaned some pleasure from this. To fantasise that he lived and enjoyed his days as other men might have had wont to do.

Lara had learned to see past the oddity of his routine, having visited him almost every day for five years. A quietly charming woman now in her early thirties, she relieved the role from her mother – the original housekeeper – when she fell ill. On each encounter, without fail, Alec still asked after the woman's health. Naturally, she had long since recovered from the common cold. Their family was of Italian origin. Dark hair, brown eyes, bronzed skin; all the colours that Alec was not.

It was nearly nine o'clock; the hour – or more accurately, the number – that Alec held above all others. *The beginning and the end.* Lara had already prepared him his evening meal and delivered him a single brandy. Provided that he abided by this tried-and-tested practice, then Alec was always occupied. Otherwise, he thought too much and his hands began to fidget. And that wasn't good for the chair's leather.

The window shutters had rolled down before nightfall, as programmed. There was a time when his home had to be locked down manually like a fortress besieged by the stars. He still recalled his father setting those wooden boards into each frame. No easy feat given their length and the man's weakness for the drink. Thankfully, owing to new technologies, those days were no more. Mankind's affection for comfort inspires all manner of invention. The technician who installed the system set it so that it adapted to the seasons, always activating at precisely the right time. Alec didn't need to know how it worked. He was content to simply know that it did.

On Sunday, the clocks would fall back. This was perhaps an insignificant day for most, but not Alec. His days were short enough without trimming off another hour. The shutters would adjust accordingly.

His study provided adequate distraction to pass these long nights. The lion's share of his time was occupied by the room's library, aligned along the southern wall from the floor to the ceiling. New books populated its shelves each month. Good reads and old editions were kept, whilst others were removed.

Though its air of antiquity had been carefully guarded over the years, more contemporary means of entertainment now inhabited the room. Alec considered them an eyesore, similar in effect to a gaudy neon sign on an old Parisian street. Not that travel was ever an option for the man. At least the house cat never knew what it was missing.

A flat-screen television had been set at the far wall facing his desk; a needless addition that Alec oft considered removing. Any news from the world outside was sourced from the broadsheet that Lara delivered to him each day. Other *popular* programmes and feature lengths were of no interest to him. Alec felt an envious disconnect with their characters and dialogue. Even those dramatic pieces mimicking real life were too fictive and implausible to be enjoyed, leaving him feeling all the more alienated.

His laptop lived on the desk adjacent to the wall of book spines, where towers of documents and historical papers had grown around it like a fragile city. The tablet he had purchased on an inquisitive whim was discarded the day it arrived. It was too sleek, and its inner workings far too baffling. And though he thought its female voice to be quite mellifluous at first, the spell was quickly broken when she requested to know his location. That wasn't information Alec shared without good reason for doing so.

Wooden speakers were set discreetly in the study's four corners. Musically speaking, the man's taste in the classical suited the ambience of the room. His interest was, however, entirely superficial. The music would play at a humble volume and he would hear it, caring nothing for the composer's identity or the key to the piece. Music was a distraction, no more. And Alec could happily live without it so long as the flaming timbers cracked.

The study's every aspect was warm and comforting, like a candle in a crimson room. Lighting was soft and a glossed mahogany prevailed throughout its fixtures and fittings. The shutters were hidden behind heavy burgundy curtains. Their lustre had faded over the years, but they were far too tall and too many to merit replacement. The framed artwork adorning the walls had not been changed since before Alec was born, and so he neither saw nor appreciated them, but they filled the blank spaces.

The clock chimed nine times, ringing in the hour. Lara would leave once his bedroom had been prepared and the windows inspected. The crackle of logs on the fire would then constitute his only company: the welcome delusions of a lonely man. He would sit for another hour before retiring.

A gentle knock came from the door, audible only to the expectant ear. Lara entered, closing it behind her. Alec turned in his chair to bid her a good night, as was customary, but knew from the lost expression on her face that something was awry. Any digression from the norm was overtly conspicuous in Alec's life.

'I'm afraid we have a problem, Doctor,' she said, her voice like that of a child.

He had asked Lara countless times to call him Alec but her mother wouldn't allow it. With a frown and a nod, he urged her to explain.

'One of the window shutters in the master bedroom has not come down. There must be a fault in the security system.'

'A fault, you say?' he replied, his fingers gripping into the leather.

'Yes, I believe so.'

'All of the other shutters are working correctly, yes?' he asked.

'Yes.'

Lara waited patiently for further instruction. There had never been such an issue in the past. Although she couldn't have understood the reasons behind the doctor's odd aversion to the night, she knew that he wouldn't set foot inside any room unless the shutters were locked in place.

'Shall I prepare another bedroom for you?' she asked.

'Would you mind? I'll see to it that you're compensated for staying on so late.'

'It's no problem,' Lara said, retreating quietly. 'It won't take me a moment, Doctor.'

She truly bore the most wonderful likeness to her mother, standing by the side – metaphorically speaking – of a man who had no one else; no remaining family, no friends, not even a hound hard-wired to sit by his legs like a painted ceramic. Such loyalty, he liked to believe, was not evoked by salary. That's partly why he never spoke to Lara or her mother about their genuine regard for him as a person rather than their employer. Some hopes, especially ones so desperate, were best left unexplored.

He would make a phone call first thing in the morning. Such malfunctions were unacceptable. It had cost Alec a small fortune to upgrade every window in his home. The technicians had thought him strange. Why would someone wilfully imprison themselves in their home night after night? They misunderstood the man's motivation. The purpose of the shutters was never to keep anything *in*.

After another timid rap on the door, Lara returned, wearing her yellow raincoat, and holding a woollen hat in her hands. Alec rose from his chair and looked to her for some report. So seldom did the doctor speak to another person that he never quite knew what to say. He was aware that he came across as old-fashioned. Speaking informally was a skill he had never mastered. The same could be said for smiling.

'I've prepared the room at the end of the hall,' Lara said. 'And I've closed the door to the master bedroom. You might wish to lock it before retiring. Is there anything else I can do for you before I go?'

'No, no,' he replied, 'you've done more than enough, thank you.'

Alec walked over to the large door leading from the study to the main entrance. His legs were stiff from sitting too long. It was as though they cracked in complaint whenever carried away from the fire's warmth. Lara stood patiently as he opened the inner door and gestured her to step through. This was how they bid each other goodnight. She would stand in that room, between two doors, and only when Alec closed the one adjoining the study would she open the main door, leading outside. This she would lock behind her.

'Goodnight, Doctor,' Lara said, pulling her hat down over her head.

'Goodnight, Lara,' he said, before closing the door behind her. 'Do pass my wishes on to your mother when you see her.'

Alec waited a moment, allowing the silence to resettle around him.

He had sat for quite long enough and his thoughts were too harried to return to his reading. A nightcap might best calm his nerves. Just the one. First, however, he would lock the master bedroom as Lara had suggested. Alec had inherited so much from his father, but not the old man's carelessness.

9

The rain came during the night. A gentle pitter-patter at first before it fell in torrents, thundering on their tent, causing its dome to bulge inwards like a fat belly. Chloe was entombed in her sleeping bag, crystalline pale, covered in any layers that Ben could spare, and still she trembled. The cold seemed to have filled her bones. From the marrow it plotted its campaign of conquest, colonising every part of her from her fingers to her toes.

He had stayed awake for as long as he could, massaging the short hairs on Chloe's head as she slept, watching over her the same way teddy bears guard children when they sleep. His two glassy eyes were fixed on the zip hanging from the door, as though it were the only weak point in a nylon tent.

Searching the surrounding fields had proven futile. Ben's torchlight was but a fissure in the black, leaving too little seen and too much uncertain. Everywhere, he imagined glimpses of the one that had followed them, as a memory haunts the mind – intangible, inescapable, and somehow worse than its reality.

At one point Chloe roused and a soporose twitch slapped Ben's hand away from her head. She turned over and plunged deeper into her bed. He hadn't really given a thought to what he was doing. It was how he helped Aoife relax whenever she was restless.

Eventually he faded. Exhaustion engulfed him like a slow drug and he slept, arms folded tight against the cold, with no sound but the rain.

When Ben awoke, a faint drizzle was playing against the tent like TV static. Hours might have passed, but it felt as though he had just rested his eyes. He sat up on his elbows. To his surprise, the nylon was dry. He must have dreamt the raindrops trickling down from the ceiling, like a leak in his subconscious. The air was cold, but fusty with sweat and tuna breath. It was bright enough to make out the silhouettes of their rucksacks in the corner, but the world was still ruled by black shapes and a lingering feeling of night.

Mornings made Ben physically nauseous. His body always revolted when called to crawl out of bed. It made working a nine-to-five job feel like a five-day working hell. This morning was no different – the denial, the rage, the sad acceptance. He had to shake off the sleep like an addict sweating out his poison.

'Chloe,' he whispered.

She buried her face out of sight and muttered what sounded like, 'Five more minutes.'

Ben's worries had interlaced overnight and now they tightened at the thought of returning home empty-handed. The villagers had given him nothing to work with. Their ignorance was calculated and their answers succinct. It was never a promising sign when the questions occupied more reel than the answers. He needed more, anything to bulk up his side of Sparling's report. Otherwise, the whole trip could have been for nothing. Ben would have to strap himself in for another year of retail-themed perdition. He imagined black mornings, black coffees, and a big black space where his hopes and dreams used to be.

They had set up camp east of where they entered the village. The church couldn't have been far, and it wasn't quite yet dawn. Ben had time. He hadn't the foggiest notion of what he would do when he got there, but he knew he had time to do it.

'I'm going to pop out for a moment,' he said. 'Will you be okay here by yourself?'

Chloe let out a little groan.

'You'll be fine,' he added.

Ben raised the zip with slow, steady care so as to not disturb her. He would be back before she even realised he was gone. His face was met with the lightest spray of rain, as if a wave had crashed against the field's wall. Given the hour, the air was still cold as night, and so he looped his scarf tight around his neck and buried his chin.

Daylight was gradually diluting the dark in the east. The surrounding lands were dissimilar to Ben's memories – those colourless flashes of torchlight. All had been black, or white as bone. The trees, once so monstrous, were now fragile and weather-beaten. Tins were scattered around their campfire, its stone rink a flooded pool of ash and twigs. Their field was smaller than he remembered. The night had confused him. And now, so too had the day.

With Chloe sealed inside the tent, Ben scanned the outlying

fields. Their grasses were grey as stone, almost merging with the misty sky. All that mattered was that they were empty. He stood for a moment, reluctant to leave her alone, but she was perfectly safe. He wouldn't be gone long.

'Okay,' he whispered, stuffing both hands into his pockets and stealing one last glance back at their tent, 'time for church.'

Chloe had already identified the building's features and peculiarities, dissecting it with an educated eye. Ben's gut just told him that there was something else. There had to be. Or maybe he was still half asleep and this hope was but a dream he hadn't snapped out of yet.

The lane was an uneven gully of puddles. Runnels of rainwater trickled through its ditches, by every dip and rise. The mud was thick, as if some deranged villager had taken a whisk to it overnight. Sunrise would hopefully cheer the world up when it came, though judging by the sky their trek back to the car was going to be a wet one. The church's triangular tip eventually rose above the treetops as Ben neared the crest of a hill.

'There you are,' he said. 'Thought you could hide from Benny Boy, did you?'

A small gate sagged from its hinges like a dislocated limb. An archway of vine had grown over it, offering some shelter from the rain that clung to Ben's face like a light sweat. No tool had tamed back the grounds for years. It was abound with briars and weeds, leaving only the narrowest pathway to reach the church. As Ben approached its doorway, he could hear the wind whistling within.

A flagstone floor led to the altar, where a fine rain misted the air, wheeling through skinny window frames and blowing leaves into every crook and corner. More weeds lined its cracks, clawing up to the light, only to die in a church that felt more like a tomb. A section of the northern wall had collapsed outward, leaving an opening that Chloe could probably fit through at a squeeze.

At the altar steps, Ben found what remained of the stone cross. Its stem was wider than he had expected. To shatter it in such way, as to leave only its base, must have taken great time and effort, and good reason for investing both. The area around it had been cleared. Chloe was right: the church wasn't as abandoned as the villagers had led him to believe. Someone had removed the debris from when the ceiling collapsed. There were white tracks like chalk where it had been dragged across the floor. Too cumbersome for the arms of a single man, this was a group effort, and hard work at that.

Ben found the angels protruding from the walls on either side, their faces disfigured. No features remained, merely a cavity, like a gunshot wound at point-blank range. He ran a finger over their injuries, trying to imagine that childish innocence before it was brutalised. A chisel or similar tool had mutilated them but left their torsos intact instead of removing the carvings outright. The act wasn't enough. They left just enough evidence to memorialise *why* they had done it – the very question that played on Ben's mind.

It was such a desolate place; broken, cold, and dark. A house of worship should inspire hope. The skeletal remains of Tír Mallacht's church served only to drain it.

'Well, that was a waste of time,' he muttered as he turned to leave.

He flinched back when his eyes raised to the door.

Someone had followed him.

Through the restless haze, Ben watched as the figure approached the church – like the last believer of a forgotten faith. It couldn't have been Chloe. Whoever it was didn't have a furry collar sprouting from their shoulders. They looked to be wearing a hood. A flurry of rain spun through the church, howling through cracks and breathing life into all those dead leaves. Ben shielded his face and when his eyes reopened, Nu was standing there, framed by the door's arched stone, shawl pulled tight over her skull. Ben could see where its damp wool had fallen in the folds of her skull. Bare legs and feet were tarred in mud, trembling in the morning air.

'Nu, are you okay?'

Her golden eyes were drawn by the raindrops rolling overhead like a ghostly murmuration.

'Would you like me to take you back to the village?' he asked.

Nu stared at him, so sadly that the rain could have passed for tears on her cheeks. 'She told you, didn't she? You should have left here when I asked you to. I've told her before not to talk about him, but she doesn't listen to me. I don't think she listens to anyone. She's bold.'

'Were you around our campsite last night, Nu?'

'No,' she replied, looking down at the muck lodged between her toes. 'She's so bold.'

'Someone was,' Ben said. 'Do you know why they followed us?'

'I'm not allowed to talk about him.'

Here we go again. This was abuse; plain and simple. Nu didn't have the capacity to extract the horror stories that the others had drilled into her head. She would always retain that childish innocence, no matter how many years she collected.

'Are you talking about the creeper, Nu?' he asked. 'It's a fairy tale, okay? You need to understand that. You've no reason to be afraid. He's just a man.'

'He *was* a long time ago,' she replied, retreating out the door. 'I'm sorry that she told you about him.'

Ben watched as she paced down the path, fading into the grey as though they were one.

'See you later,' he whispered, pitying her like all the others; he couldn't help it.

The villagers were obviously early risers. Hopefully they hadn't gone for a family stroll and happened upon Chloe in their tent. Her nerves were fraught enough without meeting their faces first thing in the morning.

Ben had one place left to check before returning to her. Sparling's map had tagged a cemetery a few paces north of the church. He couldn't recall if it fell within the grounds but it was close by. He never thought to ask Chloe about it. But the fact that she hadn't brought it into the conversation didn't heighten his optimism.

After retracing his steps through the church's doorway, Ben sidled in close to its wall where the brambles dragged across his jacket, soaking what was already wet. The stone path that lined the building offered just enough space to reach the northern side of the churchyard. But without the memory of Sparling's map, he would never have found it.

The tombstones varied in size and shape, with some no larger than a shoebox. Most had sunken at odd angles as though the dead had pulled them down from beneath. Engravings were no longer legible; smoothed out of existence by too many hard winters. Decomposed leaves layered the earth like old skin and everywhere the land was unkempt.

In the cemetery's farthest corner, there was a low mound of earth, recently patted down; it was more a pit than a grave. Ben didn't like to look at it. He was ambling by its perimeter – gleaning what shelter he could from the surrounding trees, admiring the bleakness of it all – when his boot crunched on something. Had it not been so hauntingly quiet he might not have heard it.

'And what have we got here?' Ben said, pinching the sunglasses from the black soil and, still kneeling, examining them before the brightening sky.

Aviators; Ben used to have a pair just like them. A lens had cracked under his weight but other than that they were in surprisingly good condition. He had found what he didn't know he was looking for, and in the most unlikely of places.

Ben brushed past the briars and left the church behind him. Its walls sank below the trees as he broke into a light jog down the hill, all the while toying with the *why*. Why was the church left to fall into ruin? Why were its carvings disfeatured? Why pretend as though it never existed? And now a new question presented itself. Why, if others had been to Tír Mallacht before them, did no record of the place survive?

Dawn had broken when Ben reached the field. He rested on its wall for a moment to catch his breath, waiting for the shapeless colours to fade from his vision. Something gluey had leeched onto his eyelid. He smeared it away only to realise that his jacket was polka-dotted in that same slime he had splashed through like a clumsy foal. He looked to their campsite. The tent was still up. He'd hoped that Chloe would have been ready to go.

The sun was lost to the muddied sky, but its light signalled their departure. They were already behind time thanks to his little solo outing. He felt bad for having left Chloe alone, especially considering how freaked out she'd been the night before.

He stopped dead when he rounded the side of their tent. One of its sides had been slashed open. Ben crept over to where its nylon flapped like a flag in the breeze and peered inside. Their rucksacks were in its corner. But there was no Chloe. The sleeping bags had been rolled and packed. Their belongings had been tidied away, awaiting his return, but he had been too late.

Nu hadn't walked alone. The villagers must have returned. They had crawled – stooped and twisted – from their hovels, in search of those that didn't belong, and they had found Chloe.

Had she heard their approach? Did her dawning consciousness expect Ben to zip open the tent, only to watch in horror – trapped on all sides – as their silhouettes darkened the maiden light of day.

Ben knew they had followed them to the campsite. And still he had left her. A ball of worry rose in the back of his throat, like some gristle he couldn't keep down.

He needed to get help.

Ben kneaded his fingers into his temples, trying to think, but ultimately he just found himself staring into space. He had no clue how to get home. And his phone battery wouldn't last long enough to guide him back as far as the bells. That is to assume its GPS still worked. Without Chloe, he wasn't just alone, Ben was utterly and hopelessly lost.

'Morning, Benny Boy,' Chloe said, approaching him from the trees. 'Where'd you go to?'

The sudden sight of her startled him more than her absence. His legs felt weak.

'Where did *you* go?' he gasped, the panic venting out of him like a balloon deflating.

'I was taking a pee over in the trees.'

She looked spent. Her eyes were at half rest and she carried herself as though still cold.

'What happened to our tent?' he asked.

'I'm not taking that thing down in the rain,' she replied, fixing her parka's hood tight around her head. 'I haven't the energy. And there's no chance I'm leaving an expensive piece of gear like that behind for the Tír Mallachts. I'd burn it if it weren't pissing down.'

Ben just stared at her. *You don't even realise the fright you gave me.*

'So, where'd you go?' she repeated.

He produced the sunglasses from his pocket and held them out to her.

'I found these in the graveyard.'

She examined them in both hands, drawing them right up to her eyes as if searching for some clue he had overlooked. Ben watched those smooth lips pout in deep but inconclusive thought. Eventually, her head lifted, and that wicked smile was back where it belonged.

'*This*,' she said, holding the sunglasses up, 'is huge.'

'I know, right? It means that we're not the first to come here.'

'It *means*,' she replied, handing them back, 'that everyone has been lying to us. And you found them in the graveyard?'

'Yeah,' he said, 'just on the ground, as if somebody dropped them by accident.'

'There's only one type of person who would hang out in a graveyard.'

'And who's that?'

'Archaeologists,' she replied with a wink. 'I told you I wasn't the first one.'

10

The rucksack was back on Ben's shoulders. It was a part of him now, like the pain and the cold, and that second skin of mud that seemed to grow back whenever he wiped himself clean. Another blast of rain rendered him blind, like wet splinters against his face. The once crisp leaves were as mulch, all mixed into a gritty quicksand that never settled. The rainwater had soaked the earth overnight, fattening it to its brim. Now it flooded in unseen pools hidden beneath the tall grasses.

When they reached the treeline, Chloe grabbed the tripwire and wrenched it back and forth. Even amidst the wind and the rain, the bells' toll was ear-splitting. A few of them fell like coconuts amidst the droplets; their rusty shells silenced on impact. She didn't say anything. She didn't even look back at Ben. It was an act of catharsis – a clamorous declaration to the world that they were leaving and they sure as hell wouldn't be coming back.

There was no banter between them. No smiles. No excitement to bolster their spirits. Not this time.

Ben could see Chloe's backpack bobbing in the distance, swaying as the wind whipped around her. They had set out before either one of them could speak of the prior night. No pedestal was given to common sense. Ben wondered if she'd drawn parallels to the little girl's story. It was all superstitious nonsense, of course, probably invented to keep their children indoors after dark. Folk tales were a cruel breed, always relying on fear to hammer home their message. But Ben knew how easily they were believed, even by those who should have known better. People yearned for the impossible. They would sooner trust their lives to magic than face the ennui of reality.

Ben had an aunt once, Patricia. A self-professed clairvoyant with a keen eye for future happenings. Hers was the classic Nostradamus style of premonition – spinning riddles so loose that hindsight could wrap them around any event and say they fit. She was his father's only sibling and a black leaf on the family tree that always looked out of place. Patricia had cameoed in Ben's childhood; a handful of encounters, each one tinged with crystals and vague, poetic ramblings. And yet if memories were sand slipping through Ben's fingers, then Aunt Patricia was the rock that sank into his palm. He could still feel its weight, even after all those years.

Patricia had lived and died in black. Ben recalled those long, floor-sweeping skirts swishing around him like a hundred whispered voices. Whenever he did see her feet, they were always bare, even when it rained, when kids knew to wear shoes. Her lipstick was the darkest he'd ever seen, and her mouth so slender that its colour always bled onto the skin. The woman's hair had prematurely greyed. It draped down to her waist in lifeless, silver strands, and framed her face like a cowl. She wasn't old then, and she wasn't old when she passed away.

Both parents regarded Patricia as a nuisance. Ben remembered hearing his mother refer to "that woman" in the days prior to his aunt's arrival on their doorstep. He had innocently wondered why they kept on forgetting her name. Whenever she was visiting, every window in the house was left ajar, even in winter. And so Ben learned to relocate his toys to the fireplace, where his fingers didn't ache from the cold. It was as though instead of washing her clothes, Aunt Patricia simply hung them over some smoking sage to purify the stains. No room escaped her odour and it would hang in the air for days after.

Being an only child with too few friends, Ben was scared of most things. He'd crept downstairs after his bedtime one night and caught a glance of *Jaws* on television. Quint was coughing up blood, staring down at where his legs should have been. Of course, it had to be that scene. Ben's parents became aware of his nocturnal movements some hours later, when they were called to his room to cleanse its shadows of sharks.

Aunt Patricia didn't inspire the same terror as *Jaws*. Not initially. She was just different to what Ben was used to, and so he was more wary than he was afraid. It was as though the woman chose to accentuate her eccentricities whenever he was watching. She would glide across the floor with arms aloft by her sides like some wind-up ballerina. Her right hand habitually held something that she would rub with her thumb, usually a stone or a piece of jewellery. Ben had once seen her clutching one of his toys – a *Transformer*, its body half-humanoid and half-tank, stolen away before it could fully commit to either form. He hadn't the courage to rescue it.

Sometimes, her whole body would stiffen and both eyes would grow wide as plates. She'd suck in her lungs and stare aghast at the wall. Ben had followed her eyes and never noted anything extraordinary. But then, her *gift* wasn't for the likes of him. These feats and more had made Aunt Patricia a nuisance in the French household. And this was before *that* night.

It happened in October, with Halloween looming days away. Ben's imagination was already on high alert. Patricia had landed in on top of them unannounced, as she was known to do, much to his mother's chagrin. The windows were flung open. Not a care given to the cold. Together with his parents, they'd sat in the sitting room after dinner, sharing an awkward silence that Patricia seemed oblivious to. Eventually, Ben's mother and father made some flimsy excuse to leave; be it neglected chores or something less convincing, it didn't matter. What mattered was that he was left alone with his aunt. She'd spent the evening shuffling a deck of colossal tarot cards, all the while eyeing Ben as though he owed her money.

'Come here to me,' she whispered, gently placing her cards down on the floor.

Ben was sat by the fireplace, trying to keep as still as possible for fear that something like this might happen. When he didn't react, Patricia instead came to him, floating as she always did.

'Something's wrong,' she said, listening for a moment, possibly to make sure that his parents weren't nearby. 'Do you hear that?' she asked nervously.

Ben shook his head. 'Hear what?'

Hopefully it was his parents returning to rescue him.

Patricia drew a finger to her lips. 'A voice,' she whispered as she lowered onto her knees.

'What are you doing?' he asked, shrinking back, but the woman had fallen into one of her trances.

'Everyone, back,' she said, her head twisting around the room as if she had heard someone else speaking. 'He's doing this alone.'

Ben was starting to worry where his parents had gotten to. He thought to call out to them. But Patricia seized him by the shoulders and drew him towards her, exorcising him of any free will. It became hard to breathe as his aunt's mustiness was more potent up close.

'On your knees, like this,' she snapped as she set him in front of her.

Ben didn't argue. He clenched his eyes shut as tight as he could and tried not to move.

'What are you waiting for?' he heard Patricia whisper, but he could tell from her voice that she was looking elsewhere. 'Kill him?' she asked. 'Kill who? Who are you?'

Patricia's hands clamped around Ben's neck. His eyes opened. The tears erupted as though they were being wrung out of him like a sodden cloth. This was worse than that time with the sharks. He tried to scream but his voice couldn't rise between her fingers. He was absolutely terrified, certain in that second that his aunt meant to strangle him. But she wasn't even looking at Ben. Patricia was staring over his shoulder, her face frozen in an expression so terrorised as to rival his own. She was shaking her head, utterly revulsed by whatever vision her so-called gift had conjured behind him.

'What have you done?' she shrieked, louder than Ben had

ever heard her speak. 'Her face. Oh my God! What did you do to her, you devils?'

Ben hadn't heard his father's approach, so loud were his aunt's screams. The man was suddenly between them, prying Patricia's hands from his weeping son's neck. That was the first and only time Ben had ever seen his father angry, and that was his last memory of his Aunt Patricia. His mother helped him up to his room, where he was put to bed. There were voices downstairs for a while. His father's, mostly. And then the front door slammed and the smell of sage was banished from the house forever.

With Aunt Patricia gone, so too was anything remotely bordering on make-believe. Entertaining such things had invited only trouble thus far in Ben's childhood and, going forward, his upbringing was to lead a more rational path. Movies weren't real. His father would show him behind-the-scenes footage; actors not acting and monsters out of costume, not monstering. Vampires, werewolves, fairies – all of them fictitious. Santa Claus died around that time, too. Ben's parents sold this mindset to him as something lofty, as if he were too clever to believe – never mind enjoy – anything that wasn't real. And whatever it was that Aunt Patricia had seen that night was never spoken of. Eventually his parents probably hoped that he had forgotten it even happened. People always assume children to be forgetful. Nothing could be further from the truth.

Whenever Ben remembered his Aunt Patricia, he would instinctively touch his neck like a prisoner who'd felt the noose. It wasn't the act of being choked that stuck with him. It was her face, so honest and terror-stricken. He would often wonder what it was that she had seen. What horrors had her mind projected onto the space behind him?

The rain eased off eventually, but it wasn't the water above their heads that slowed Ben and Chloe's pace to a crawl. Parcels of dry land were rare. Tír Mallacht was ringed with swampland, making every step a roll of the dice. And Ben's luck was borderline cursed.

He couldn't shake the feeling that they were being followed. His suspicions, like himself, lacked solid ground to stand on. But the wasp had been so keen to see the back of them. He might have sent someone to make sure they did as they were told. Shadows shifted like stealthy bodies in the periphery of his vision. But it was just his eyes playing tricks on him. Ben knew that. He was tired and easy prey for those fears and doubts that roamed the land so freely.

What was it that Mary had said? *Everyone is safe so long as we stay here, and that's what matters.* They could stay where they were. The world was better off without them.

Ben imagined sitting into the rental's faux leather, the dull tap of rain on its roof, the click of the door and the milestone it signified. He wanted it more than anything – that *modern* sense of security. The comfort of the now, instead of the painful primitiveness they'd just escaped. From there, the journey would be a breeze. Nothing like the gale that had chased them since daybreak. All they had to do was reach the car, that flagpole on the mountaintop bending in the wind.

He tried to visualise exactly how he had left it. His worries seized the brush, painting a car submerged up to its windscreen in Tír Mallacht's signature brand of ooze. Between the excitement and hauling their equipment out of the boot,

Ben hadn't paid due attention to his parking. He wouldn't have put all four tyres on the ditch, would he? Surely some silent alarm would have stopped him. If they were stuck, he'd call for help. That is to assume that one of their phones still held any charge. How would he even begin to describe where they were?

'Please,' Ben muttered to himself, 'don't tell me I fucked this up.'

Chloe reached the gate first. She had kept her lead the entire way, stalling her stride here and there so as not to lose him, like a lover teasing his advances. Her arms lifted in tired celebration before she clambered onto the other side, winning another gold medal for the mantelpiece. Ben wasn't rejoicing just yet.

'Let's never do that again,' she said to him, breathless, watching him throw a leg over the gate, its steel cold and slick in his hands.

He cast a discreet eye in the direction of the ditch and let out a sigh of relief that Chloe probably mistook for one of exhaustion. The wheels hadn't sunk.

'Hey, stop,' Chloe shouted, 'look at this!'

She was looking down at the earth beyond the gate, shirking back as though the cold wind had touched her for the first time. There they were, embedded fresh with no effort made to lighten their dent – footprints. There was no reason to travel this way unless hikers or those living close by had a mind to ramble. But Ben knew from their journey that there were no houses for miles. They were far removed from the world, its people and their comforts. The steps grouped around the car but stretched no further. Whoever was responsible hadn't followed the same narrow lane that Ben had driven the day prior. They must have come from the field, and from the direction of Tír Mallacht.

'Holy shit,' Chloe said, 'look at the car.'

Ben pried his eyes from the ground and saw the scratches across its side. From the front door, reaching far as the back wheel, were symbols, like those in Chloe's sketchbook. They lacked the contours and curves that flow naturally from the wrist. These were carved into the paint job with great force, defacing the car whose rental company still held their deposit.

'Jesus fucking Christ,' Ben gasped, hands on his head. 'Those motherfuckers!'

He knelt down and ran his fingers along one of the gashes. They were so deep and so many. A dent could be talked around or even hidden. But this was going to cost someone a small fortune and Ben was damned if he was going to bear the brunt of it. Sparling told them to park the car here, so the good doctor could pay the fine.

'Why would they do this?' Chloe asked him, hugging her shoulders as she stepped back towards the gate.

'It's just mind games. Look, that lad in the field told us as much when we arrived. We were never welcome here. This is their way of telling us not to come back.'

'The car's ruined,' she said, approaching it cautiously, as though the villagers had boobytrapped it with more bells.

'Let Sparling worry about that,' Ben said as he threw his rucksack into the back seat. 'We got what we came for.'

11

'I've been thinking about last night,' Ben said.

Chloe's eyes were closed, her face at rest. She had reclined the seat and jerked it back like a lounger. The air was warm and dusty from the fan, and the wipers' hypnotic meter was steadily putting her under.

'What were you thinking about last night?' she replied lazily, succumbing to the lullaby of a homeward-bound car.

Don't scare her – that was his priority. Wherever Chloe's thoughts and fears had landed, Ben wanted to guide them to brighter territories.

'I was thinking about that bastard from the village who was spying on us,' he said. 'He must be dying of a cold after standing out there for as long as he did.'

'But you saw him, didn't you?' she asked, opening her eyes.

'It was so dark. I'm not sure what I saw.'

'Oh, come on,' she said. 'If I saw him, then you saw him. He didn't look right.'

'He was too far away to look like anything.'

'And you remember what the kid said to us. *Three times you see him. The first night he's far, far away.*'

'Chloe,' he said firmly, 'don't tell me you believe all that? I've heard these stories a hundred times and that's all they are. The Tír Mallachts sent him out into the field to fuck with us.'

'Maybe,' she replied, sinking lower into her seat like a sulking child, 'maybe not.'

'They're just stories, trust me.'

'I trust you, Benny Boy,' she said through a yawn. 'I trust you to wake me when we're home, okay?'

The rain cleared eventually, leaving the flat surfaces dark and damp with a dove-grey sky that hinted at a second round. The warmth from the heater had returned some colour to Chloe's cheeks. But she still looked like a porcelain doll thrown on the passenger seat.

Ben hoped she had taken more from Tír Mallacht than he had. The church's desecration and the symbols should have been enough to keep the doctor entertained, even if his dreams of a lost civilisation had yet to be realised. No doubt there was more, too, that she hadn't shared with him. Ben felt like a weak link, undeserving of his share.

Her face had turned towards him in her sleep; lips were slightly parted, revealing the tiniest white of her teeth. Ben set his tape recorder on the dashboard, arranging it so that it wouldn't slide off at the next roundabout. His interviews wouldn't make for the most riveting of listens but it was time to make a start, and he'd keep the volume low so as to not disturb Chloe.

'Let's find out how bad these really are,' he whispered, reaching forward to press play.

Testing, testing, interview one.

Ben recalled all those hopeful expectations yet to be disappointed. Ideally, he would have stopped the tape between each interview. That *off-the-record* moment was a great opportunity to sneak in some last questions. But because he had to keep the recorder hidden, it had been allowed to run, listening in when no one was around. He would have to fast-forward through the interludes, hopefully without crashing the car.

Mary's feet scrunched over the bark. The wooden board was set in place. Ben heard a short rustle as he adjusted the recorder's hiding place, poking it further under his jacket's collar.

Now, Mary. Thanks for volunteering to go first. I honestly don't know what I would do without you.

'Yeah, thanks a lot, Mary,' he mumbled.

Ben always enjoyed listening to past interviews – the anticipation of that perfect question and the subtle press, encouraging the speaker to elaborate, guiding them into divulging their secrets. But he was dreading these.

As the tape played, however, and the interviewees came and left, he started to suspect that he had done everything he could. If one line of questioning reached a conversational cul-de-sac, he had segued into another. His questions were well timed. His demeanour was friendly and receptive. He had played his part and the evidence was on the reel.

Now then, John, make yourself comfortable and we can get started.

The man's age was baffling, as from a distance he could have been mistaken for a child. It was as though he hadn't grown but he had aged, and not particularly well.

No matter the question, John would wheel the conversation back to the land, speaking erratically about the crops and the soil, his legs twitching as though he was about to break into a sprint. None of his stories stretched back further than last season's harvest.

When it became apparent that the man was an empty source, Ben asked him directly about the creeper. He had nothing to lose.

Who told you that name?

The man's years manifested in that second, and there was nothing childlike about him.

It's a common enough superstition, John. You'll find it in most parts of the country, if you ask around for it.

It wasn't as though the Tír Mallachts would know any different. But John rejected the lie.

You made a big mistake coming here.

Luckily, Chloe was still passed out and hadn't heard that closing line.

Ben listened to his own steps crunch towards the door. John had already shifted the board aside with his little marsupial hands and stormed out. A long sigh of frustration was heard and Ben pictured himself alone in that grimy stable. He would never forget *that* feeling.

'Hang in there, Benny Boy,' he said, looking at the recorder on the dashboard.

It had shifted out of reach and become wedged under the windscreen. He would have to wait out the silence until his past self recruited another villager for interrogation. Ben's footsteps faded into the distance. If only he had had the good mind to pause the tape after John left. It's not as though anyone would have seen him.

He pushed his shoulders back into his seat to ease the aching, glancing enviously over at Chloe, out cold. *Lucky for some.* Ben thrummed his fingers on the wheel, listening out for his return to the stable.

And then he heard it, something that nearly made him swerve into the other lane.

'What *is* that?' he whispered, now staring at his recorder instead of the road ahead, trying to visualise what the hell he was hearing.

Someone was breathing over his jacket. It was a slow, heavy snarl. So loud that whoever it was must have had their face right down by the recorder. But Ben had hidden it so well.

He listened to every hoarse breath, imagining the empty stable, where there was nowhere for anyone to hide. It was a dog. It had to be. Ben counted himself lucky that it hadn't chewed his recorder to bits. But then the breathing grew fainter, as the one responsible stood to their feet and slowly walked away.

Ben heard his own voice approaching.

If you would like to take a seat over there, Nora, I'll just close the door behind us.

There was only the sound of the woman padding across the bark and Ben putting the board back in place. He took his seat beside her and the interview began. There had been no one else in the room. There couldn't have been. His skin ran cold as if its every inch were wrapped in frozen lace.

Chloe was stirring beside him. Ben's hands were tensed around the wheel. What had he just heard? If there had been someone or something in the stable, he would have seen them.

Should he have told Chloe? Maybe together they could have purged the facts of falsity. But what if it meddled with their report? Ben needed Sparling's money more than he needed answers.

It was nothing, just a fault in the reel. His recorder was long past its best. And besides, it had happened before; a day's worth of interviews garbled and lost because he hadn't loaded the cassette properly. There was no logical reason to fear it. The sound was merely an excuse for those who wanted to believe, as a door moving in a draught is proof of a presence.

It was some mutt or one of those androgynous kids from the village. When they weren't admiring each other's dresses, they were probably out for mischief. The logical explanations far outweighed the absurd.

'Where are we?' Chloe asked, wiping her eyes.

'And there was me thinking my co-pilot was going to sleep

the entire way,' he replied, fronting a smile as best he could. 'We've a long way to go yet.'

'You *did* volunteer to be my driver, you know.'

'Did you just say *your* driver?' he asked.

'I don't see anybody else in the car, do you?'

The creeper must have derived from another folk tale. That's how it worked. Stories changed from place to place, between villages and counties, like a criminal seeking a new identity. Details were omitted. New ideas were added in. Landmarks and local names were attached, and in time the provenance was forgotten. Ben had said as much in his thesis.

He wanted to substantiate Sparling's report with some theories as to its origin but his mind was running on fumes. The early tremors of a headache rumbled somewhere in the back of his skull. A name like the creeper would have survived. It was too distinctive. And if it had reached anywhere beyond Tír Mallacht, Ben would have encountered it. Since turning the key in the ignition it's all he had thought about, and he could feel his ideas leaking like oil with every mile.

Three times you see him.

'Always with the number three,' he whispered, rubbing the tiredness from his eyes as he stared at the taillights stretching ahead like a landing strip.

What Ben saw the night before went against the grain of convention. The villagers had sent someone to scare them into thinking that the creeper was real. But if they believed in his existence, why would they impersonate him?

None of it mattered. They had gone to Tír Mallacht to gather information. This they had done to the best of their ability and the proof of their efforts would be in Sparling's report. And what Ben heard on that recording was probably the cassette again. Maybe it was time for an upgrade.

Chloe looked to be in a trance, staring at the ladders of rain trembling across the window. She had slid down even deeper into the seat. Her discarded parka cradled her like a nest. Muddy boots had been kicked off, and her feet were up by the windshield, both legs at full stretch just to reach it.

The traffic was at a crawl, less than two miles from the city. The wipers slicked back and forth. Between their squeak and chatter, two lint-laden speakers hummed a song too low to hear. Ben had been sitting too long. No matter how he shifted his weight there was discomfort, as though his bones carried bruises.

'How do you suppose Sparling knew to ask about the creeper?' he asked.

It felt an age since either of them had spoken.

'I was thinking the same,' Chloe replied. 'He definitely knows more than he'd like us to believe. I just don't understand why he sent us to that place. Like, honestly, there's nothing there, and that much was obvious from the million maps he showed us.'

'What do we care? We're getting paid, aren't we?'

'I suppose,' she sighed. 'It's weird though.'

'What is?'

'*Everything*, Benny Boy. I regret to politely break it to you that *everything* about this is fucking weird.'

There was so much that they didn't know. Ben hadn't even read his contract. He had nodded his head like a money-starved idiot as Sparling spouted *facts* that he knew couldn't be true. Who even was Doctor Alec Sparling? They hadn't enquired as to his profession or academic history.

Ben knew the man's name. That's all, because that's all he had told them.

'Have you any battery left in your phone?' he asked.

'Yeah, I turned it off once we reached the car. Why?'

'Look up the office number for my old supervisor, Joe Cunningham. He's the lad who recommended me to Sparling. It should be on the university's website.'

'Yes, sir,' she replied, digging around in her jacket.

He should have researched Sparling sooner. It wasn't like him to be so lackadaisical. Ben liked to reserve his negligence strictly for the realms of retail and parenthood. The financial reward that Sparling repeatedly alluded to had obviously blindsided his better judgement.

'It's ringing,' Chloe said, holding the phone over to him.

Ben hadn't spoken to his supervisor since finishing his thesis. But they had shared a well-disposed rapport throughout. Cunningham recognised the hours he put in and probably played some part in Ben receiving the grade that he did. The man himself was extensively published and well connected in his field. His word could be trusted.

Ben was nervous as he listened to the dial tone. He hated talking on loudspeaker.

'Hello,' said a slow, slightly gruff voice.

'Joe, it's Ben French, long time no talk.'

They had always spoken casually. It was one of the reasons why Ben enjoyed their meetings. He had wanted to take him for a few pints after his master's was completed, like soldiers catching up on past victories. But time got away from him and soon the idea – like everything – became history.

'It *has* been some time. Where are you working these days?'

There was that question again, only now Ben had an answer.

'That's why I'm calling you, Joe. I'm about to write up a report for Doctor Alec Sparling. He told me that you're the one who recommended me to him.'

'Alec Sparling,' he repeated, and Ben could imagine him creaking back in his chair, fingers tugging at his beard.

'Yeah,' Ben confirmed, 'he was assembling a team for a survey.'

'And he told you that he spoke with *me*?'

Ben and Chloe looked at one another.

'That's right, Joe. That's what he told me.'

'I've never heard of the man, Ben, and I've certainly never spoken to him. Besides, if I were to put your name forward for any work, I would always contact you to let you know.'

'That's what I thought.'

No, Benny Boy, there wasn't a thought in your head when you signed that contract.

'What work are you doing for him exactly?'

'Well, that's the strangest thing. He made us sign confidentiality agreements, so I'm not allowed to talk about it. Not until he gives me the all-clear to do so. It's a research gig, historically and archaeologically speaking.'

'That *is* strange.'

Ben could tell the man was thinking. Cunningham's gears turned slowly but they always produced worthwhile results; a machine that prided itself on quality over quantity.

'I *have* heard that name before,' he said eventually.

'You have?' Ben asked, as both he and Chloe leaned in closer to the phone between them.

'Oh, it must be two years ago now. One of my students told me that she had been approached by a Doctor Sparling.'

'What was her name?'

'Oh,' he said, as the cogs turned again, 'Carol Fortune, I believe it was. Yes, such a rare surname. How could I forget?'

'Do you know what Sparling wanted from her?'

'Unfortunately, no. She was a history graduate and I thought she might go for the master's, as you did, but I didn't see her after that. She was a clever girl, I remember. I must actually chase her down and see where she ended up.'

'So, Alec Sparling isn't an academic?'

'I can assure you, Ben, if he were, I would know about it. I make it my business to keep up with these things.'

'Okay,' he said, eyes locked with Chloe's in concern, 'thanks for your time, Joe.'

The car ahead had pulled away without either of them noticing. It was Chloe who voiced what they both were thinking.

'So what the fuck is he?'

12

Chloe lived at the end of a cul-de-sac. It was one of those quiet, suburban semicircles where every car was eyed with suspicion. Curtains shifted aside. Old eyes peered out, committing the registration to memory. Ben had rented a room somewhere similar before. The long-term residents distrusted the blow-ins because they were too loud, too modern, and too young. And these new additions to the street were none too pleased that their lives were under twenty-four-hour surveillance. Whenever they came and went, somebody was watching, clocking their movements. One cul-de-sac, two factions locked in a silent, passive-aggressive war that no one elsewhere either knew or cared about.

Like any outmoded estate, it wasn't difficult to pick out the rented properties. Driveways cracked. Recesses blackened with grime until they were, quite simply, black. Scratches on wood became dents and in some places split. Net curtains were eternally fashionable. Gardens were grass or nothing at all. Without a fresh coat or a few flower beds, their colours drained over time, looking even more neglected when set between the more privileged homes with their brightly painted doors and window boxes. They were the ugly, less-favoured siblings in the housing family.

It was already after five o'clock. Their odyssey across acres of bog-land had been laboured and slow, and the final hurdle of back-to-back traffic hadn't reclaimed any lost time. The city seemed darker than its hour. Swarthy clouds had devoured the daylight too soon like a hungry dog. A delicate drizzle tinkled on the car's roof after Ben killed the engine. His senses had accustomed to its hum and the vibrations of the gearstick in the ball of his palm. Without the engine's drone, the silence felt hollow and carried with it a sense of loneliness when it should have instead brought peace.

The day seemed to pass so quickly. Without some event to punctuate the idle hours of travel they all melded into a single, expendable memory. Years spent in Tír Mallacht must gather in a similarly indistinguishable heap, with no variety or event to identify one from another. No past that they want to speak of and no future unlike the present.

Chloe lived with one other housemate and he was out of town until the end of the week. It was she who proposed to use her home as their base of operations. It was by far the better of two options. Ben's poky apartment came with two deadbeat housemates who occupied the sitting room like taxidermy. The furniture and carpet were leavened with the funk of weed. They smoked day and night, indifferent to either.

Ben and Chloe sat at opposing sides of the kitchen table; a rectangular, austere slab of wood whose dark lacquer had faded in its centre. It was probably an original element of the house like an organ in a body, growing old together, inseparable until the reaper comes a-calling in the guise of a wrecking ball.

A sickly filter covered the entire room. The maple cabinets and fittings had blenched to a yellowish off-white. The same could be said for the magnolia walls, and the floor tiles whose grouting resembled a fisherman's net.

'It's the bulb,' Chloe said, looking up from her laptop. 'My housemate picked up a replacement when the old one fizzled out. *No*, you're not losing your mind. And *yes*, everything is fucking yellow.'

A sliding glass door exhibited their reflections but stored the back garden in the dark. Night had fallen the second Ben turned his back on it, between the front door and the kitchen. He could make out the distant square of a neighbour's window like a glowing frame hung from a star, but nothing else. His reflection – that bedraggled-looking imposter – was always in the way.

He rolled his knuckles over his eyelids. Whatever focus he thought he had was fading fast.

Chloe's fingers tapped in rapid bursts. A heart surgeon wouldn't have looked so preoccupied. Ben had yet to begin. As his technological demands were deemed as trifling, he was given the lofty honour of using Chloe's old laptop. It was still booting up after ten minutes, its fan humming like a plane set for take-off.

'What are you working on first?' he asked, slouching over the table.

'What am I working on first?' she repeated slowly, making every syllable sound, still squinting at the screen, typing away.

Chloe spun her laptop around like a magician revealing the

card she had told you to remember. Ben leaned forward to get a closer look. A rough 3D church comprised of blue lines was on the screen. Ben recognised the shape of its altar and the narrow window frames. Red letters were suspended over points of interest, probably as links to notes or photographs. In its digital format the whole building looked too clean. There were no weeds or imperfections. And no *feeling* to it which he knew, having stood within its walls, was not true. There was a very particular type of sadness there: old and silent, but very much alive.

'How did you throw that together so quickly?' he asked, pivoting the laptop back to face her.

'This isn't my first church, Benny Boy. All I had to do was input the measurements and tweak it a little. You historians wouldn't understand.'

A resounding ping came from Ben's laptop, a touch too loud and slightly distorted.

'It actually turned on?' Chloe said, grinning at him.

'Why do you sound so surprised?'

This was it. The age of procrastination was over.

Ben eyed up his recorder on the table. It must have been quite the machine back in its day. Ahead of its time until time left it behind; such was life. The transcriptions would have to wait until morning. He didn't want Chloe to overhear that breathing on the tape until he could rationalise who or what was responsible.

'Oh, and another thing,' she said, 'I've been trying and failing to figure out what those symbols mean. There isn't a single spiral amongst them. No pentacles. No moons. They aren't pagan. I don't know what they are. They were in crevices and at the base of its wall, as if they weren't meant to be seen. But why bother then? The whole point is to have them on show.'

'Could the children have done them?' Ben asked.

'Maybe, but I doubt Sparling's going to get too excited about some kids' art project. I'll keep looking and find something to keep him happy.'

'Find *something*?'

'Well, yeah. This isn't an academic paper. All we have to do is keep the doctor happy.'

Ben's plan was to approach the report like a college assignment. But they weren't chasing high grades. They just had to impress Sparling enough to justify their fee. The creeper was what the doctor wanted, and Ben would give it to him, even if he had to bend the truth a little. And so, he wrote.

The creeper myth is unique to the village of Tír Mallacht. Common tropes abound in the field of superstition, especially where the oral tradition is the chief mode of transference. These include, but are not limited to, the recurrence of the number three and the ominous implications of the titular character's appearance. However, comparable motifs serve merely to classify, not to strip a superstition of its singularity. Having personally collected folk tales and fables across the island of Ireland, I can credibly argue that the myth has never left Tír Mallacht – the location of its conception. The village's isolation and the social restrictions adhered to by its residents are likely responsible for its anchored state, whilst their lack of education has secured the superstition's roots in their community.

'I wish I'd recorded that kid,' Ben said.

'The *uh-oh* one?'

'Yeah, her little song and dance about the creeper is all I have for Sparling. Without a recording it's going to sound like I made the whole thing up.'

'Tell him to go to Tír Mallacht himself if he doesn't believe you,' Chloe said. 'He'll have a great time with all his fucking maps.'

Superstitions often rely on rhyme or verse to survive the passage of time. These are respected in that specific community and only receive alteration in cases where they are adopted by another people for the sake of personalisation.

'Should I change anything about what the girl said to us?' Ben asked.

'Why would you?' Chloe replied without looking up for her screen. 'It's perfectly creepy as it is.'

'I don't know. It sounds very childish or something. Will I keep the *uh-oh*?'

'If you remove the *uh-oh*,' she said, staring at him now, 'I'll never talk to you again.'

The creeper is more than a superstition to the people of Tír Mallacht. Its collective belief – and the effects of such – has limited their social and working lives to the daylight hours. Each family retires to their home come nightfall, bringing with them all they need to abide indoors until dawn. Their reasons are, like all facets of their community, guarded. However, one can assume that the creeper's nocturnal movements are responsible. Their acceptance of this communal curfew hints at the superstition being exceptionally old, so ingrained in their lifestyle that it is respected without question or complaint, as if there is no alternative. Its foundations are not built upon worship or autocratic ruling, but fear.

'Would you find those wooden window hatches anywhere else in the country?' Ben asked.

'Maybe here and there, but they wouldn't be as secure as the ones in Tír Mallacht. Those things were bolted down.'

Although window panels can be found on dwellings throughout the country, in Tír Mallacht they are a staple feature of every cottage. However, whereas the function of these hatches elsewhere was to forfeit the elements and secure warmth on cold nights, here they are a means of security. Their locks are designed to keep something out, most likely the ill-defined creeper entity. Given the size of these apertures, it would be impossible for anything larger than a small animal to enter. And so, it would seem that it is the very sight of the creeper that they wish to avoid.

'Jesus,' Ben sighed, drawing his hands down his face, 'I hope Sparling buys all this. I'm basing this entire report on what that little kid told us in thirty seconds.'

'*Uh-oh*,' Chloe replied, winking at him. 'Embellish, Benny Boy. You historians are masters of fluffing things up.'

Ben's internal battery had switched to power-saving mode, restricting his vision to that jaundiced hue that was everywhere he looked. He couldn't blink or wipe it away, and any moisture in the corners of his eyes stung like vinegar.

'On second thought, can we take a break from this?' he asked, pointing towards the bulb hanging from the ceiling.

'The lemony light? Yeah, it gets a bit surreal after a while. Come on, we'll take a breather in the sitting room.'

The room was just off the kitchen, through a door with half a dozen coats bunched across its two pegs. Chloe stepped into the black, leaving Ben to dither in the yellow. She switched on a tall uplighter in the corner, its bulb no brighter than a lit match. The carpet was old and worn. A narrow step of beige tiles affronted the fireplace where an empty crisp packet awaited cremation. There was a coffee table and a couch in the centre of the room. The couch was covered in fleecy throws and blankets in a variety of sombre colours, indiscernible in the dim light. The cushions had slumped and spread over the years.

Chloe sank into its corner and threw up her legs.

'I love this couch,' she said, stretching her arms toward the ceiling. 'It's comfier than any bed I've ever slept in. Just don't go peering under any of these blankets. It's probably pure filth.'

Behind the open curtains sagging in folds on the floor, a window faced out towards the cul-de-sac. Its pavement was lined with tall amber streetlights. Distant dots peppered the surrounding estate like candles in dead air. Ben paid them a tired glance before collapsing into the couch's other corner. The car seat had been discomforting and the kitchen chair Spartan like its kind, but the couch almost made it all better. Like a drowning man at sea, he submerged into its softness, letting the throws rise around him like waves.

'How are you still awake?' Chloe asked.

'Am I?' he replied, his voice a croaky whisper. 'I don't know what I am anymore.'

Chloe heaved herself off the couch. The bones in her feet cracked as she walked across the hard carpet, towards the open curtains. Ben folded both arms over the couch's backrest.

'Lovely,' Chloe whispered, standing before the bird shit that had streaked the window, 'just lovely.'

'That's good luck, you know?'

'For a lad who doesn't believe in superstitions,' she replied, 'you certainly do keep going on about them.'

Chloe dragged the left curtain into place, its rings swishing across a pole whose screws were coming away from the wall.

'Would you look at that,' she said. 'Any day now, the whole thing is going to collapse. The landlady would want to replace them,' she added, leaning in to sniff the curtain. 'Ugh, and these too.'

Ben had zoned out. He was staring past her. Memories of the village rallied under the moonlight. Chloe's suburban dead end – with its concrete, symmetry, and artificial light – couldn't have felt any farther from Tír Mallacht. Here there was comfort and security. Her house wasn't exactly palatial but the rent probably didn't leave too deep a dent in her pocket. And it seemed to abide by the classic *all mod cons included* mantra. There weren't many modern conveniences two hundred years ago, and there certainly weren't any in Tír Mallacht now. What if Sparling had been right after all?

Chloe was still stood where she was, primed to drag the other curtain into place. Outside, all was calm like an abandoned cemetery with mausoleums the size of houses. The last drops of rain had dried. The wind had given up its chase, or else it had simply run out of breath. Even thinking about the miles they had walked was enough to dim the light behind Ben's eyes.

Chloe's fingers suddenly tensed around the curtain's cloth, as if something had caught her eye on the street. She snapped it closed and staggered backwards, both hands searching blindly for the couch.

'Ben,' she tried to call out, but the word came no louder than a whisper.

He was slumped over the backrest, eyes finally at rest. His revival was slow, like an old fluorescent light flickering into uncertain action. Chloe's fingers clinched around his shoulder bone.

'Ben,' she repeated, shaking him awake. 'Ben, please.'

'What's wrong?' he asked, sitting back.

'He's outside.'

Ben rose to his feet, head spilling with sleep. He looked to her – to the whitest eyes he had ever seen, so flushed with fear that he knew who had to be responsible.

'That's not possible,' he said disbelievingly.

Chloe had to be mistaken. Whoever she had seen was probably just a neighbour out for an evening stroll. Ben rounded the couch and approached the window. Chloe stayed back. She stared at the curtains, seeing past them, to the impossible sight seared into her mind.

'What does he want?' she asked. 'Why did he follow us?'

'It can't be the same person, Chloe. How would he even get here?'

'Open it,' she said, taking a timorous step forward. 'See him for yourself, if you don't believe me.'

Ben threw the curtains open with a sharp wrench of his arm.

There, in the centre of the street, not forty yards away – his scrawny black shape illumed in orange light, as still and sinister as the night before – was the man from the far field.

In the shadows that fell by his face, Ben could feel the eyes that had all the while been watching them.

'No,' he whispered. 'That's impossible.'

It *was* the same man.

His was the only body on that deserted street. It was too spindly and disproportionate to be anyone but him. The streetlights overhead brushed his shape with the faintest gloss of copper, but the darkness kept the features of his form a mystery.

'I told you,' Chloe whispered. '*And then the next night he's closer. So close that you can see him, and he can—*'

'Stop,' Ben interjected, so loudly that he startled himself.

They had abandoned Tír Mallacht at first light with the dawn still breaking over the rain-swept trees. By foot and by car they had travelled, leaving it all behind. Nobody could have caught them. The man outside the window couldn't be there.

It was a cruel joke and it had gone on for long enough. Ben stormed away from the window, fists clenched, nostrils flaring like a warhorse at full gallop. Chloe reached for him, but he had already crossed the room, simmering with a rage that he couldn't contain. Not while she suffered at the hands of the Tír Mallachts and their fucking creeper.

'What are you doing?' she shouted, following him into the hallway.

'I'm putting a stop to this. It's just a man, Chloe, and I'm going to prove it to you.'

Ben threw open the door and charged outside, never second-guessing what he was about to do. To think was to hesitate, and his anger wouldn't allow it. Cold air raced into the hallway as the door handle knocked against the wall. The silence was broken only by Ben's footsteps as he paced towards the pavement, and there he stopped.

The man was gone.

There was no sound to be heard or movement to be seen. The whole estate had the eerie air of an abandoned film set.

'Where'd he go?' Ben said, walking onto the road, his neck all the while turning, searching, but finding nothing. 'He couldn't have just...' He stopped himself from saying it.

Chloe came to stand in the doorway. There she watched Ben walk out to the centre of the cul-de-sac, facing where the stranger had stood, where the memory of him still did. Ben had his hands on his head, scratching at its short hairs. Out there, alone, on that orange-coloured concrete he resembled an astronaut on some alien planet, seeking desperately for life.

'What do you want?' he shouted.

His voice echoed to nowhere. Behind a curtained window, a neighbour's light came on, and then another, like dead souls stirring from their slumber.

Ben made a beeline for the house two doors down. He was never the kind to go knocking on strangers' doors after dark but someone had to have seen their stalker running from the scene. There was no dithering on the doorstep. Ben slammed down its knocker as though he'd seen their pursuer close the door behind him. He listened as a chain was slid into place. The door clicked. It peeled open so slightly that the chain's links weren't tested. From within, there peered the face of a woman, elderly and understandably apprehensive. Of all the houses, he had to pick this one. He fought the urge to apologise and bid her a good night.

'What do you want?' she asked, holding up a phone for him to see. 'Don't think that I won't call the Guards.'

Perhaps that's what Ben should have done. Wasn't there a law against staring in people's windows? There was probably also one that didn't smile too kindly on terrorising grannies after hours.

'There's no need to do that,' he said, taking a step back. 'I was wondering if you saw anyone outside. He was standing right there,' he added, pointing back to the street. 'He was tall. Dressed all in black. You couldn't have missed him.'

'I just saw *you*,' she replied, 'shouting your head off.'

'Please,' Ben pressed, 'did you see him? Or did you see someone running from here? I need to know where he went.'

'This is a quiet estate and that's the way we like it. If I hear you outside again, I'll call the Guards.' Here she advertised her phone for the second time. 'I know where you live. I've seen your friend with the hair.'

The door closed before Ben could respond. The woman was probably still stood in the same spot, listening for the sound of his retreat. Other houses had awakened. A dog was barking somewhere. The whole street seemed hypersensitive to every noise. Ben couldn't bring himself to knock on another door. He was surprised that he hadn't already heard the distant siren of a Garda squad car.

'Where did he go?' Chloe asked as he approached her.

'I don't know,' he replied, shaking, his frustration more restless than before.

She looked to him, waiting for more – some explanation for what she had seen – but Ben had no words to comfort her. The truth was that there was nowhere the man could have gone. Dark bodies shifted by their curtains as he stepped inside and locked the door behind him, sliding its chain in place. It had taken him mere seconds to get from the window to the door, and in that time the man had disappeared.

13

Music *had* been playing. In the background of Alec's thoughts there had been strings and possibly piano, comforting in their distance like the ebb and flow of an unseen ocean. Now there was only the cadent tick of the clock and the crackling of hot logs on the fire, its light shivering across the rug as far the armchair's back legs. He reached for his brandy, deliberated for a moment, and then withdrew his fingers back to their locked position. Alec hadn't been listening to the music. But the realisation of its absence further accentuated his sense of loneliness. During these fugitive and altogether futile moments he would often reflect upon his parents and the fraction of a life they had given him.

Alec had no children. In light of his life's experience the man viewed having a family as an act of cruelty. It was no better than adopting a dog only to throw it into a cage. He had never broached the topic with his parents when they had been alive. But he would often ponder how exactly they had deemed it admissible to have a child. What selfish lies had been shared between them? Was it love or simplicity that sealed his fate? They knew of the horror that he stood to inherit, of the curse that was not his doing but his to suffer all the same. Cruelty was too tame a word.

His mother was the first to go. She thought that she could live with it but the restrictions became too much. Alec remembered only her silence and short temper, and the way she used to stare down at him like a metal ball chained to her freedom. The woman's anger eventually turned to distrust. She came to doubt if any of it was necessary. Her death was proof enough for Alec. He still recalled her screams with crystal clarity, and the turmoil of that night when they were cut short.

His father persevered for some years after, but he was never the same man. The memories he clung to – of a love and companionship never to be repeated – turned cancerous, blighting whatever happiness his life might have held thereafter. He taught Alec how to survive – inspiring in him the fear that was essential – and saw to it that his son was financially self-reliant in the event of his death. That had been the man's ultimate plan all along: to die, but by his own doing. A rare feat for any Sparling. He drank too much. He ate too little. Eventually, he became reckless and as a result his plan never came to fruition. He didn't scream like Alec's mother had done. He went quietly and without complaint, as might a drunk who had lingered after hours by the bar, all too aware that he had outstayed his welcome.

Mr French and Ms Coogan had been carefully chosen from a long list. Alec predicted that their financial circumstances would ink their contracts without great debate. Neither of them had any children. And they each possessed the essential skills that he had been searching for. On paper they were the perfect candidates.

His only regret in his handling of this project was that he hadn't organised it sooner in the year. Other matters had demanded his attention, as choppy waters call the captain to the quarterdeck until he sails again through the calm. This storm had, unfortunately, lasted late into the summer. Alec emerged from it unscathed. But the long evenings had been squandered. Daylight truly was more valuable than gold, and one of the few luxuries that Alec's commanding wealth could not buy.

The October days were too short. With any luck, Mr French had the know-how to organise his interviews before nightfall. Otherwise, it would all have been for nothing. The man's master's thesis had certainly shown some promise, and judging by his focus during Alec's presentation, he also shared a keen eye for cartography. Nevertheless, it bothered Alec like a loose marble rolling between his thoughts.

Alec was only a boy of seven years the first time he saw him. It wasn't an act of disobedience, nor was it truly his parents' fault. At that age and having demonstrated the care that would come to define his life, they assumed that he was safe to be left alone. But he was still a child and still susceptible to childish curiosity. It took something as simple as a noise he didn't recognise to draw his eyes outside, into the night, where he saw him standing at the edge of their estate. Strike one, and he hadn't even hit puberty. Panels were added to the windows shortly after, becoming a staple of Alec's life from that point onward.

The second mishap occurred fifteen years later. His father was still alive. Alec had to visit the university for the sake of sitting an examination. It was scheduled to finish later than the hour he would have liked to be home, but there was no evading the issue. The university had already been accommodating enough, and Alec was confident that he would be safely indoors before dark. Of course, the car's unprecedented breakdown could never have been foreseen.

His home was isolated as per his father's design, and Alec ran for miles, racing against the sun. When he climbed the front steps and fell against the door, there was still time. But a mountain of sand had slipped through the hourglass. He had made it, though only barely. He hammered down the knocker until its iron almost split. No response came from within. All windows had already been sealed with their wooden defences, denying any points of entry. Alec's father was in the study, passed out drunk, leaving his son outside in the night for the first time in his life. Strike two, and Alec hadn't seen the darkness since.

He slouched back in his chair and cast a disappointed eye over his lot in life – the room that had, since birth, been his prison. It was a solemn place. A sepulchre of unwanted memories. Every year it felt a little smaller as though its four walls were constantly shifting inward ever so slightly. Given the lifetime that Alec had spent there, it was a wonder he hadn't been crushed alive already. Where had the years gone? His hands were those of an old man; veins and grey-skinned bone. He had never known love or meaningful friendship. The world's offering was denied to him. If it was pity he deserved, then there was no one to give it to him.

He knew that his father would never have approved of what he had done. But then, every Sparling eventually cracked in some way or other. Addiction, depression, even madness; they were as common to his blood as the curse that sired them. For Alec, it was his obsession with escaping his fate, to do what his father had deemed impossible. So many had been sacrificed by his own self-concern and cowardice. And still it remained, as contagious as the day it was first spoken.

It never changed. Not since it had been created. It didn't age. It didn't die.

'Bedtime,' Alec said as he raised himself to his feet, quitting those thoughts, flinching slightly from that rusty feeling in his lower back. He walked over to the fireplace and shifted its iron guard in place. His shadow came to stand in the cage now strewn across the floor. There was still a spit of brandy in the glass beside his armchair. Memories of his father tainted even that simple pleasure. The grandfather clock read half past ten. Its eleven chimes would be loud and long, and he would rather not be around to hear them.

The repairmen had come that afternoon to service the faulty shutter in the master bedroom. Although they had other appointments to attend that day, the persuasive power of Alec's pocket convinced them to inspect every security feature on the premises. They spoke to him as though he were odd or eccentric, sharing jokes at his expense. Their camaraderie wasn't something that Alec could relate to, and the laughter between them seemed far too forthcoming to be genuine, he thought. Perhaps falsities were simply the social norm.

This was the only occasion that Alec could recall Lara donning a frown. Such were her reasons for doing so that it left him feeling quite flattered. She had obviously overheard the mechanics deriding her employer. Far from subtlety were these men born. They were the crass, mouth-breathing sort and the Italian blood must have simmered in her veins at the impertinence of it all.

Lara had subsequently checked each room by Alec's request. She was the only person he enjoyed any regular contact with. He trusted her above all others because there were no others. Not that Lara was any the wiser, but upon Alec's death she stood to inherit a handsome sum. A posthumous gesture of his appreciation as he could never truly find the right words to say in life.

The hallway was lined with lamplight. A dark green runner covered its length, leaving only the narrowest strip of mahogany on either side. There were no windows, paintings, or other ornamentation. Its only function – for Alec at least – was to access the stairs. These Lara swept each day and polished occasionally.

Upstairs, doors stretched down to the far wall; rooms that Alec had no use for. These included the bedroom once belonging to his parents, and his old nursery, windowless but well ventilated. His mother's perfume still haunted the air where her dressing table – like all furniture – had been concealed for decades under white sheets. Its smell didn't trigger any fond, nostalgic reminiscence. Instead, it caused Alec to pity his youthful past self, with all those idle years laid out before him, not quite understanding back then how or why his life was different.

His steps carried him quietly to his bedroom. Big houses never felt empty. They stored too many memories. He would often pause and listen, and hope – more than fancy – that he wasn't alone. And then he would enter, closing the door quietly behind him.

Alec's room was always well lit. Lamps occupied its

four corners and his bedside cabinet. The fear instilled in him throughout his formative years had embedded in his psyche a terrible indisposition to the dark. The curtains had, as expected, been drawn. Behind them the shutters had automatically locked in place. Lara had left a glass of water by his bed and a single tablet to aid his sleeping. His pyjamas were neatly folded atop his pillow. It was always the same.

One more mistake – one more sighting – and his miserable, lonely life was done for. Would that really be such a terrible thing? Nobody would miss him. Not even Lara, his only friend, though he doubted that she saw him as such.

Alec sank his head into the pillow and lay, staring at the ceiling. The pills had helped for a while. But sleep had grown more and more elusive, his body more tolerant to the drug's effect. His nights were plagued by the same thoughts – the same image. He knew that behind the shutter *he* stood with his face inches from the glass, smiling, and waiting for strike three.

14

The clink of a plate was the first sound he remembered. And then the weightier clunk of a mug on the coffee table. Ben could feel the blanket's tassels, itchy under his chin. Chloe must have draped it over him while he slept. He listened to her light step move into the kitchen. A chair moaned across the tiles like worn brakes on a bicycle. There was a clatter of cutlery followed by a sudden gush of water. The tap squeaked off. Ben's eyes hadn't opened yet. The world didn't know he was awake. Nothing would be asked of his aching body if he stayed still. The patter of Chloe's feet passed quickly from tiles to carpet, and another plate and mug found their homes on the table. He felt a tap upon his knee and turned to look at her, squinting lazily, as though he had just woken up.

'Good morning,' she said, her voice's volume turned down to near silence. 'I made us some breakfast.'

Ben could feel the cold air on his cheeks and ears, and on his nose especially. No wonder she had tucked him in. Thin windows, light walls; expense had been spared and so too had the warmth. The steam from their mugs clouded above the coffee table like two chimney pots. On the plates there were toasted sandwiches cut into triangles. Ben spied some bacon poking out from between the bread. A light spread of ketchup lined the lower slice, spilling out onto the plate like a bloody wound. His body yearned for something warm. He sat forward and pulled the blanket down to his lap. Chloe passed his plate over to him and shifted his mug to the edge of the table. Ben couldn't recall the last time somebody made him breakfast.

'What time is it?' he asked.

'It's just after eleven.'

'Jesus,' he said, wiping something brittle from his eye. 'Sorry, I didn't mean to sleep in so late.'

'Don't worry about it,' she replied. 'It's good for you. Eat some food and you'll feel better.'

Neither spoke as they ate. There was only the crisp bite and the chew, and the slurp of coffee that slipped down Ben's throat like a life-giving elixir. It was the same sound Aoife made with every drink. She had always been of the opinion, in her three long years of life, that everything tasted better when slurped. They had put it to the test one weekend. First water and then orange juice, and finally a cup of Coke was brought into the experiment. Consistent with past findings, the Coke was determined the winner. In the days after she went back to Donegal, Ben still slurped his drinks in private.

Chloe was so quiet. It didn't take a mind reader to know why. She'd locked the house down as soon as he returned indoors. Ben hadn't argued. He hadn't really said much of anything. Windows had their clasps tested, doubted, and tested again. Curtains and blinds were drawn in every room. He had wanted to keep an eye on the street outside in case the man returned, but Chloe wanted to sit together, to wait for the dawn, sharing the couch like a vessel on icy water. The curtains, whether he liked it or not, had stayed shut.

Ben hadn't lain down with the intent to sleep and had no recollection of closing his eyes. He remembered sitting beside her, both buried into their respective corners, and then nothing else. Sleep clicked its fingers like a hypnotist and it was eleven o'clock the next day.

'I did some research while you were sleeping,' Chloe said, returning her plate of crumbs to the table. 'I thought I'd see what I could find out about Carol Fortune. You know, the girl your friend Joe told us about.'

'The one Sparling had been in touch with?'

'Yeah,' she replied, 'that's the one. Well, it turns out that there's a good reason why Joe hasn't heard from her since then.'

Ben looked to her as he stole another sip from his coffee. He knew what was coming next. Chloe was biting her lip as though she didn't want to say it.

'Go on,' he said, 'tell me.'

'She went missing two years ago. No one has seen or heard from her since. There was an investigation and everything.'

Before Ben could react, Chloe was up and pacing into the kitchen. He reached forward to put his mug down. A splash of coffee puddled on the table. His wasn't the first offence. Its wood was already streaked with stains. There were even lacerations on its side where someone had gone at it with a knife to occupy their boredom.

Chloe returned with her open laptop and sat back down beside him, their bodies sinking together. He dragged some of the blanket over her legs as though they were an old couple in a nursing home. Her unease was most noticeable around her restless fingers, and the feet that wouldn't stay still, even when sitting.

'That's her,' Chloe said, guiding his attention to the screen. 'She was a history student, like you. She was only twenty-one.'

Carol Fortune somehow looked even younger. She had turned to face the camera, smiling, as though the photographer had caught her by surprise. Her shoulder-length dark hair had slipped behind her ear. She didn't look lost or missing. Ben might have passed her on the street. She would have been another face in the crowd, too young to imagine the short time she had been given. The photograph was from a newspaper; a quarter page soliciting any information on her whereabouts. Ben had only seen missing person posters in movies. They were the same. Her brief description – the physical traits and the clothes she was last seen wearing.

How many days and weeks had they printed it before giving up hope? When does a missing person die if they're never found?

'Don't *they* look familiar?' Chloe said, pointing to Carol Fortune's T-shirt.

A folded pair of sunglasses hung from its neck – aviators, identical to those discovered in Tír Mallacht's cemetery. While Ben was passed out on the couch, Chloe had been busy concocting conspiracy theories in the kitchen.

'They're everywhere,' he explained. 'I've probably something similar in a drawer back home.'

'But Sparling contacted her before she disappeared,' Chloe reminded him. 'Maybe it was some other little *project* of his. I don't think it's a coincidence that she was studying history either.'

The coincidences weren't the worst part of it. Ben still couldn't explain the breathing on the tape. And Nu's words, as throwaway as he deemed them at the time, seemed to have stuck. The creeper *was* a man, she had told him. Well, if that's the case, what the fuck is he *now*?

Ben had to be stronger than this, for Chloe and himself.

'So, you're telling me that Sparling sent Carol Fortune to Tír Mallacht?' he asked. 'But why would he? Like you said yesterday, there's absolutely nothing there.'

'Then why is someone following us?'

Ben shuddered at the question. He was quick to rub his palms together, unconvincingly ascribing his convulsion to the cold. Chloe must have seen right through it. Had it been the day before, she might have poked some fun at him. But not now. So much had changed in two nights.

Memories hounded Ben like a dodged subpoena; that black effigy, so thriftly brushed with light, had appeared even more disjointed than the first sighting. Those arms – skeletally thin and braced by his sides – must have reached down to his damned knees. And those fingers – inhuman in spread and length – were the stuff of nightmares.

Was that it? Had he dreamt of their stalker without realising it?

The bastard must have crawled into his skull whilst he slept. Ben could visualise him running, as if he had seen it with his own eyes. But the man's stillness on both occasions was indisputable. He had dreamt of him passing through a fog, its mesh of weblike strands aglow in the moonlight. He could hear bones cracking; limbs, jagged in their movements, forcing the stranger forward. Ben was running. But there was nowhere to escape to. The man was gaining on him, his grey form darkening to black as he tore through that crystal mist.

It was a nightmare, that was all. But Ben saw it now as clear as his own reflection. He stared ahead, seeing something where there was nothing, like his Aunt Patricia used to do. Maybe the madness was in his blood, too.

'It's like the kid told us,' Chloe said. 'You see him three times, remember? Well, now we've already seen him twice. *And on the third night his big ugly face is at your window.*'

'Chloe,' he said, calmly as he could, 'these things don't exist. It's just a story.'

It *was* the same man from the village. But Ben couldn't water down his conviction in front of her. Doubts and misgivings were par for the course when the questions outweighed the answers.

'If we see him again, we'll call the Guards,' he said. 'How about that? They can arrest your creeper and put him up in court for harassment.'

She didn't laugh. She didn't even break a smile. Instead her eyes scrolled down the screen, to the first column about Carol Fortune, printed only a few days after her disappearance.

'There,' Chloe said, drawing her finger to the screen. '*Detective Eamon Barry* was in charge of the case. Maybe he's still around.'

'*Or* how about we call Sparling? We can tell him that we're back and that we've nearly finished writing up his report.'

'Do we have his number?' she asked.

'Yeah, I'm sure it's in that folder he gave us. I'll give him a call. Once his money is in our pockets, we'll never have to speak of the Tír Mallachts again, okay?'

'Okay,' Chloe replied, crossing her arms, and sinking back into the couch. 'Call him.'

Ben emptied the folder onto the kitchen table. There were the doctor's beloved maps; each one a different stage of their journey. It didn't seem so far on paper. Other pages held general particulars concerning the project and its purpose, all fluff and filler. There was no contact number. There was no information pertaining to Doctor Alec Sparling at all. Even his name was absent. They had each given him their numbers that day on campus. One would have assumed that the doctor had included his own amidst the papers in case of any complications.

Chloe pulled out a chair across from him. Her pearl-grey eyes carried a hint of pink, as though she had spent the night in a smoky jazz bar. Her oversized black jumper reached down to her thighs. Its sleeves were bundled back to the elbows. She leant forward on the table, watching Ben rifle through the pages. She watched him find nothing.

'Okay,' he said, 'it would seem I was wrong.'

'These fucking maps,' Chloe said, holding one up in frustration. '*Two hundred years*, my arse! I'll email him. There's not much more we can do.'

The laptop was jerked open like a bear trap. She was far too livid for the usual formalities. Her fingers stabbed the keys as though they were Alec Sparling's eyes.

'Doctor Sparling,' she read aloud, 'contact me ASAP. You have my number. We don't have yours. We need to talk. Ms Coogan.'

'Is that it?' Ben asked.

'That's it,' she said, and after one last tap she pushed her laptop aside.

No sooner had it sent when an automated response landed back into Chloe's inbox. They both knew what that meant. The email address no longer existed.

'Fuck this,' she said. 'I'm not doing a tap of work on his project until I talk to him. This is bullshit, Ben. We have some fucker following us from Tír Mallacht and a missing girl Sparling spoke to who, for all we know, was killed by whoever or whatever was outside last night. And if he thinks for a—'

Her mobile phone began to shudder on the table. They leant over to peer at its screen – *private number*. Ben's phone was still buried somewhere in the bottom of his rucksack.

'Nobody ever calls me,' Chloe said, taking the phone and letting its charging cable slip down to the tiles like a snake retreating. 'Seriously, I don't give my number to anyone.'

'But you did though. It has to be him.'

Ben opened Chloe's old computer to have some notes at the ready. Its inner workings began to hum and grind like last time, as if it were operated by cogs and sticky gears.

Chloe held the phone like a bomb seconds away from detonation, 'Hello?' she said, staring at Ben.

'Ms Coogan,' came Sparling's familiar voice. 'I see that you have returned safely from your expedition.'

How did he guess so confidently where they were? Wasn't it possible that they could still be in Tír Mallacht or anywhere in between?

Ben imagined that insipid little smile on the doctor's face. His memories of him were monochrome. He was so dull – so uniquely forgettable – that Ben strained to recall any feature but his smile.

'Uh, yeah,' she replied. 'We've been working on the project since we got back. Ben is beside me. We've got you on loudspeaker.'

'Ah, I see. Good afternoon, Mr French.'

'Hey,' Ben said, awkwardly looking to Chloe as he waved at the phone held between them.

The laptop was still booting up. But he knew enough if Sparling tried to gauge the return on his investment. Ben was missing a week's work for this. He couldn't afford to walk away with nothing.

'Tell me, Mr French,' Sparling said, 'did your interviewees tell you anything of note?'

Ben considered stepping over the truth. But the lie would be too precarious, especially with the likes of Sparling – a stickler for detail who seemed to know more than he declared.

'Well, Alec,' he replied, feigning fellowship to soften the blow, 'the villagers went out of their way not to tell me very much at all. And it was made quite clear to us that we weren't welcome. So much so, unfortunately, that we were asked to leave the following morning.'

'I see,' he said.

Sparling hadn't enquired about his two-hundred-year-old theory. Surely his first question should have concerned whether he had been right or not. If they *had* found his Atlantis, then he was only asking questions about the fish that swam there.

'Not a single person that you spoke to mentioned anything about the creeper?' the doctor asked.

'Well, not exactly,' Ben replied. 'There was a child.'

'What did they tell you?' Sparling asked, slowly and intensely.

Ben's memory hadn't quite woken up yet, and the laptop was proving just as slow. He looked to Chloe for support.

'Three times you see him,' she began, reciting what the girl had said, word for word.

Never had a child's joke been treated with such earnestness. Ben had belittled the superstition whenever it crept into conversation and now he felt almost embarrassed listening to it again. They were meant to be academics – *the perfect candidates*. The kid's story made them sound like amateurs.

'She told you that?' Sparling asked after Chloe had finished. '*That's when the creeper kills you,*' he repeated. 'This *child* said that to you?'

'Yeah,' Chloe replied.

'And did you see him? That night did you see him?'

'Yeah,' she said. 'Someone followed us back to our campsite. And then, last night—'

'You saw him again?' he interjected excitedly.

'He was outside my house.'

'I see,' Sparling replied, and then all was silent over the line save for his breathing.

'Who is he?' Chloe asked. 'What does he want?'

Click.

The man had hung up.

15

Ben splashed his face with tap water; so cold it burned. Now he rested against the counter, dabbing his eyes with a dishcloth. The kitchen had been so obnoxiously yellow the night before. The sunlight exposed its true palette of dirty browns and a stale biscuit colour that might have been cream or even white before he'd been born.

Chloe had sleep-walked out of the room without a word. By the creak of her step on the stairs and the slam of a door, Ben guessed that she had gone for a lie-down. Any dream was better than this nightmare.

From his podium, Sparling had sold them his theories like a used-car salesman born into the trade. He used all the shiny things at his disposal – money, adventure, enlightenment – and Ben had champed at the bit. The bastard set him up. He had sent them to Tír Mallacht knowing full well that some local head-case would follow them back to the city. But why?

Ben shuffled over to the back door and pressed his forehead against its glass. Grey blocks were stacked tall on all three sides of the yard; a private prison to contain his misery. On the cracked patio between the weeds and the door there was a cereal bowl full to its brim with rainwater. Maybe Chloe fed a cat. Her relic of a laptop finally snapped out of its slumber with another shrill ping. It had been booting up since Sparling rang. Ben felt obliged to use it now, considering the trouble it had gone through just to turn on. He peeled his head from the glass and his reflection came into focus. Both eyelids were jammed halfway down like two broken blinds.

Ben had one lead to follow – Detective Barry. Their only link to Carol Fortune and the truth behind her disappearance. Alec Sparling was a ghost. But his hauntings hadn't passed unchecked. A quick internet search told Ben that Barry was still active. More importantly, it offered up the man's contact number.

Chloe had left her phone on the table. If it were unlocked, he would make the call himself. Ben figured the detective might take him more seriously if he spoke to him one-to-one. Having two voices jumping in and out of the loudspeaker wasn't exactly the deftest approach to conversation.

The phone lit up without need for a passcode. Behind its icons was a photograph of Chloe and a woman who Ben guessed to be her mother. They were cuddling into each other on a wicker sofa, tanned and holidaying somewhere warm by the looks of it. Their big eyes and matching smiles sparkled in the sun like a cheesy cosmetics ad. The woman could have passed for her older sister, such was her youth and likeness. Chloe looked so different. Her hair was a light, chestnut brown and trailed past her shoulders. And she was laughing like she had when they first met.

Ben's hand carried a slight tremor as he inputted the

number, his eyes twitching between the phone and the laptop with every digit.

The man answered almost immediately.

'Barry,' said the cheerless voice.

Ben hadn't registered what he was doing until the onus was on him to speak.

'Detective, my name is Benjamin French. I was hoping that maybe you could help me.'

'I would suggest you call the station, Mr French, and explain to them the nature of your problem. They'll be far better equipped to help you than I can.'

'Actually, it's *you* I wanted to talk to.'

'Okay,' Barry replied after a long sigh, airing his disinterest, 'what is it that *I* can do for you?'

'I was hoping you could tell me who Doctor Alec Sparling is?'

Silence. That told Ben all he needed to know.

'And what makes you think I know *that* name?' the detective replied, a hint of what could have been spite garnishing his words.

'You worked the Carol Fortune case two years ago, didn't you?'

'I did.'

'Well, the thing is that…'

'Mr French,' Barry interrupted, 'if this is another podcast or true crime piece, then I'm sorry to disappoint you. I'm not at liberty to discuss cases with every—'

'No,' Ben put in, 'it's not that. I'm an historian, like she was. And like her I've been contacted by Alec Sparling.'

'You're saying that this doctor of yours knew Carol Fortune.'

'Yes, I know for a fact that he did. Carol Fortune and I attended the same university. And I think that...'

How could Ben explain what they were experiencing? There was no way that one of the Tír Mallachts could have followed them back to Chloe's home. And yet he had seen him with his own eyes.

'You think what exactly?' Barry pressed.

'I think that what happened to Carol Fortune might be happening to us.'

'And who's us?'

'Chloe Coogan. She's an archaeology student, doing her master's. Sparling emailed both of us.'

'Archaeology, you say?' Barry said thoughtfully.

Ben heard some rummaging, as though the detective was reorganising his desk. Pages were being turned. Was he consulting a file?

'Tell me, Mr French, why did Doctor Sparling contact you?' Barry asked.

To hell with the non-disclosure agreement. Ben told him about the meeting, the contracts, and the trip to Tír Mallacht. To save his own embarrassment, he omitted the kid's little song and dance at sundown. He shared their first sighting of the man in the far field, but not his appearance outside Chloe's home. He still couldn't explain it to himself, never mind somebody else.

Barry listened. He scratched down notes. Ben would have liked to have had Chloe by his side, but maybe it was for the best. Too much talk of the creeper might have crippled the detective's trust in him. It was unlikely that the Guards had a fairy-tale division for apprehending disorderly superstitions.

'I *have* had some dealings with Alec Sparling,' Barry said.

'I'm sure you understand that I can't go into any further details. These are sensitive matters, Mr French. What exactly is it that you're accusing him of doing? From what you've just told me, the man isn't guilty of any crime.'

'I don't know yet,' Ben replied. 'I just want to talk to him.'

'I see. I suppose there isn't much harm in that.'

Ben realised how ridiculous he must have sounded. He had agreed to work for someone without checking their credentials and now that man had backed out of their arrangement. It hardly merited contacting a detective. He was like a teary-eyed schoolboy, whining that the other kids weren't playing fair.

'Okay,' Barry said, 'here's what we're going to do. I'm going to give you Alec Sparling's address, and in return for this I want you to keep our talk today to yourself. Don't mention to the man that you even know who I am. Do you understand?'

'Yes, Detective, I get you.'

'And you'll contact me immediately afterwards, won't you?' he added.

'Yes, immediately afterwards,' Ben agreed.

'Alec Sparling is an unusually private man. It's all very well giving you the coordinates to his home but that doesn't guarantee that you're going to get past the front gate.'

'Okay, good to know. We'll find a way.'

'A way that won't have you up in court for trespassing, I hope,' Barry said.

'No, nothing like that, Detective,' Ben said unconvincingly. 'I'm sure he'll let us in for a chat. He doesn't seem so bad.'

'That's where I think, Mr French, you would be very much mistaken.'

★ ★ ★

Ben rapped faintly on the door, 'Chloe,' he called in a loud whisper.

When no answer came, he cracked it open an inch and peeped inside. Soft daylight filtered through the curtains. The bedroom's walls were bare. A mound of clothes sat shapelessly in a chair beside a chest of drawers. There was a framed photo of Chloe when she was just a kid sitting on her mother's lap. Her smile looked even bigger, as though she'd grown into it as an adult. Books were stacked on the floor beside the boots she'd kicked off.

'Chloe,' he repeated, the word steadily losing sense.

She was hidden beneath the duvet. Only a foot could be seen poking out. Floorboards creaked as Ben tiptoed over to her. He sat on the edge of the bed and gently shook her awake. The foot retracted back into the warmth. She turned with a sigh, sleepy-eyed, with the tiniest weight of a frown, no doubt expecting more bad news.

'Get your boots back on,' Ben said. 'We're going to see the doctor.'

16

The car jerked to a stop, lurching Chloe against her seatbelt. The brick wall had stretched on for what felt like miles, but there was finally a break.

'Is that it?' she asked.

'I don't know,' Ben replied. 'I suppose it must be.'

'It doesn't look very welcoming, does it?'

The gate wasn't the decorative, wrought-iron variety common to moneyed estates. There was no frill or embellishment, and no obvious means to open it. Vertical bars stood like an armoury of eight-foot spears, glossy black and reinforced with a cross-brace that marked the entrance with an X. A monstrosity of this size wasn't designed for residential use. And yet there it was, surrounded on both sides by red-brick walls garlanded with coils of wire; silver thorns in the sunlight.

Barry's coordinates had pinpointed their destination. But none of the roads leading there were deemed travel-worthy by Chloe's GPS, and so they drove blind. Sparling's home wasn't too far divorced from civilisation. But there was nothing there except for some scraggy meadows and clumps of trees that made negotiating its serpentine lanes even more puzzling. Eventually they found themselves driving by the shadow of a brick wall, and then the world's most intimidating gate came into view.

'This is where Barry told us to go,' Ben said, nodding at Chloe's phone, 'and we haven't seen another house for miles.'

'Why is it that when I'm with you I always end up in the arse end of nowhere?' she said.

'I could say the same about you.'

Ben pulled the car up to the gate, where the coarse road turned smooth. He had expected to find a house, not a fortress. Between the bars, the driveway veered off through a spinney of old oak. The answers they sought were in there somewhere. But Barry may have underplayed just how *unusually private* Alec Sparling was when they had spoken.

'There,' Chloe said, pointing to the right of the gate, where an electronic panel was set into the wall. 'Maybe you want to try climbing over the top, but I'm thinking the bell would be easier.'

'And what do I say?' he asked.

'I don't know. Aren't you supposed to *have a way with people?*'

Ben clicked the door open with a sigh. His *way with people* was about as believable as the fucking creeper at this stage. He heaved his legs out of the car and crossed the tarmac to the intercom. Chloe followed. Her parka hung open; its furry hood draped back over her shoulders like a pelt.

It was nearly three o'clock. The black clouds had fallen away like quarried stone, and fissures of sky now gleamed sapphire blue. A musky-sweet smell pervaded the air; autumn's decay, like cremated ashes thrown to the wind.

Ben pressed his finger into a circular button. A dial tone rang out; high-pitched, low volume. Chloe shifted in beside him. There was probably a camera somewhere watching them but Ben couldn't see it. He imagined himself, recorded from an odd angle in black and white grainy footage, leaning his shoulder against the wall, eyes locked with Chloe's as they waited for a response like two Bible pushers determined to spread the faith.

'Can I help you?' asked a female voice carrying a hint of an accent.

'We're here to see Doctor Sparling,' Ben replied.

'I'm afraid that Doctor Sparling isn't receiving visitors.'

'Tell him, please, that Mr French and Ms Coogan would like a moment of his time. And if this gate doesn't open, we're coming over the wall.'

Chloe slapped him on the back and revealed that toothy smile of hers, as if to say *look at you go*. She let her hand rest on his shoulder, massaging her fingers into it. She'd obviously learned by now how anxious he got whenever a conversation took an impolite turn.

'One moment,' the woman answered sharply, and the intercom clicked off.

Ben watched Chloe's lips pucker up like they always did when she was thinking. Was scaling the wall really their backup plan? Hoisting her up on his shoulders wouldn't be too difficult. The boots were the heaviest part of her. Not getting her tangled in barbed wire or impaled on a spearhead could, however, have presented a few problems.

Still they waited. Ben suspected that Sparling was avoiding his perfect candidates.

'Fuck it,' Chloe said, 'if this bastard's not going to—'

'Hello,' Sparling interrupted, to which she covered her mouth in embarrassment.

Ben was surprised to hear the man's voice. He had expected the woman to return, sending them off like an overprotective mother. *Doctor Sparling can't come out to play today.*

'We need to talk, Alec,' he said.

'Yes, I suppose we do, Mr French.' Sparling replied. 'Follow the driveway and Lara will greet you at the front door. I'll be waiting for you in my study.'

The gate proceeded to slide slowly behind the wall, its gears buzzing like a beehive.

Sparling's home was a stark block of stone – a dull, characterless building not unlike the man himself, and reminiscent of the Anglo-Irish manors of the sixteenth century. Two storeys were lined with evenly set window frames, tall and slim, befitting a lofty ceiling and a fondness for light. Above them, in the attic, were smaller panes granting fractional fresh air to the old servants' quarters. Its grey walls had bruised over the centuries. Never painted, never washed. The double-leaf door with its pillared awning was flanked on both sides by flares of bottle-green ivy, ravelling out the higher it climbed.

'Sparling isn't shy a few euro, is he?' Chloe said, leaning forward in her seat.

The estate was large but lacking in features. Its lawn was sprinkled here and there with coppered leaves and had grown just tall enough to look untidy. There were no shrubs or flowering buds. Its upkeep would have been a soft affair for any gardener. Ben couldn't imagine Sparling donning a pair of gloves to tear up some weeds. *Did they even make gardening gloves in black?*

There was someone standing at the front door, waiting for them, presumably Lara. Her olive complexion and dark, wavy hair was decidedly continental. If she was a maid or housekeeper, then Sparling wasn't strict regarding uniform, as she was dressed casually in jeans and a laurel-green sweater.

'Check out the windows,' Chloe said. 'It looks like Alec's had some work done.'

Atop each frame was a white rectangular block; a modern mechanism that didn't aesthetically belong. They stood out against the dirty, stone walls. Ben had worked in enough shops to know a roller shutter when he saw one. They had to have been steel or aluminium. But security features like that were designed for jewellers and banks, not country manors.

There were no CCTV cameras. It would seem that Sparling had no interest in looking outside once those shutters dropped.

'I agree with you now,' Ben said, causing Chloe to frown in confusion. 'Everything *is* fucking weird.'

'I told you so.'

He parked the car facing the front steps. The woman didn't move to greet them. She watched their approach with quiet apprehension, her brown eyes tarrying on Chloe's hair.

'If you will both follow me,' she said before Ben could offer a greeting, 'Doctor Sparling will see you in his study.'

'Okay,' he replied awkwardly, glancing back at Chloe who seemed to share the suspicion that the woman wasn't accustomed to unexpected callers.

They followed her up the steps and through a windowless porch. Ben felt like an inmate being transferred to a stately prison. Chloe shifted in closer to him as Sparling's home opened out before them like a cavern. There was no grand hallway. There were no stairs to be seen anywhere. They stepped directly into the man's study; a room that seemed to occupy most of the ground floor. The smell of wood smoke was heavy in the air, as was a warm feeling of antiquity. Beneath a wall of books stood Alec Sparling, behind his desk, with two chairs facing him.

Ben had known something was wrong that day on campus. His first impressions never missed their mark. There *was* something remarkable about Alec Sparling; Ben had felt it when he hesitated by the door. It was a coldness – an apathy towards others, so absolute as to make the man dangerous. It was so obvious now. *Little late, Benny Boy.*

'Lara,' he said, addressing the woman who had just closed the front door behind them, 'I think it's best if I talk to Mr French and Ms Coogan alone.'

'Of course, Doctor,' she replied before disappearing through the only other door that Ben could see.

'Please,' Sparling said, beckoning them to sit and then doing so himself.

He was dressed in his drab ensemble of shirt and slacks. He looked the same as he had the day they had met, but that perplexing smile of his was absent on this occasion. In fact the man's face upheld no distinguishable emotion. Even the eyes were blank. Only when he peeled back his cuff to check the time was he seen to faintly frown.

'How did you find me?' he asked, looking up from under his brow.

'We have our ways,' Ben replied.

'Maybe I have grown careless in my old age. And what is it that you want? Money, such as the sum we agreed upon?'

'*I* want to know who the fuck is following us,' Chloe put in.

'I fear, Ms Coogan, that's not so easy to explain.'

'You'd better try,' she said. 'He was outside my home. Do you've any idea what that's like, to have someone staring in your fucking window?' Here she glanced outside, towards the high brick wall in the distance. 'No, I don't suppose you do.'

The tips of Sparling's fingers were pressed together in thought. 'You suppose incorrectly, Ms Coogan.'

Ben's memory recalled the doctor's eyes as blue, but now they seemed drained of even the weakest tincture. They watched Chloe intently as though she were the only other person in the room.

'Why did you send us to that place?' Ben asked, drawing the man's attention.

'Why, indeed, Mr French,' Sparling replied. 'You must forgive me. I haven't been entirely honest with you both. The truth is that I needed to know if the people of Tír Mallacht still lived as prisoners. *That* is why I sent you there.'

'And what does the village have to do with you?'

'Something happened there a long time ago and it has been the bane of my family ever since. It is the reason why its people don't leave and the reason why they were so reluctant to speak to you.'

'The creeper,' Chloe whispered.

'Correct, Ms Coogan. You have been paying attention.'

'Please—' Ben laughed mockingly '—don't start with this superstitious shit again.'

'I regret to inform you, Mr French,' Sparling said impassively, 'that this is no superstition. I can assure you that if it were, you and I would not be sitting here having this conversation.'

'You actually think it's real, don't you?' Ben asked, grinning in disbelief. 'Jesus Christ, Alec, you're an adult. It might be time to quit believing in fairy tales.'

There were still so many unknowns – those inexplicable happenings – niggling at the bedrock of Ben's beliefs. But, nevertheless, he held that grin as best he could.

'I understand you're something of an expert in that realm, Mr French, but it's made you sceptical. I should imagine that there are very few things you believe in anymore.'

'I believe in facts and *findings*,' he replied. 'Maybe you can explain these to me?'

Ben produced the sunglasses from his pocket and tossed them onto the desk. He guided the doctor to examine them, which he did, holding them tenderly between thumb and index finger as though they were made of the finest crystal.

'And what do you suggest I do with these, Mr French?' he asked. 'Aside from being broken, I see no reason to hide the sun's beauty behind a lens.'

'I found them,' Ben said smugly, 'in Tír Mallacht's cemetery. You knew that others had been to that village before us, didn't you?'

'Of course,' Sparling replied calmly, handing back the glasses. 'I'm the one who sent them there.'

'Then why should we believe a word you say now when everything you've told us has been a lie?'

'Because, Mr French,' he said with a fleck of impatience to

his voice, 'if you don't believe what I'm about to tell you, then you won't survive to see next week.'

Chloe's hand reached across and touched Ben's thigh. *Cool it, Benny Boy.* After a lifetime of eschewing every argument, he finally wanted to let loose.

'Okay,' Ben said, patting her hand as he held Sparling's gaze, 'I'll listen to what you have to say, but don't imagine for a second that I'm going to believe a word of it. At this stage, Alec, I just want my money.'

'Ben, please,' Chloe said, 'let him talk.'

'Fine, if that's what you want?' he asked her.

'It is,' she replied. 'This is why we came here, isn't it? You wanted the truth.'

Ben nodded his head and looked back to Sparling.

'You had better not lie to her.'

17

There was no tremble to Alec Sparling's hands. No nervous glances about the room. No stilted formality. In his own home, in this room, the doctor was perfectly calm.

'I've never told this to anyone,' he said, eyes narrowed pensively towards the window. 'I was forbidden to do so for reasons that you'll come to understand. Taking into consideration what you both know and what you've seen, the irreparable damage has already been done.'

'I think you might be overestimating how much we know,' Ben said.

'You know enough, Mr French, unfortunately,' he replied, letting his gaze linger on him.

Sparling pulled his chair in tighter to the desk. He fixed his posture, as one preparing for a long and uncomfortable journey. Next, the man straightened his shirt collar and fixed both cuffs tight over his wrists. He then cast an eye over his desk. Its contents all passed inspection. Only a single pen was adjusted slightly so that it was now aligned symmetrically beside a leather-bound diary. The doctor looked to Chloe and then to Ben. The grandfather clock's steady pulse counted the silence between them. This was how he wanted them to listen, without interruption, and with their full, undivided attention. Satisfied, Alec Sparling began.

'My ancestor was Tír Mallacht's clergyman. He also holds the distinguished honour of being the last of my family to die there. That church you would have examined, Ms Coogan, was once his house of worship. Brendan was his name. He had a wife and son as permitted by the Church of Ireland, and in his role as priest he cared tirelessly for his community; resolving disputes, prompting vows, offering advice on all matters spiritual or otherwise. Such was the man's compassion and patience that he planned his week around visiting every home, leaving none wanting for company.

'There was one man, however, whom the priest never met. He had lived alone on the outskirts of the village for as long as the oldest amongst them could recall. Months had gone by without anyone so much as seeing him. It was believed that he had either passed away or passed on elsewhere. But despite these rumours, Brendan still visited his home each week. The priest wished only to befriend him, to encourage the man to join his congregation if only to remedy the loneliness that had, no doubt, become his stock and store.

'Tír Mallacht was fortunate in that it hadn't suffered the woes of famine or illness common to the country at large. I theorise that their isolation kept them safe. They were a self-sufficient people and practised no contact with other communities. Survival of the narrow-minded, you might say, but they fared better than most. The young grew old and only then did their souls depart, leaving behind them families and fond memories, and a sense of loss that could in time be accepted.

'All good things, however, as I'm sure you both know, cannot last forever. It is one of life's painful little truths, I dare say.

'Tír Mallacht was no exception in this regard. And there came a time of unprecedented sadness, when death was not reserved strictly for the aged. In a few short weeks, six lives were lost without any recognisable ailment. Naturally, they feared that disease had finally found them. The more devout turned to their priest for answers as though God's will were accountable.

'So often in those weeks, he would spend his evening hours giving counsel to those in need. There were times – as he departed their homes – that Brendan marked a presence; the silhouette of another trespassing on their land. Each sighting preceded another loss of life. It was the only element that tied these tragedies together.

'His body was tall and spindly. The head, though impossible to discern by the moonlight alone, was without hair. The man didn't resemble anyone that the priest knew to live in the village. Not anyone that he had met, that is.

'He kept vigil over the man's home in the hope of resolving his suspicions face to face. He was certain – as only a man of good faith could be – that there had to be an innocent explanation.

'Good people see the good in others. They search for it, even when it isn't there. You could say that Brendan was a shepherd who didn't believe in black sheep.

'But days passed and the stranger neither came nor went. The priest's fears began to fester. So many lives had already been lost. Would God have forgiven him if another were to die because he had failed to act?

'Atop his pulpit, facing a full church, he aired his wariness of the stranger, beseeching the opinions of all those present, confident that someone could put his fears to rest. The man was a fool, so desperate for reassurance that he spoke without a thought ceded to consequence. His parishioners trusted his word without question. Each one eager to share and support his suspicions.

'Worried whispers passed between the pews until a child made her voice heard. The girl's mother urged her to speak. Everyone listened, their priest included, still ignorant as to the events he had now set in motion.

'Two nights earlier, the child had seen him standing at the far end of her family's land where the willows weep over a low wall. There could be no doubting who it was by her description. The mother held her child close and asked if that was the only time the man had visited her. The girl shook her nest of strawberry blonde hair. She had seen him again the night after, closer than before. She had waved at him but the man did not wave back. He didn't move at all.

'Brendan was probably as curious as everyone else. But that's hardly an excuse for letting a child speak so freely and to so many without first considering the repercussions. As you have no doubt guessed, any hopes the priest may have had of dealing with the man discreetly were quashed in that instant.

'The child's father demanded that the assembly – with their prayers spoken and their sins forgiven – confront the stranger at once. Brendan had vilified a man he knew nothing of; not the most Christian of behaviour, I'm sure you can agree. His pleas for peace and order were lost amidst the bustle, and soon everyone was storming towards the man's cottage. Though perhaps *cottage* is a poor choice of word.

'It was a windowless hovel on a hill with all the hallmarks of dereliction. As Brendan had hoped and learned to expect, nobody was home. But this did little to appease the mob. Their priest's voice – that which gave them solace in that darkest of times – was ignored, and they took God's wrath into their own hands, rending the door from its hinges.

'The men recoiled back from the stench that escaped from within; a putrid miasma that envenomed the senses, causing a few bystanders to retch. The stranger's home shocked a silence from the crowd. By the scant daylight that crossed the threshold, blood stained its floor, in gruesome puddles and crude finger paintings on its walls; symbols unknown to the Christians who eyed them. Scraps of parchment blackened with etchings lay strewn throughout. But of the man himself, there was no trace. No clothes. No food. No water. Not even the basest necessity.

'Every man, woman, and child clung together as one on their return to the village, as though a single consciousness mulling over a terrifying mystery. These people, familiar with their faith and its grace alone, could never have understood the evil that they had affronted.

'Brendan prayed that the man had abandoned Tír Mallacht for good; guided perhaps by the sudden exposure of his wickedness. If he was, as the priest suspected, in some way responsible for the tragedies of those weeks, then God would forgive his people their moment of weakness.

'But that night, as Brendan drew his curtain shut, he caught sight of a figure standing at his garden's far wall. Who knows what my dear old ancestor hoped to achieve when he rushed outside. Whatever the fight – be it for the sake of the stranger's soul or to simply chase him off his land – when the priest met the open air, he was gone.

'Not wishing to foster any further disquiet in the community, Brendan kept his sighting a secret. The villagers carried on as though having fulfilled God's will they now sat in his favour and the happiness they once shared could return. They assumed that they had rid Tír Mallacht of the evil forever. Their priest, of course, knew otherwise.

'The following night, with his appetite stifled by fear and secrecy, Brendan sat with his family. His wife and child sipped soup and broke bread in a peace that was uneasy to the priest alone. The curtain was drawn before dusk. The door – always open, always welcoming visitors at any hour – was locked. It would seem that black sheep existed after all.

'After his family retired to bed, Brendan remained, eyes transfixed on the covered window, imagining the other standing behind it. His chair creaked, though he strained to stay still. He needed to know if his family was safe. And so Brendan spied out into the night.

'We three are some of the few on this earth who can appreciate the exquisite horror of that second sighting. It stays with you, I regret to say. Even after all these years, I remember it as though it were yesterday.

'That chilling silhouette had returned – the one whose presence promises only death. Worse still, it had crept menacingly closer to all the priest held dear, and now stood, unmoving, watching from the darkness like a scarecrow gifted life.

'Brendan had no choice but to return to that wretched cottage whose symbolised walls and abandonments might have held some means to save the ones he loved. There, he procured any writings he could find, crawling through the shadows and the many fears they now awoke in him. It was an ungodly place and home only to ungodly things.

'The pages were laid on the floor of the priest's home and much time was spent in applying some order to them. The handwriting differed dramatically, ranging from the legible to the downright maniacal.

'The earliest passage – deemed so due to its ease of readability – was written in a tongue common to the area. It spoke of age and sickness. The man was, at the time of writing, fearful for his life. He reviled the slow corruption of his body and sought out a means to cheat death, to reverse the years so intent on destroying him. No price was too high. He pleaded with dark powers that Brendan was unfamiliar with. These weren't devils or demons – those known and repelled by his Christian teachings. In his desperation the man had turned to something else.

'His penmanship deteriorated and the language, evident on a single entry, turned archaic and indecipherable. So frantic were his movements that blood from his hand spotted the page. Like a puppet, the evil had wielded him into writing their contract; signed and sealed without hope or consent.

'One harrowing entry wrote of his betrayal, of a hidden clause in his soul's agreement, of a vanity mocked and spoiled. The evil had left him deformed and hideous to the eye. He became an immortal and a slave cursed to never know love or society for time eternal. He became what we now know as the creeper.

'The man was charged with stealing the lives of the innocent. But the kill was only part of it. His means lack the simplicity of mere murder. I suppose it was the evil's requisite for fear and its desire to toy with our kind that set the rules. Three nights its thrall visits their home. Each time that he is seen he draws closer, until on the third they bear witness to his face. Three sightings seal their fate. The night that follows is always their last. There is nowhere that the evil won't find them.

'The creeper *was* a man. But I fear that now he is something else entirely. It doesn't suffer the same restrictions as you and I. I wonder if it even retains a corporeal state at all times. How it moves so far and freely – manifesting where it pleases – is beyond me.

'Brendan burned the writings before his family returned home. If the contract held the man as its prisoner, maybe its destruction could repeal his servitude. Desperate acts from a now desperate man. The cottage was secured before dark. As his wife prepared their meal, Brendan sat anxiously, his eyes straying towards the cloth guarding his window.

'I don't doubt that the secret of the two sightings had grown inside the man like a tumour. You'll both come to understand that feeling – that fearful awareness of the sun's path across the sky and of the night that is inevitable.

'The priest stayed in his chair after his family were asleep. In the dregs of a whiskey jar he found his courage, and with a lamentable sigh and his tired body atremble, he opened the curtain ever so slightly. Maybe he thought that the stranger's writings were but records of his madness; idle impressions left by an ill mind.

'I won't tell you what he saw. Trust me, you don't want to know. All I'll say is that even the priest's most diabolical of expectations couldn't have conjured those eyes, inches from his own, mesmerised by the very sight of him. He recoiled in terror, fumbling for a God that had seemingly deserted him.

'Brendan lay down beside his wife and son to await the dawn. His boy's face twitched into a smile born from some wonderful dream. They needed to know. But he would let them have that last sleep and that last dream before the nightmares came.

'The next day, arrangements were made for his family to travel overseas. Their savings were gathered up, as were any light possessions of value. Brendan shared with his wife all that he had learned about the creeper, only so that she might understand. She would go, taking their son with her, and Brendan would stay. The shore was a day's journey. He hoped that an ocean could guard his family from the horrors he had invited into their lives.

'His last act as Tír Mallacht's clergyman was to warn those whose souls were his responsibility to protect. He summoned them together, the old and the young – every family that had a home there – and he told them of the creeper's existence. He told them everything. In their eager innocence they listened. The man had never led them wrong in the past, but in this act – however well intended – he doomed them to the life you have seen with your own eyes.

'It was through the priest's voice that the creeper was exposed, and it is through our voices that his evil is spread. To be told of his existence – to anticipate the three sightings – is to suffer his curse.

'I have spent a lifetime trying to understand it. And I can tell you no more than that.

'Without a priest, the villagers' faith over time diminished. I assume he waited for the creeper to come for him; a noble sacrifice of sorts to save his family. But he was wrong to think that the evil sought only him, that his death would bring an end to it all.

'The ship sailed at dusk. Some travelled alone, others with any family or friends who could fund the passage. Tears were shed for those left behind. There were some who had already made peace with the land they once called home. They busied themselves folding blankets into beds and preparing what needed preparing for the journey ahead. The priest's wife and son – my family – gazed back toward the shrinking shoreline, hoping perhaps that Brendan had raced after them, that the man who cared for them above and beyond all other things had come to take them home.

'Alas, by the bank – his long, cadaverous limbs shrouded in black – stood the creeper, watching them.'

'It followed his family?' Chloe whispered.

'My ancestors learned to avoid the night. The rules for survival have been passed down for generations. You're allowed two mistakes, that's all. It's a wonder my bloodline has gotten this far.'

'But we've already seen him twice,' Chloe said.

Sparling sighed and leaned forward, resting both elbows on his desk.

'Then I'm afraid you must live as I have done if you want to live at all, Ms Coogan.'

'Why did you send us there?' she asked him.

'Like I told you, I needed you to discover if they still feared him,' he said. 'It's the only way I can know if the creeper still exists and if I, too, am still his prisoner.'

'And what do you expect us to do?' Chloe asked, her voice faltering.

'There's only one thing you can do, Ms Coogan.'

'And what's that?' Ben interjected, glowering at the man.

'Fear him,' Sparling replied with the deadest eyes. 'It's the only way to stay alive, I assure you. Take it from one who knows. Live cautiously and live alone. Forsake any hope of having a family. Children born from either of you will suffer the same.'

Children? The word closed its teeth around Ben's heart. Sparling couldn't have known about Aoife. So why would he say that? Ben tried to suppress any reaction that might please the bastard.

'Ben,' Chloe said, 'what about Aoife?'

'And who, may I ask, is Aoife?' Sparling asked, sitting back.

'She's my daughter.'

'I see,' the doctor sighed, rubbing his fingers into his eyelids as if suddenly stricken with a wave of exhaustion. 'I do wish that you had told me the truth when we spoke on Tuesday, Mr French.'

'And why's that?'

'I'm terribly sorry for your daughter. I truly am.'

18

Ben milled around the room, phone held to his ear, waiting
for Jess to interrupt its dial tone. She was always slow to
answer his calls. Most of the time she didn't and most of the
time he didn't care. It was like waiting for a bus that – if it
came – was never on time. And the journey that followed was
not something that Ben ever enjoyed.

They barely knew each other. And yet she knew how to
hurt him. Her words were few, but they were precise, and
they never missed the heart.

Ben hated the act of airing some credence to Sparling's
fairy tale and he had played up the absurdity of it all. And
yet some unsung parental part of him still needed to know
that Aoife was safe. It would be a short conversation. They
always were.

He passed by the armchair and ran a hand over its leather.
His boots sank into the largest rug he had ever seen, and
probably the most expensive judging by the bastard's wealth.
Sunlight hung in a haze by the westerly windows. There were
paintings on the wall; uninspired landscapes with pigments

so thick that Ben would have loved to scrape them off like a scab. They were all the same – nondescript trees and hills, and skies of dull cloud, as if the artist loathed the sight of nature instead of admiring it. Still the phone rang. *Come on, Jess, pick up.* The curtains were tall, musty towers of velvet, and wouldn't have looked out of place dangling above a theatre stage. Maybe that's what all this shit was – gaudy props masquerading as the real deal.

There was no obvious pageant of wealth that Ben could find. No trinkets adorned the tabletops. There were no silver salvers or tea sets gleaming in a glass cabinet. The antiquated furniture was long overdue upholstering, and patterns once held by the carpet and wallpapering had faded to resemble more a mishmash of man's stains than his artistry.

Sparling and Chloe were sitting silently by the wall of books, probably bought in bulk at a second-hand sale. Surely there must have been a psychological term for adults who believed everything they were told. Still searching the night's sky for sleigh bells or dreaming of a shiny coin with a tooth under their pillow.

The phone clicked.

'Hey, Ben,' came Jess's disinterested voice, 'now's not really a good time.'

There was never a good time; one of many reasons why they so rarely spoke. Even now, Ben couldn't shake off the embarrassment, the regret, and the shame of his parents' reaction. The sound of her voice brought it all back to the present.

'I know and I'm sorry. I won't keep you for a second. I was just calling to see how Aoife is?'

'She's fine. She's watching cartoons.'

'Okay,' Ben said, letting the relief rinse over him; not that he expected Jess to elaborate any further, especially regarding skinny men standing outside her window at night.

She communicated mostly through sighs or in those whispered words under her breath that he never quite heard. The worst was that sharp intake of air when she said *yeah, yeah* whenever he invented some novel excuse for sending Aoife less than he promised. He always pictured Jess rubbing her tired eyes in frustration whenever he rang, as if the sound of his voice were enough to induce a headache.

'Ben, I've told you already that you can't call me out of the blue whenever you remember that you've a kid.'

'What?' he replied. 'Jess, that's not fair. I was worried, that's all.'

'Something wrong?' she asked.

'No, of course not. Everything's fine. Listen, would it be okay if I talked to her for a moment?'

'Ben, every time you call, she starts asking me where her dad is and why he isn't here, and I'm sick of making excuses for you.'

'I'm working on that,' he said. 'I've some money coming—'

'When?' she snapped. 'Amazing how you seemed to produce money out of nowhere when I told you I was pregnant.'

'That was never going to happen,' he said, trying to keep his voice down. 'I thought we got over this.'

'Yeah, Ben.' She sighed. 'Let's just forget every shitty thing you've done so you can start pretending to be Aoife's dad, like you've been telling me for three years now.'

'We're not having this conversation again. I just wanted to talk to my daughter. It doesn't matter. I've got to go.'

Ben ended the call.

'Okay,' he whispered under his breath, 'I should *not* have done that.'

He couldn't have asked her. He refused to. Good fathers are meant to chase the bogeyman from the closet, not invite him in.

Chloe turned expectantly as Ben returned to the desk. He already regretted hanging up on Jess so abruptly. It added more fuel to the pyre that she kept aflame. Chloe hadn't overheard his conversation. He had made quite sure of that. Ben took care to affect a smile. Aoife was safe and everything was fine. Why should his face say any differently?

'What did Jess say?' Chloe asked him.

'Like I told you,' Ben replied, ignoring the doctor entirely, 'there's no creeper coming after us or Aoife. She's perfectly safe. She's watching cartoons.'

'And what age is your child, Mr French?' Sparling asked.

'She's three.'

'Three years old,' he repeated, inferring some significance. 'I should imagine that your daughter isn't in the habit of looking out her bedroom window at night. At such a young age she's probably sound asleep by then.'

'I wouldn't know,' Ben replied.

That tightness in the chest, the sweaty palms, that lump in the back of his throat; all the tell-tale signs were there, including that familiar indecision to swing a clumsy fist or break down in tears. Some people thrived on conflict. Ben hated it. But maybe – just maybe – he hated Alec Sparling more.

Chloe fidgeted constantly, biting her thumbnail down to the quick. One leg was crossed over the other with a boot quivering above the floor like a dead body dangling from a noose, convulsing from the trauma of its final seconds. This was Sparling's doing. He had wormed his way inside her head. Ben watched as her lips parted to talk, only to clamp shut again.

'What happened to the others?' she asked, finding her voice, but it all came out too fast, her words exploding like trapped air pressure.

'And who, Ms Coogan, are you referring to when you say *the others*?'

'Carol Fortune,' Ben said before she could answer, 'and the other perfect candidates that you failed to tell us about.'

'Mr French,' Sparling replied, accenting his surprise. 'You know much more than you're letting on, don't you? Wherever did you hear *that* name?'

'Cut the shit, Alec,' he snapped back. 'What happened to her?'

'Ms Fortune and the others met with the same *misfortune*. There was always someone who couldn't keep their mouth shut. One wouldn't be blamed for thinking that the villagers *want* the curse to spread. But I assure you, that is certainly not the case.

'The adults don't talk of him. They know better. Well, most of them do. It's difficult to hold the tongues of those born with some defect of the mind, and Tír Mallacht has its fair share of those. It's the inbreeding, you see – it presents myriad complications. The children were to blame on almost every occasion. Mischievous little things, as I'm sure you know, Mr French.

'That was how Ms Fortune encountered the curse, through the whispered warnings of a child who found fun in sharing secrets. It attached to her as it has attached to you.

She didn't call for help like some of the others did. Maybe, like you, Mr French, she thought it was some practical joke in the poorest taste. I never did discover where Ms Fortune was on her last night when the creeper came for her. Her body is still missing. After so much time we can assume it will never be found.'

'My God,' Chloe whispered, lowering her face into her hands.

'Don't believe a word of it,' Ben said. 'Let's just take the money that—'

'No,' she replied, standing up, sending the chair falling back onto the floor. 'Why won't you listen to him, Ben? This *thing* is following us! It's not going to go away because you don't fucking believe in it! How do you suppose it appeared outside my house? Can you explain that?'

'I don't know. He could have followed us. They're obviously not as backward as Alec here thinks they are. Maybe he hid in the trunk? We did throw our bags in the back seat, remember? Or what if he was under the car the entire time? Or who is to say that the Tír Mallachts don't own a fucking car?'

Sparling's grotesque little smile grew on his face like larvae. Ben balled up his fists. He had never thrown a punch in his life. He wasn't sure if he knew how.

'Mr French,' the doctor said collectedly. 'As convincing an argument as you make, I can tell you with absolute certainty that the creeper doesn't need a vehicle or whatever it is you're alluding to in order to find his victims. He appears. It's really that simple. And he will appear to you every night from here on out, waiting to be seen.'

'What can we do?' Chloe asked.

A bell sounded through the room. The grandfather clock

tolled up the hours. *Two o'clock, three o'clock, four o'clock*, and there it rested. Night was steadily approaching. The October days never held the sun aloft for long.

'You're welcome to spend the night here,' Sparling said, his shark eyes turning to Chloe. 'I can have Lara prepare a room. Given its modifications, my home is the safest place for you right now.'

Had this been his plan all along? Ben had kicked around different theories as to why the man was so intent on terrorising Chloe with horror stories. Why else would a grey-skinned hermit go to all that trouble?

'She's not staying here with *you*,' Ben said.

'Mr French, I think there's been a misunderstanding. The only reason I—'

'Give us our money,' he interrupted, 'and we'll be gone.'

'Ben,' Chloe said, 'can't we just—'

'Chloe, please,' he said, softening his tone, 'trust me. We're getting out of here.'

'Tell you what, Mr French,' Sparling said. 'If you wish I can pay you the fee we agreed on right now. You and Ms Coogan can leave, and you and I will never speak again. However, I have another proposition for you – take the original fee now *or* I can pay you both double that amount on Monday. Of this you have my word. You know where I live and we do, of course, have a contract together. What do you say?'

Windfalls like that come once in a lifetime. No more retail. No dingy apartment. Ben could move closer to Aoife. He could be a father. But tempting as it was, something wasn't right. It was impossible to ignore; a dissonant note that couldn't be unheard.

Alec Sparling remained a mystery. What he had told them

was the product of the man's delusions; a web so irrationally spun as to addle his own agenda. All Ben knew for certain was that affording double the original fee wouldn't trouble his private treasury in the least. He probably carried that kind of cash in his back pocket, in a black wallet, folded neatly between other colourless things.

Ben's patience for the superstitious had been bled dry. The Tír Mallachts were the worst of their kind. Enslaved by simplicity, isolated, and abandoned by civilisation, they had become dangerous, like dogs guarding their territory. They had tracked them back to their car. They had followed them to Chloe's. And in doing so they had gone too far.

Sparling was familiar with their traditions. Maybe it was a hobby of his to prey on the financially forlorn, to send them there under false pretences so that the Tír Mallachts could have their fun. Or maybe he was the lecher that Ben now suspected him to be, terrifying young women into his arms and, in turn, his bed; imprisoned in his roller-shuttered mansion until his libido yearned for other *perfect candidates*.

Sparling had been on the detective's radar. What if he was a suspect in some long-running case? How else would Barry know the private address of someone who went to such efforts to stay off the grid? If the detective wanted the dirt on the good doctor, he could have it.

Ben would fold out a deckchair across from Sparling's gate and watch him being driven away, bound in a straitjacket, fated to live out his last years in a white, padded room, reiterating the story of Father Brendan over and over as if anybody cared.

'Triple it,' Ben said, 'and you've got yourself a deal.'

Sparling nodded. 'Very well, if that's the sum you desire.'

'I'll be back on Monday,' Ben replied, 'and you had better have it ready.'

'I'll have your fee delivered to the gate, Mr French. There you may count it at your own avaricious leisure.'

Sparling re-examined his wristwatch and lifted himself to his feet. Their meeting had adjourned. He looked towards the tall windows, considered the daylight mournfully, and clasped his hands together.

'The autumn evenings are getting shorter,' he said. 'I trust you don't have too far to travel.'

'It's not really an issue,' Ben replied. 'The dark doesn't scare us like it does you.'

'Very good, Mr French,' Sparling said, insinuating the slightest smile. 'For what it's worth, I'll have your money waiting for you on Monday.'

Shadows were growing through the earth. They spread like a disease from the western wall, thinning the estate of colour. Leaves had clustered around the last step by the manor's front door and now crunched beneath Ben's boot. The fresh air hit him like a strong mint; ice against his eyes. Behind the oak, the evening sky was a cloudless, orange cocktail of light. The sun skulked between their branches like a guest slipping away from a party, not wanting to be seen.

Ben didn't look back until he was sat in the driver's seat, belt on, key in the ignition.

'Come on, Chloe,' he whispered, squeezing the wheel with both hands.

She had dithered by the door, hesitant to abandon the

safety of Sparling's home. But she was brave despite his best attempts to make her doubt herself. The engine sputtered before it growled into eager action. Ben clicked the headlights on full, illuming the lonely shape of Alec Sparling shuffling toward the front step.

Chloe sat in. Her seatbelt swished and clicked.

'You good to go?' he asked.

She nodded, biting her lips in indecision.

'It's okay,' Ben added, reaching out a hand to squeeze her shoulder.

Sparling returned their gaze, his leaden pallor bleached in the headlights. Ben had hoped the doctor would offer them some acknowledgement so he could flip him the finger as one final *fuck you*. But the man just inspected his wristwatch and stood there, watching them as though they had boarded a sinking ship.

Chloe turned to Ben. 'Are you sure about this?'

'Absolutely; there's only one creeper around here and he's standing right in front of us.'

'You really don't believe any of it?' she asked, seeking some reassurance like a kid hiding under her bed.

'Not a word,' he replied, watching Sparling return indoors.

Ben wished he could have witnessed the ritual of his lockdown, the sight of all those shutters rolling – sealing the bastard inside – like a wall of eyes closing their lids for the night. Despite his obvious intellect and perfectly ironed shirts, Sparling was no better than the Tír Mallachts – a prisoner of his own phantasms.

The smooth tarmac fell away with a thud that made the whole car rattle. It felt good to be in the open, like fresh ocean air for the soul. Just over an hour of daylight remained.

The red-brick wall smouldered in the dusk, its barbed wire gleaming.

Chloe's face was turned towards the passing fields; rising and falling, but never offering enough variety to hold her interest. Ben suspected that those big eyes stared inward, imagining only the horror that Sparling had forced upon her.

'Are you okay?' he asked.

'I don't know.' Chloe sighed, finally turning to face him. 'He believes it all, doesn't he?'

Sparling might as well have been sat in the back seat, whispering in her ear.

'He's probably spent his entire life in that house,' Ben said, 'with too much money and not enough to do. The man's lost it.'

'I know, I know. You're right. I was just thinking about the other teams that he sent there before us. What really happened to them?'

'I'll call the detective after we get our money,' Ben replied. 'Don't worry. He'll look into it.'

'And can we call him if that fucker from Tír Mallacht shows up again?'

'Absolutely.'

Common sense was the best tool for prying out Sparling's claws. Whether she honestly stood with Ben's stance or not, she would come around eventually.

What he wouldn't give to catch the creeper, to parade him in front of her like an episode of *Scooby-Doo* when the monster is revealed to be just another everyday villain, cursing the meddling kids who found him out.

They had almost arrived at Chloe's. The evening's firmament was blushed with pink. The last of its amber wash had retreated over the horizon like a low tide, and the peace of nowhere was usurped by car horns and a din with no distinctive sound. Ben had skirted around the worst of the evening traffic, and now they waited at the last set of lights before turning into her estate, where tall streetlamps burned like blown glass, sweeping the shadows from the pavement below.

It was almost six o'clock. They would be indoors before dark.

19

The shutters adjusted in harmony with the sun. October's evenings were drawing in, shaving off a little extra light with each passing day. Lara had already sealed the curtains throughout the house and the fire had been fed its meal of timber. Its flames smouldered in Alec's dark eyes. He was sat, fidgeting with the arms of his chair, deliberating over the day's proceedings and the identity of the one who had betrayed his trust.

A door opened and closed just as softly. Alec didn't turn. Lara was ghostly quiet and stepped without imprinting a sound. He knew, however, that she travelled from the door to his chair in approximately six seconds, and so he counted the pendulum's swing. Lara stood by his side in nine; later than expected. Their uninvited guests had obviously thrown the household into flux. Even the wood was slow to crackle, slapping away the flames like indecent hands.

'As it's Friday, Doctor,' she said, 'I've taken the liberty of preparing a casserole for your evening meal.'

Lara wore a white cotton apron and stood with both hands

neatly behind her. The dear girl's posture was perfect. Her hair was tied back in a bun, accentuating that sublime bone structure and those coffee eyes that swirled in the firelight.

'Thank you, Lara,' Alec replied. 'A fine choice considering the chill in the air this evening. Winter is nearly upon us.'

'It is, Doctor. Can I bring you anything else in the meantime?'

'Please, Lara, could you leave the telephone by my side. And my diary, if you would be so kind.'

'Of course, Doctor,' she replied with a subtle bow of acknowledgement.

The flames finally wooed the timber with their persistence. Alec rested his eyes for a moment, enjoying their heat against his cheeks. His study was too large a room to banish the cold completely, an oversight on his father's behalf. One of the old man's many shortcomings.

The building was practically a shell when the deed was signed. Fittings were too few to render it remotely liveable. Ivy had snaked inside through splintered doorframes and windows, inspiring the usual suspects to take up their residency: rodents, insects, birds, and beasts – poor housekeepers, all of them. So dilapidated had it become that restoration seemed a fool's errand. The previous owner assumed that it was his wish to knock it down and rebuild, and so it was auctioned off at a sliver of the market value. The estate itself – mere overgrown grass and oak – wasn't appreciated for its full worth by any man but Alec's father.

The manor's interior was eviscerated, including the grand mahogany staircase with its fluted balusters worth more than the building it was housed in. The man's vision was unique, as were his needs. Many small rooms required many small lights, whereas a large hall could be lit without great expense. In its original state, most of the study's window frames were bricked up, leaving the bare minimum to admit sufficient light during the daytime. A new corridor was constructed. This led into the kitchen and bathroom, and upstairs to the other chambers where no windows remained. The manor would have appeared derelict and unlived in from the outside, and suitably uninviting. His family never had been the sociable sort.

Alec drew the phone's receiver to his ear. The location of his home was a secret known to few. His trust in Lara remained uncompromised. Like her mother before her, she had always demonstrated absolute discretion. That left only one other: a man whose confidence Alec had paid handsomely to hold.

'Barry,' answered the voice.

'Good evening, Detective.'

Barry coughed to clear his throat. A coarse and obvious play for time. Alec got the impression that the man had been slouched quite comfortably at his desk, and that he now sat forward like a nervous bird on its perch, the pride of his profession humbled in an instant.

'Doctor Sparling,' he replied. 'I wasn't expecting to hear from you.'

Alec imitated a laugh as best he could. Much like his smile, it didn't come naturally. It was too high-pitched and false to ever convince. Not that this was his intention.

'I suppose the criminal never *expects* to get caught, does he, Detective?'

'I don't believe I understand.'

'Good heavens,' Sparling sneered. 'I would advise you

not to waste my time with this insubordination any further, Detective. Can you do that?'

'Yes,' Barry replied, his words fragile. 'Of course, Doctor.'

Alec knew the man was terrified of him. He could crush his life and livelihood in a quick morning if he so pleased.

'Today I received two visitors to my home,' Alec began. 'They knew precisely where I live because *someone* had shared with them its location. Now, as you know, Detective, I am a remarkably private man. And you will also remember that you and I have a strict arrangement. You respect my privacy and I in turn keep your dirty little secrets safe from those who, God forbid, should wish to use them to destroy you. I know it was you. Your honesty now will determine how I deal with your betrayal. So, Detective, tell me, what information exactly did you share despite my most inflexible of wishes?'

Barry told him about Benjamin French and how he and a student by the name of Chloe Coogan suspected some link between Sparling and the disappearance of Carol Fortune. He was patently honest, upfront, and repeated the conversation as best as his mind could recall.

'Why would they have connected you to her disappearance?' he asked, bested by curiosity as weak men so often are.

'Careful, Detective,' Alec replied. 'You would be wise to avoid matters that do not concern you.'

'When we first met, I asked you what your interest was in—'

'Must I repeat myself?' Alec interjected. 'I'm willing to forgive, if not forget, your indiscretion on this occasion. But I will not be so lenient should this ever happen again. Do I make myself clear?'

'Yes, Doctor,' Barry replied sheepishly.

'In the event of either Mr French or Ms Coogan contacting you, I want you to feign action. Let them believe that you will aid them with any issue. But – and I cannot state the importance of this enough, Detective – you will do *nothing*. You will tell me of any such development. But you will tell no one else. If you go against my wishes, I can guarantee that your life will be altered greatly and not for the better. Do you understand?'

'Yes, Doctor.'

'And one final request,' Alec added. 'Mr French and Ms Coogan are currently in possession of some documents that I have commissioned. I should imagine, seeing as they spent last night in Ms Coogan's home, that this is where you'll find them. Collect them all, Detective, and any computers or devices on the premises and bring them to me. But wait until Monday. By then I should imagine that the house will be empty.'

'What's her address?' Barry asked.

'You're a Detective, for Christ's sake. I'm sure you can find that out without my help.'

'Of course, I'll get on it right away.'

'Then I'll bid you a good night. Don't disappoint me.'

The receiver clicked back into place.

Alec returned his hands to the armchair's leather. He had been displeased with the detective's behaviour. The truth was, however, that he was just as dissatisfied with his own. Maybe when a man has survived for as long as he had, he derived some deluded sense of invincibility from his years. But that was no excuse. He had told Mr French and Ms Coogan too much. After a lifetime of silent suffering, perhaps he had hoped it would ease his burden to finally share his plight with another. On the contrary, it served only to add to his worriment.

How would they each react to what was coming? It was perfectly reasonable – expected even – for one of them to call for help, as Ms Quinn had done. On listening back to that phone call, he could tell that the poor girl was terrified. She had blurted out so much that even the emergency services operator disappeared within the week.

The rumour mill churned out its own fairy-tale ending that Alec knew to disbelieve. Those who worked with the call taker said that he had been planning a grand escape abroad. Thailand or Vietnam, or somewhere comparably muggy. Innocence and ignorance were so often indistinguishable.

Ms Coogan was aptly fearful. Not even the most gifted actor could mimic such candid, hopeless despair. She would speak of the creeper to no one. Mr French could, however, prove problematic for two reasons. Firstly, his hatred for Alec was undeniable, bridled only by greed. Secondly, the man's scepticism was inconvincible. So familiar was he with Ireland's superstitious offering that he disbelieved anything bordering on the extraordinary.

Luckily, Mr French's narrow-mindedness would expedite his expiration. Whatever money he thought awaited him, the man wouldn't live as far as Monday to receive it.

20

Grey concrete rolled under the headlights. The cul-de-sac was as lonesome as last time. A curtain shifted aside as Ben slowed the car to a stop. Same registration, same bizarre scratches on its paint, same two culprits, same reckless inconsideration for the lives of others. The rumour mill had creaked to life, marrying what they knew with what they didn't, conceiving due cause for concern.

Chloe's boots thundered upstairs, sending a tattoo of tremors through the house. Floorboards groaned and cried. Curtains were called on every pane. Somewhere, cups chimed in a hidden cupboard. Sounds were oblivious to the walls around them. A heavy step in an upstairs bedroom landed just as loudly in the sitting room below, leaving no creak unheard and no peace undisturbed. It was as though the old house was a nocturnal sentient waking for the night ahead, wiping the sleep from its windows and stretching its aching beams.

Ben walked through to the kitchen. Its bulb was even more nauseating having come from Sparling's low-lit study, where the hearth held the brightest light and its sombre fittings melded seamlessly with the shadows. Chloe was stomping around in the sitting room now, swishing its curtains together. Ben – playing his part – lowered the blind above the sink and drew the slatted curtain across the back door, dusty to the touch with ends discoloured from damp.

He peered out between the slats where the last cinders of dusk burned in the black. Chloe's backyard was surrounded by similarly miserable enclosures. So tall were the walls dividing them that the creeper would want to be in the shape of his life if he planned on staring into Chloe's kitchen.

As inventive as these superstitions were, they fell apart when examined too closely. It was more convenient to muddy the details or to breeze over them completely. The creeper must have rented a room in a neighbour's house if he planned on *appearing* seven nights a week. Maybe he was the one watching them from the window, sipping on a steaming mug of coffee, bracing himself for another night standing out in the cold.

It had been decided during the drive that Ben would stay over. Chloe hadn't asked but he knew that Sparling's scare tactics had left their stain on her, and so he had volunteered, casually and without inconvenience.

Under no circumstances was he leaving her alone. There was one truth that they could both corroborate. Someone – a man, not a curse – had spied on them the two nights prior. Ben wanted to be there in case he returned, to disprove the myth once and for all and, in doing so, expose Alec Sparling as the fucked-up liar he knew him to be. He was still seething over his invitation to Chloe. Ben wished he had copped on to the doctor's sordid little plan sooner. He would have landed his first punch for sure, right in that sickly smile of his.

The laptops were on the kitchen table, surrounded by scatterings of paper and Ben's mug of stale coffee – mementos of a project that would never be completed; one that never really existed. Not that he cared anymore. On Monday, he would be the wealthiest he'd ever been.

He began tidying Sparling's precious maps into a pile, soon to be reduced to tinder.

'What are you doing?' Chloe asked him, appearing in the doorframe.

With eyes that big there was no disguising her tiredness. The night before, Ben had conked out without a fight, the journey to and from Tír Mallacht having left him a hollow husk of a human being. A week's worth of sleep wouldn't replenish what he had spent. Chloe had probably sat till sunrise, watching over them, as he had tried to do in the tent.

'I'm going to burn every trace of Alec Sparling and Tír Mallacht,' he replied. 'And we're going to celebrate, okay? On Monday we're rich. Have you anything to drink? I should have stopped by an off-licence.'

'I *always* have something to drink,' she said, her smile fragile as a rose in a storm. 'There are briquettes inside, and wood from a cabinet that we broke up. Just don't tell the landlady. There's so much shitty furniture in this house that I reckon we've enough firewood to last us until Christmas.'

Ben couldn't have been prouder of her. She was no more intrepid than a child who had sat through a marathon of horror movies. But she was forcing all those senseless fears to the back of her thoughts.

The sitting room felt somehow colder than the street outside. Ben stood by the coffee table for a moment, blowing air into his cupped hands, eyeballing the sealed curtains like forbidden fruit, chewing over that same seed of doubt. What if it *was* real? What if just one of those superstitions were true?

The curtains were suddenly illumed by the headlights of a car turning at the end of the cul-de-sac, like a lighthouse beacon warning distant ships to steer their course to safer shores.

'That'd be the creeper now,' he whispered to no one, 'running late as usual.'

The uplighter was too dim to dispel the room of darkness. It served only to draw attention to the black spots of mould that sagged down in the corner of the ceiling. These weren't isolated lumps. This cancer ran deep. Ben laid down the briquettes and went about assembling the shattered memories of Chloe's bedside cabinet into a pyramid.

He regretted calling Jess earlier. *Jesus, what if she thought I'd been drinking?* Any impoliteness on his part would be construed by Aoife's mother as an act of war. And she was more formidable than any creeper.

Ben had wanted to tell Jess about the job and the money, but he couldn't exactly do that with Sparling sitting across the room. When eventually they spoke again, the reality would be carefully dressed up to best impress. *He had been headhunted for a research position.* Not too far removed from the truth. The pay should be false proof enough. It had certainly duped Ben into believing it. Everything would be better with a few more digits in his bank account.

And Aoife was fine. She was perfectly safe. Then why, whenever Ben thought of his daughter, did he imagine her standing within the creeper's gangly shadow, unaware of those long fingers reaching for her neck?

★ ★ ★

They were soon ensconced on the couch's swamp of throws and blankets, glasses in hands, with Chloe's laptop on the coffee table beside them. Ben faked familiarity with its music; some instrumental metal band whose distorted riff had been on a loop for the past five minutes. The briquettes were ablaze, and the landlady's cabinet was slowly catching up, cracking away as cheap wood always does. Now and again, one would catch the other glancing towards the curtains and they would each pose a smile.

'What a day,' Chloe sighed, her legs curled into the couch's corner.

'What a *day*?' Ben scoffed. 'This whole week has been insane.'

'It wasn't exactly what we signed up for, was it, Mr French?'

'Never a truer word spoken, Ms Coogan. To think that I believed him. I thought this was the beginning of my brilliant new career as an historian-slash-adventurer.'

'That's not even a thing,' Chloe said. 'Historians don't go on adventures. But to be fair, it was pretty convincing. I know I called shenanigans on his *untouched for two centuries* theory, but I kind of hoped we'd find something. I guess that's the archaeologist's dream – to discover a lost piece of our past before anybody else.'

She never seemed overly interested in the money. Not like Ben.

'What are you going to spend your *financial reward* on?' he asked. 'Bearing in mind now, we're getting thrice what we thought we were.'

'People still say *thrice*?' Chloe replied, savouring a sip. 'I reckon a holiday is overdue. There are a few sites that every archaeologist worth their salt should see. And sure, I'll bring you along. You can drive me around and spy on me whenever I'm taking my pants off.'

'I'll drink to a holiday.' Ben laughed, raising his glass. 'And that was an accident, just so you know.'

'Any holiday would do,' she replied, toasting him back. 'Maybe I need a break for a while. I've not taken any time off since...' She seemed to lose her train of thought. 'What about you?'

'I don't know,' he replied, frowning down at his wine. 'I need to see more of Aoife. She's three years old and I feel like she hardly knows me. It's my own fault. I've not been the best dad in the world.'

'You'll be great, don't worry. You're already doing a better job than my dad ever did.'

'Really?' he asked, looking for the truth in her eyes.

'Absolutely,' she replied. 'Look, your whole world changed and that's not easy, Benny Boy. Maybe for a while you didn't want to change with it. But look at you now. You *want* to be a dad.'

'You don't think I'm a lost cause?' Ben asked.

'No way. You're going to be amazing.'

'I could move to Donegal and start afresh. I'm not exactly leaving too much behind me here, am I? I hate my job. I hate my house.'

'You could always buy a little cottage in Tír Mallacht.'

'Yeah, I should renovate that black one on the hill.'

Chloe's smile dissolved at the mention of it.

'What's wrong?' he asked.

'Do you think that that's the cottage Sparling told us about?'

Ben hadn't made the connection himself. But it was there that Chloe had discovered the symbols, on a house set apart from the rest of the community, like the creeper's cottage in Sparling's story.

'It's a coincidence,' he replied quickly, hoping to trim back the idea's thorns, 'or else Sparling probably picked it out from one of his maps.'

'Ben,' she said sharply, 'everything that he told us checks out with everything we've seen. The secrecy, the shutters, even that man's reaction when the kid told us about the creeper. You're so convinced that Sparling is lying to us. But we've seen it all with our own eyes.'

'Chloe, please,' he said. 'Curses and creepers don't—'

'You've seen him yourself,' she snapped, interrupting him. '*Three times you see him.* You remember what she told us? *On the third night his big ugly face is at your window.*'

Ben drained his glass and slammed it down on the table. With fingers pressed to his lips – not wanting to say something he might regret – he stared at Chloe from across the couch. *That fucking kid!* He couldn't listen to it anymore. Every mention of the creeper's *big ugly face* was an attack on his patience. It had to stop. He struggled off the couch and muted the laptop.

The silence was essential. He needed Chloe to listen.

'It's the third night,' he said, standing before her, wreathed in firelight.

She burrowed into the couch like a tick.

'What are you doing?' she asked uneasily. 'Sit down, will you?'

If that bastard from the far field *was* outside somewhere, Ben would prove to Chloe that he was just a man. Why was the truth so hard to believe?

'It's the only way you're going to believe me,' he said, pacing towards the window.

'Ben, stop. You don't have to do this.'

He spread his arms wide, resembling some cheap, street-side showman teasing a reveal behind the curtain. If only Ben could have seen himself. Chloe needed reassurance. She needed a friend. Instead he was parading in front of her as though she were a child and he the all-knowing adult.

'This is all Sparling's handiwork,' Ben said, wagging his finger as he took a step back. 'He's gotten inside your head, Chloe.'

'Ben,' she shouted, rising to her feet, 'don't you dare open that.'

'Why? So we can keep on believing in the creeper or Count Dracula or whoever else you think is out there. Chloe, listen to me. None of it's real.'

This was for all those believers, the gullible and the deceived, and every scared little kid crying into their pillow. But most of all, though Ben would never admit it in a thousand lifetimes, this was for himself. This was proof that he had been right all along.

'Ben, please. Don't...'

He gripped the curtain in a balled-up fist and ripped it back; so swift and simple an action.

The horror nearly brought Ben to his knees. He staggered

back into the room, staring in terrified disbelief at the face that stared back at him.

Its smile was unflinching; stretched impossibly wide as though the cheekbones had been shattered and reformed. Teeth were rooted in black gums, each one pared and veined with decay. The skin was ghostly white. Eyes, like the malformed mouth, were sickeningly caricatured; bloated like pus-filled sores bulging out from their sockets. The head was hairless, crooked and cracked, with a chinbone split beneath the skin, torn apart by the sheer force of that smile. Ears were absent, with only flays of skin remaining. The nose looked to have been smashed and pulled as putty into a point; like the face's every aspect – mutilated and hideous to behold.

Ben's body pressed against the back of the couch. The room around him dissolved into a fog, leaving nothing, just those soulless, shivering eyes.

It wasn't a man. What now stood with its face practically pressed against the glass wasn't human, if ever it could have been.

'Make it go away!' Chloe screamed. 'Make it stop staring at us!'

Ben snapped back to the moment like a dog whose collar just got wrenched. He couldn't catch his breath. That feeling of helplessness, of confusion, and the suffocating terror of that moment had left him weak. He faltered forward, willing himself to approach that which eyed him with all the fiery darkness of a devil. Every alarm in his head called for him to scream, but his voice had abandoned him. He kept his footing, though he couldn't feel the ground. Ben reached for the curtain and suffered those eyes one last time before snapping it closed. His legs gave way immediately. And he dragged his body away, across the carpet.

He pressed his shoulders into the couch and sat, stupefied. That face was burned into his brain. It was all he could see. There was nothing else. He listened to Chloe weeping behind him on the couch, the only sound save for the terror that screamed from within them both.

'It can't be,' he tried to say, but the words were just a feeling in his throat. 'It's not possible.'

The creeper was real. All that Alec Sparling had told them was true.

21

What have I done?

The consequences barraged Ben in a torrent of tales and warnings, all spoken in Sparling's voice. Never had he felt so foolish nor so destructive. Worse still, the repercussions were not his alone to suffer. *That* he could have lived with.

'Chloe,' he called out.

When no answer came, Ben struggled to his feet. He found her dug into the blankets, like something broken beyond repair.

'Chloe,' he repeated, 'I'm sorry. I didn't know.'

The excuse sounded more pathetic than he expected. How could she ever forgive him?

Chloe reached for his hand and drew him down beside her. The firelight gleamed atop the table, glinting through his glass and the bloody puddle above its stem. Ben felt sick. The wine had risen as far as his throat, but he forced it back down, burning like acid all the way.

'It's okay,' Chloe said, squeezing his hand. 'It's not your fault.'

Ben imagined a missing person's poster like Carol Fortune's. Only now, Chloe's face occupied the frame, pleading with everyone and anyone to find her.

Nobody would know their last movements or what had happened to them. No names, no places, not a single loose link to tie him to the terrible truth. They would vanish like the others and Alec Sparling alone would know why. He would live on to repeat the process all over again with another team. Ben took out his phone, hands twitching.

'What are you doing?' Chloe asked.

'Barry,' he replied, swiping through his contacts, trying to focus his mind to perform a task as simple as making a call. Ben didn't know how he was going to explain it to him. But he had to try.

'It'll be okay,' Ben said, drawing the phone to his ear.

He had no time to think. The phone rang twice and the man answered with his customary, 'Barry.'

'I need your help,' Ben said, trying to temper his words. 'I didn't tell you because I knew you wouldn't believe me, but it's all true. Sparling tried to warn me.'

'Slow down,' Barry said. 'You're not making any sense. What's the matter?'

'He's outside.'

'Who's outside?'

There was so much the detective needed to know for any of this to make sense. As panic-stricken as Ben was, he needed to decompress.

'Who's outside?' Barry repeated impatiently.

That question would have to wait. Ben knew first-hand the intolerance of a sceptical mind.

'We went to see him,' Ben explained. 'I was right. Sparling's responsible for Carol Fortune's murder. There were other teams, too, and they're all gone, dead, missing; whatever you want to call it.'

'Did you say Carol Fortune's *murder*? You're telling me that Alec Sparling killed her.'

'No,' Ben replied, 'the one that killed her is outside. He's standing outside the window.'

'Benjamin,' Barry said, 'is this a joke? You do realise that it's a—'

'It's not a joke,' Ben interrupted, his voice raising out of his control. 'We're in a lot of trouble. We need your help. Please, I don't know what to do. I thought it wasn't real, but...'

'Okay, leave it to me. Don't contact anyone else. Not even the station. Do you understand? I'll take care of this myself. Did you call anyone before me?'

'No, you're the only person I've spoken to.'

'Good, let's keep it that way.'

'What do you want us to do?' Ben asked.

'Just stay where you are, and don't contact anyone.' Barry hung up.

Had he listened to a word Ben told him? The conversation seemed to end just as it had begun. And how did Barry know where he was? He'd never asked for Chloe's address.

Ben sat on the couch – rigid, remote – staring vacantly at the flames, imagining everything he knew burning around him with the creeper standing atop the ashes. He might as well have just slouched into an electric chair. His life was over, and he would happily pull the lever himself.

The creeper would find his daughter. She would suffer those same eyes. The horror that had knocked Ben to the floor would be unleashed on the innocence of a three-year old; his child – the one human being in his selfish world that he was supposed to take care of.

If only he had told Sparling the truth, he would never have been recruited. Perfect candidates didn't have kids.

Ben jumped back to his feet, legs wobbling on a floor that seemed to sway beneath them.

'What are you doing now?' Chloe asked him, drying her cheeks with the sleeves of her jumper.

'I don't know,' he replied, staring at his phone. 'I need to tell Jess. I don't know how but she can keep Aoife safe.'

He dialled her number and roamed back and forth between the table and the fireplace. His eyes kept returning to where he knew the creeper still stood. It couldn't have known about his daughter. Even the all-knowing Alec Sparling had been ignorant of her birth. He wanted to run, to scream, to shout, but all he could do was wait and listen to that dial tone.

'Come on, come on. Pick up the phone.'

It rang and it rang, and eventually it stopped.

You have reached the voicemail inbox of...

'Fuck it,' he shouted, hanging up, squeezing the phone near to the point of fracture. 'She never answers! What do I do?'

'I don't know,' Chloe whispered, painfully aware of the one standing outside her window. 'She still has time.'

'Still has time?'

'You have to see him three times. That's what Sparling told us.'

'Three times,' Ben repeated, despairing, 'and what happens then?'

Chloe spoke through trembling fingers, '*Uh-oh.*'

Ben lurched back to the couch and peered timidly over his shoulder, towards the thing that threatened to destroy everything he loved. He looked down at the phone in his hand, resisting the urge to fling it into the fireplace.

'Do you want to call anyone?' he said, holding it out to Chloe.

She shook her head.

'What about your mum?' he asked.

'My mam died two years ago,' she replied, sniffing back the tears.

Ben stared at her; breathless, speechless, hopeless.

How could he have been so selfish? It was as though no one else mattered. There were only his problems, his daughter, and his natural-born ability to let everybody down.

'I'm sorry,' Ben whispered, placing the phone between them.

That's all he ever said, as if *sorry* could fix all the damage he had done. Ben held his head in his hands and waited for the tears that never came.

The curtains had lightened, as had the walls on either side, though only a keen eye would have noticed the change. Ben was sat on the edge of the coffee table, hands holding his heavy head upright like a marble statue, his countenance as stoic.

Chloe was asleep. One moment they were talking and the next they weren't. He couldn't remember the last thing she said. Her voice had lulled to a low whisper, the words trickling slow and few from her lips, and then there wasn't a sound; just Ben's thoughts, tangled and torn.

Detective Barry never showed up. After their conversation,

Ben kept expecting his headlights to flash across the curtain. Seconds became minutes, and then hours. The longest of his life. Every call thereafter rang out. No response was still a response. Help wasn't coming.

One day left and that didn't include the night. Ben considered his options like a death-row inmate choosing his last meal. He was screwed either way. That much was a given. But fate had forced his hand to make a choice.

Driving to Donegal to see Aoife one last time was a hot contender. He could visit his parents on the way to thank them for all they had done for him and to apologise for all that he had not. The *Benjamin French Farewell Tour* wouldn't be the worst way to close out his life.

Night would fall. He would die and the curse would remain.

Ben could have thrown himself at Sparling's feet, begging for forgiveness, pleading with the man to grant them sanctuary. Any kindness on the doctor's part was unlikely, especially after their last encounter. And even if the gates did open and he welcomed them in with open arms, Aoife was still out there.

Ben's parents were creatures of habit. His father, especially, was predictable down to the minute. His mobile would be charging by his chair in the conservatory, where it lived tethered to the wall like a landline. Ben's mother, on the other hand, kept her phone by the bedside, always available – the family's twenty-four-hour helpline. He couldn't remember a time when she hadn't answered one of his calls, and that fact alone stirred the tears in his eyes. How many times had he not answered hers? She was only ever calling to hear his voice. She got lonely like everyone else.

She would be so surprised to see his name flash up on the

screen. And worried, of course, as was her knee-jerk reaction. He was calling to say goodbye, that's all; to hear their voices one last time. The less he told them, the safer they were.

'Ben?' she answered croakily. 'Is everything okay?'

'Yeah, Mum,' he replied, holding his breath to keep from welling up. 'Everything's fine.'

'What's wrong?' he heard his father ask, waking in the bed beside her.

'Honestly, there's nothing to worry about. I'm just calling to say hello.'

'It's a strange time to call, Ben,' his mother said, as he heard her propping her shoulders up against a stack of pillows.

'Does he need some money?' his father was heard to say, not surprising considering the cause and effect of Ben's usual phone calls.

'I'm okay for money.' He chuckled, sniffing back the sadness as best he could.

'How's your project going?' his mother asked. 'Your father and I can't wait to hear all about it.'

'It's going good, Mum. It's going really good.'

He couldn't tell them the truth. Sparling didn't know how to lift the creeper's curse but he knew how to keep it contained. Silence was the key. And should that fail, solitude. The safest option was to simply disappear completely.

'I'm sorry to call so early,' Ben said, pinching the bridge of his nose, eyes closed, imagining their heads leaning in to listen. 'I just wanted thank you. Jesus, I want to thank both of you so much. You've always been so good to me. And I've been so—' he dabbed his cheek dry '—just so bad at saying thank you.'

'You've always tried your best,' his father put in.

If only that were true. But he knew the old man honestly believed it. There was no message he could pass to his parents that could save Aoife. The creeper was coming for her. Hopefully, *his best* would be enough to stand in its way.

'This is going to sound a little strange,' Ben said, 'but if anything should happen to me, will you look out for Aoife? Maybe tell her about me. I'd be worried about what Jess says. She might grow up thinking that I didn't love her. And if I disappeared, then...'

That's enough, Benny Boy.

'Whatever's brought this on?' his mother asked.

'Nothing,' Ben lied. 'Sorry, I think I'm just tired, Mum, that's all.'

'Go back to bed,' she said. 'Sleep makes everything better, isn't that right?'

'That's right,' his father confirmed.

Ben laughed but he could feel himself falling apart. 'I love you guys,' he said, before it became too obvious.

'We love you too.'

And that was that.

There was no choice but to return to Tír Mallacht. One day, one shot. That's all Ben had left. He stood up from the table, every bone and muscle already anticipating the journey ahead. Light had edged further onto the wall and now leaked across the floor like spilled silver.

'Okay,' he said, steeling himself for the inevitable. 'Let's get this over with.'

After a whole night worrying about his daughter, Ben's own wellbeing no longer concerned him. There was nothing like turning over a new leaf on the last day of your life.

He whipped the curtain open. Daylight blinded him.

Such an ordinary sight and yet startlingly comforting in that moment. A misty rain spiralled soundlessly in the air. Ben pressed a palm against the pane, looking out at a world that had changed in a single night. His last unless he did something about it.

'What time is it?' Chloe asked, her squinty face emerging from the couch.

'It's time to go.'

22

The hum of the shutters signified the beginning of Alec's day. He would always awaken early and lie awhile, listening to them rise amidst the soft lamplight of the room. No happiness awaited him. No laughter, no friendship, no surprises. In a mere ten hours the security system would lower them again. The night was a guillotine suspended. These dark and dismally short autumn days were not something he cared for. But he had learned to endure them. They made the mornings all the more special.

Alec set his mug down on the desk and went about his ritual of drawing back the curtains. There was no misdoing more unforgivable than a morning wasted. Some days, elements permitting, he was known to venture outside and steal a few steps from his front door, breathing in deep the fresh air denied to him during the night. On this autumnal day, however, given its inclemency, he was content to open the window closest to his desk and sit there while he enjoyed his coffee. Simple chores such as preparing his own French press and the daily admittance of daylight gave the man a wonderful sense of independence.

Ribbons of light spiralled through the trees, dribbling across the lawn like honey. Clouds were as gunpowder, sprinkled here and there amidst the mellow blues and pinks of a sky now awoken. Sunlight and rain were a near magical sight to behold. Moments like these, Alec remembered. Few men appreciated every sunrise as he did. He felt, always, as a prisoner released, for a few hours at least.

Alec brought his mug to his lips as he eyed the myriad books beside him, their every spine coated in a fine veneer of powder grey. There was order to the man's library, akin to all facets of his life. The uppermost shelves were reachable only by ladder, and so here he had placed the books that he wished to keep, but not for the purpose of reading again: rare titles, rarely touched. Some shelves were dedicated to the classics. Valuable editions had been collected over the years as a hobby of sorts. Alec enjoyed more so the chase than the capture. Others dealt with the realms of science, history, and astronomy. And there was the largest section of them all – the one that drew his eyes now as it did every morning, calling to him, taunting him. Here he kept the books that few reputable libraries would ever list in their catalogues and each one had been procured by Alec at great expense.

Such dark knowledge was not to be studied without due caution. It could corrupt just as easily as it might enlighten. Volumes encompassed beliefs both ancient and dissolute. They detailed experiments and theories that civilisations had burned for centuries, and yet had survived nonetheless, as man's penchant for evil wills it so. These books Alec would return to often. Year after lonely year had been dedicated to examining and re-examining their pages, searching for answers, finding only more questions.

Numbers had long proved a lasting play on Alec's mind. The more he researched, the more his obsession grew. The creeper had always respected, be it by duress or obeisance, the three sightings. This number alone was too complex to unravel in a single lifetime. The devil tempted Jesus three times; a messiah who in turn held the threefold office of prophet, priest, and king. Judaism called for three daily prayers. Shabbat ended when three stars were visible in the sky. Religion and moral decency be damned, soldiers in the trenches shunned the flame if they were the third to spark their cigarette from the same match. Everywhere the number three commanded some mystifying power.

But of all the numbers – that never-ending puzzle expanding beyond space and time – Alec's fascination was drawn to the number nine. Pythagoras identified it as the beginning and the end. If Alec's life was one such cycle then he sought that end like a drowning man yearned for air.

Hell was home to nine circles. Likewise, the Mayan and Aztec underworlds each descended nine levels. Norse mythology divided the universe into nine worlds. Beliefs were invented. But there must have been some cause for such widespread effect. Christ died, or so it was written, at the ninth hour. Nine represented completion, derived from the Trinitarian and Divine number three. It was the culmination of wisdom and experience. It *was* the beginning and the end. But it was not yet the answer.

The creeper was once a man – flesh and blood like any other – corrupted centuries ago by something truly malevolent, enslaved and mutilated in both body and mind. If only Alec knew what was responsible, maybe then he could conceive some means to release its curse. However, after a lifetime of intellectual pursuance, he sat beside his wall of books none the wiser, sipping coffee that was still too hot.

The creeper's legacy of menace and murder escaped every tome and decrepit journal in Alec's possession. At times, the man felt a rising madness, a self-doubt brought to bear by the singularity of his plight. Had no other man of words and mind ever suffered the same horror? Such was the man's obsession that he saw the creeper everywhere, during his dreams and all waking hours.

Countless towns and villages in Ireland's troubled history had fallen foul to misfortune. Populations were ravaged. Over the course of a single week, whole communities ceased to be. Disease and famine were the obvious explanations. But what if this wasn't the case? Should knowledge of the creeper have spread to an unknowing society, then they could be wiped out in a few short nights. Fear would disseminate through every household. The curse would spread through their voices, and all knowledge of it would die with them. Alec often found himself in this wildering predicament – too many questions, not enough answers.

The rotary phone chimed. Alec correctly supposed the caller's identity.

'Good morning, Detective,' he said. 'You know that I don't appreciate being disturbed in the morning unless it's absolutely necessary.'

'Yes, Doctor, I know, and I do apologise, but it's regarding what we spoke about yesterday evening.'

'Did they contact you as I anticipated?'

'They did,' Barry replied.

'And what did you do?' Alec asked him.

'I did as you said.'

'Which was *to do nothing*, yes?'

'Not exactly,' the detective said nervously. 'I drove to the housing estate where Chloe Coogan lives and I parked by its entrance, just to keep an eye on their movements.'

'I see, and were there any *movements*?'

'They left the city at first light. I followed them for a while, at a distance, naturally.'

Barry relayed the route that Mr French and Ms Coogan had taken up until he lost sight of their car. Of course, Alec knew it well. It was the exact journey that he had marked out for them.

This was a first for any team. The difference being that he had shared with them the creeper's origin. Why hadn't he thought of this sooner? Mr French and Ms Coogan were industriously seeking out a means to subvert the inevitable. What other reason would have drawn them back to Tír Mallacht? They were doing his work for him.

'Very good, Detective,' Alec said, taking a wary sip of his coffee. 'I would like to commend you on demonstrating such welcome initiative. Your efforts of this morning shan't be forgotten, I assure you. And in view of this intelligence, you can collect any documents and devices from Ms Coogan's household as soon a time as it suits you.'

'Didn't you want me to wait until Monday?'

'Oh, I don't think that will be necessary anymore. Good day to you, Detective,' Alec said, dismissing the man. 'I will expect to see you at a time when you know you are welcome.'

The phone's receiver was returned to its home before Barry

could disturb the morning any further. It was a hallowed time for peace and reflection.

Alec let his old bones ease into his chair. He listened to the rain playing timorously against the windows. It had become a common practice of his to send a team to Tír Mallacht every two years. But now, given this latest revelation, his excitement wouldn't wait. The following year, in the spring, he would try again.

'Whatever is he planning?' he whispered, watching the steam rise from his mug.

Mr French's scepticism had obviously been rattled the night before. Alec could only assume that they had both beheld the creeper's face and the fear of it had instigated their departure. He was acquainted with its many descriptions, from his father and past recruits. But he had never seen it up close himself. To do so was to die, of course, and so Alec was content to make do with the accounts of others. And yet, throughout his life, his curiosity regarding the creeper's appearance never waned. Could it possibly be as terrifying as they say?

Success was highly unlikely, and it was reasonable to assume that Mr French and Ms Coogan were doomed to die that night. The villagers would prove as disobliging as ever. And with such scant daylight to keep them safe, Alec couldn't imagine any action on their part that would benefit his own circumstances. The next team, however, would prove more promising.

23

The engine was still running. A soundless rain peppered the windscreen between wipes. This was where the road ended and where the hardest part of the journey began. The gate's wet steel shone like polished bone in the headlights. Ben stared into the field beyond, dreading the gauntlet that lay ahead of them. Grasses rippled like dirty hair; greens and browns, with the rarest vein of red. The sombre sky had been all but squeezed dry, leaving the land sodden. He could already feel the mud squelching and hear the cool wind whistling by his ears.

The lane was pockmarked with potholes, but none too deep. Few wheels came this way to grind them down. Ben rested his chin on the steering wheel, imagining the slippery feel of the gate against his skin. A chain held it shut. Its links were scabbed with rust. The car could have broken through it if he found the speed, but how far would they get? Its wheels would sink in seconds.

'This is the worst idea you've had in a long time,' Chloe said, shrunken into her seat.

Try as she might to veil it, Ben knew she was terrified, and with good reason. A voice inside his head hadn't quit screaming since seeing that *thing* outside her window. Whenever he closed his eyes, its pale face glowed in the dark of his thoughts, patrolling their perimeter; so clear that Ben could count its teeth.

Chloe had spoken only to guide the way with her GPS. She couldn't stop shivering. Ben had turned the heater up. It didn't help. Instead, it made the air sparse and heavy to breathe as though they were both trapped in a coffin, sharing the last of its oxygen. He recalled most of the twists and turns without need for a co-pilot but thought it best to let the journey distract her from their destination. Now that they had arrived, he felt guilty for letting her come. Still selfish, no matter how he tried.

'You don't have to do this, you know?' Ben said.

She nodded, staring absently at the field ahead. 'I want to,' was all she whispered before her jaw tightened up like a stiff lever turning off the tears.

Ben tugged at the nub of his beard and pressed his skull into the headrest. He clicked off the wipers. Then he cut the engine. There was peace in the nothingness. He listened for a moment to the rain, to his heart, to the calm before. His gaze returned to the gate like a mountain climber standing in the shadow of Mount Everest, plagued with doubts and second thoughts.

They had left Chloe's house at the crack of dawn, under steel skies and a soft haze. Ben had argued against her joining him, but there was no argument really. She was already lacing up her boots as they spoke, committed to the cause before he had told her where he was going.

Ben could hardly believe it himself. Hope and desperation became indistinguishable. Whichever one it was that guided them, they both led to Tír Mallacht and that cottage on the hill. It was there that the priest had uncovered the creeper's creation. What if, in his haste, he had overlooked some vital clue? One hidden there still, waiting to be found.

'*I'm* the archaeologist, remember?' Chloe had said as she slipped an arm into her parka. 'I can't have you playing inside some run-down cottage without me.'

'There's no point in the both of us risking our lives on this.'

'You said you wanted a chance to be a better dad, didn't you? Well, come on, get your shit together. And I'm coming because I can't trust you to do anything by yourself.'

Chloe was more like her old self back in the house. Only when Ben started the car did the colour drain from her cheeks. Words became few and forced. And that longest of journeys felt far too short. It was the thought of returning to *that* place, to the home of the very thing that wanted them dead. A sense of parting graced the air between them. Conversation wasn't necessary to know what the other was thinking. Sights and sounds were finally seen and heard for what they truly were, because there was every chance that they would never be experienced again.

Jess was probably still fuming over how he had hung up on her the day before. And there was the matter of Aoife's belated maintenance money. He had fallen behind on his payments again. Jess's phone was on silent and no text message of Ben's would be read until she saw fit.

'We'll keep on trying until we lose coverage,' Chloe had said.

'Even if she answers and even if she believes me, which isn't likely, it still doesn't save Aoife.'

Three years old and perfect in every way. A gift he now felt undeserving of. Would she even remember him? Did it matter if she did or not? So long as the creeper was out there, she would never be safe. Ben's concern was for his daughter's safety, not her memories of him.

The rain complicated matters. But this time round there were no rucksacks to weigh them down. They knew the way. They knew the obstacles that lined it. Chloe had re-examined the GPS and made a few adjustments. Ben would force his way through a field of thorns if it were deemed the quickest route. *Clear the gate and don't look back.* For Aoife and for Chloe, and for any future perfect candidates out there.

The door clicked open like a vacuum and cold air raced in around Ben's legs.

'You ready for this?' he said, turning to Chloe as he sank a boot into the mud.

'Just try to keep up this time.'

24

The rain-soaked lands surrounding Tír Mallacht were nothing like Ben remembered. His memories were lost to the dark waters flooding the low ground like black syrup, sucking their boots into its depths. The absence of their rucksacks kept them from cratering too deep. But they still had to remain mindful of every step. One twisted ankle and they would never make it to the village before nightfall.

'What do you think Sparling hoped to gain by sending us here?' Chloe asked as she snapped at fistfuls of passing grass.

'If the village is still cursed, then so is he,' Ben replied. 'The man's basically a Tír Mallacht. Maybe he's hoping that they'll find a way to lift it, though I can't see that happening. They've modelled their lives around the curse's restrictions, just like Sparling. And every time they teach a child to fear the night, they're just passing it down to the next generation, keeping the thing alive.'

'So, the...' she stopped, not wanting to speak its name '... *curse* survives because people know about it. That means if

Sparling and all the Tír Mallachts die, it's over. There'd be no one to speak about it, to spread it.'

'You're forgetting about us.'

She ran both hands through her hair and sighed. 'We're just like the Tír Mallachts now, aren't we?'

'No way, we're far better-looking.'

'Why must the beautiful always die so young?' she sang dramatically before throwing a handful of torn up grass into his face.

Ben had committed to going it alone. But he knew in his heart that if the cottage held the key, Chloe was their best shot. Her educated eye could see things that he wouldn't even know to look for. And her company was a light in the abyss that he had dragged them into.

This time, when Ben spoke to the Tír Mallachts, there would be no smiles, no gentle push or politeness. Whether the secret to their survival was in the creeper's cottage or locked away in one of their inbred heads, he needed it before dark. Otherwise, his last day of life promised to be a short one.

Chloe stopped at a wall of tumbledown rock woven with vine. She stared to the horizon, where spindly treetops split the sky, breaking around the flood like a fleet of shipwrecks.

Hours had passed since the gate. Now was good a time to ask as any.

'Are we close?' Ben called after her between breaths.

'We're here,' she replied, looking back to him, her eyes popping white against rosy cheeks.

Since they set out, Ben had visualised a blurry, ill-defined object inside the creeper's cottage, propped up neatly in its corner, gleaming for them to find. But this wasn't some *happy-ever-after* fairy tale. Where there once shone a dim light at the end of the tunnel, Ben now saw only the creeper, smiling alone in his lightless den, awaiting their arrival; the latest perfect candidates marching eagerly to their doom.

'Come on,' Chloe said to him, noticing how flushed he'd become. 'Just follow me.'

It had been a gruelling week, physically and emotionally, with too little sleep to keep either one afloat. When eventually the tears came, they would pulse out in torrents. Ben was surprised he hadn't broken down already.

They entered the woodland as before, guarding their faces lest some thorny whip should find its mark. Everything was the same but different, like a memory altered. The earth oozed under their feet and the shadows had grown fat since their last visit, as though they had gorged their fill of all that filthy water. It was darker than Ben remembered, like a dimmer switch dialled back right before the click. One more turn and they would be blundering around blind. Droplets fell from the branches above, spattering his eyes as he searched for the bells amidst the abandoned nests.

'Where are they?' he whispered. 'I can't see them.'

Ben suddenly blundered into Chloe's back.

There they were, dangling like hanged men from the highest branches; dead until summoned to sing. The tripwire was within an arm's reach of her. Had he been plodding forward any faster he might have knocked her right into it.

'Can you fit through there?' she whispered, pointing to the meagre space between the tripwire and the ground.

It was going to be tight, that was for sure. Before he had a chance to answer, Chloe had ducked under, wrenching down her parka's collar with both hands, shrinking into the smallest possible version of herself.

The bells watched on.

Ben had to drop down to his knees, letting both hands sink into soil thick like unset cement.

'I hate this place,' he whispered as his wrists plunged out of sight.

'I know,' she said, still kneeling, watching him crawl towards her. 'I'd be seriously worried about you if you didn't.'

They soon stood on the clay path, now grey and gritty with pools seeping through from the surrounding fields. The flood was mirror calm, spreading through the distant walls as far as the eye could see. Ben rested a moment, dirty hands on his thighs, suffering through the pain and those memories of the creeper's smile – like flashes of lightning in his mind. The closer they got to the village, the more frequent they became. He had tried to ignore them but now he was simply too tired to fight back. Fear had coiled around him like a snake, squeezing out whatever strength he had left.

'What time of the day is it?' he asked, trying to focus on the here and now.

'It's just past half three,' Chloe replied. 'It's as good as we could have hoped for.'

'Still though, it's not giving us much time.'

She slapped him on the back and walked on. 'Come on, the cottage isn't far.'

Ben expected that same child around every corner, but they encountered neither sight nor sound of anyone. It was like walking through the fallout of some bygone disaster. Nature's remnants had withered to the point of rot and even the air was unpleasant to breathe; a cloying dampness clung like wet powder to his sinuses.

Chloe reached the hilltop first, where they'd glimpsed the villagers idling after their day's work. But the land – still so fresh in mind – was now lost to the eye. Only the field's tallest stones could be seen, like drowning men poking their heads above the surface. The rain had consumed it, denying them the same route as last time.

They held each other as before and scraped their way downhill, into the village's slimiest reaches. No field was free of the flood. It was as though the ocean had risen to devour it. *Just like Atlantis after all.*

'Here we are,' Chloe declared, stepping off the path and onto a stream of muck that Ben hadn't noticed, and one he certainly didn't recognise.

'Where are we exactly?' he asked, looking around him.

'Isn't it a good job you brought me along? You would have wandered around this shithole until sundown with no clue where you were going.'

The penny dropped. This was where they had followed the wasp after leaving the field that day, before their lives were marked with an expiration date.

Ben had joked about Chloe being his anchor but she was that and more; never asking for anything and always giving all she got. No bullshit. No talk without honesty. And he needed that – someone to grab him like a ball of clay and mould him into something better.

They followed the dirt track with Chloe at the head of the queue, camouflaged in a collage of browns and blacks. Ben wanted to tell her how much he appreciated all she had done for him. But how do you thank a person for saving you when you can't return the favour? Hers was the hand that had reached out for his when he'd felt almost too ashamed to take it. Who else would have given him another chance after so many fuck-ups?

'There it is,' she called back to him. 'Watch your step. It gets deeper off the path.'

Most of the water had drained into the field on the far side, but still the cottage looked as though it had been built on its own private island. This explained why the whole place had been so wretchedly damp on their last outing. A stagnant stream must run beneath the village, trickling through its black depths like a sewer. All it took was a hard day's rain to invite it up onto the surface.

'Fucking typical,' Chloe muttered under her breath.

'There's nothing *typical* about this,' Ben said, looking at the island as though an ocean divided them.

'Our luck, I mean.'

'Oh, okay,' he replied. 'Yeah, this pretty much falls into line with being cursed, I suppose.'

'Let's get it over with.'

Ben dithered as always. Chloe, as he'd come to expect, did not.

She sloshed towards the cottage, wading through the brownest water he'd ever seen. Dead leaves were as boats sailing away from the maelstrom of her movements. Her arms were held high as their reach. And whatever profanities she was whispering, Ben couldn't make any sense of them. Suddenly she sank up to her neck. One unlucky step had found a hole in the earth and those heavy boots were enough to drag her right to its bottom; fazed but not fallen, she clambered up and kept on going.

'How is it?' Ben asked, once Chloe's shrieking had quietened.

'How the fuck do you think it is?' she shouted back.

He dipped a foot under the surface, letting the boot fill, imagining that sensation crawling up his body, numbing him like a liquid anaesthetic. The pain would come after, assuming he was still alive to feel it. He forced his legs reluctantly through the flood, its waters rising in increments to his thighs, and then high as his waist. The soil below was ever-changing, shifting with each uncertain step. His height would count for nothing if he fell.

The earth around the cottage was slick and fell apart in Chloe's fingers as she clawed her way up. Only when she dug in her knees like two climbing picks did she find some purchase. Ben had watched her flounder, memorising her method, dreading his own turn.

His body convulsed violently, clewing his gut, tautening muscles so tight they hurt. Mud and broken tinder had risen from the water's depths like plankton; a single entity born from a thousand parts. Ben felt every piece of it; in his boots, under his jeans, anywhere it wasn't welcome. He washed both hands in the water and saw the skin of his palms for the first time since the bells. The sight of them was short-lived. He buried in his kneecaps and hauled himself onto the knoll, scrabbling over towards Chloe who was already examining the cottage's wall.

She produced their two Maglite torches from her pocket and held one out to him.

'Good idea,' he said, embarrassed that had he travelled alone he would have forgotten them.

'Oh, and here.' Her hand sank back into her jacket and

returned holding a hammer. 'It's the only thing I could find in my house. But it should make short work of that door.'

Ben gripped the hammer, bones rising white under red skin. His hand felt its weight but not its handle. The anaesthetic was kicking in. Fingers and toes were the first to go. His heart was already thumping like an industrial pump, keeping the blood from freezing in his veins.

He left Chloe's side and dithered over to the boarded-up doorway, being careful not to step too close to the bank. Considering how useless he felt, taking a tumble back into the flood almost seemed fitting.

'There are new markings,' Chloe shouted from around the corner.

'What kind of markings?' he asked, hammer raised, committed to strike.

'Someone's painted a few more symbols. They're different from the last ones.'

'Okay,' he called back.

'Hang on, don't you want to…'

Ben struck a plank, splitting it across its centre. He stood back, wincing as maggots squirmed into sight, curling and falling, as though the wood were rotted flesh. Again, he attacked it, swinging over and over with whatever strength he had left. The first board crumbled and the most putrid air escaped from within. He kicked the ruins into the flood, wiped their filthy spray from his face, and continued his assault. Ben ignored the growing pain in his arm and swallowed back the stench that fed into his mouth like a poison. He hammered as he should have, as a man whose very life depended on it.

'Hey,' Chloe shouted, her voice a million miles away. 'Hey!'

He stopped, sweating cold, and turned. She was stood

beside him. He had zoned out entirely. Had she edged any closer he could have easily caught her with a blind swing.

'Take it easy. You're going to hurt yourself.'

'Sorry,' he replied, massaging some feeling into his arm. 'It's just, well, look for yourself.'

Chloe buried her nose in the crook of her arm. 'Jesus, that's foul.'

She slipped in beside him and together they peered into the pitch-darkness of the cottage, both leaning in to listen, as though waiting for some ancient horror to break into the light.

'What's that smell?' she asked.

'It's probably best if we don't think about it,' he replied, handing her back the hammer. 'What's the story with the symbols?'

'Not a clue. They're all low down on the wall and not especially well drawn. I think you might have been onto something when you thought that it was the kids' doing. It makes you wonder why they're hanging around the creeper's cottage if they're all so scared of it.'

'That little girl didn't seem so scared,' Ben replied.

Chloe hummed in thought. 'Good point.'

'Shall we?' he asked her, switching on his torch.

'You first,' she replied, moving further back, eyes watering from the stench. 'I need a minute.'

Ben took a wary step forward. Never, before that moment, had he been so mindful of his heart; its thud, its tempo, and the courage it strained to muster. Since daybreak he had narrowed his focus on each consecutive action, ignoring their chilling culmination. Now it was all Ben could imagine – the creeper eyeing him from the darkness.

This was where the evil had been created, where a sick and desperate soul had spoken to the shadows and from their impossible depths something spoke back.

'You all right?' Chloe asked him.

He was terrified. He was anything but *all right*.

'I'm fine.'

Ben crept inside, carefully negotiating the wreckage of his labour. He fought back the overwhelming urge to vomit, to reject the foulness that embodied the air. It bubbled below his throat as he panned his torchlight around the room. The walls within, like those outside, were blackened, as though some dark soul had left its stain upon them. He directed his beam around its corners, eyes stinging from the fumes undisturbed since its door was sealed. Wherever the white light fell he found only soil and stone.

There was nothing. They had travelled all that way – wasting their precious, last hours of life – *for nothing*.

Chloe's torchlight fluttered around the room. 'What have we got?'

'It's empty.'

'Ruins are never *empty*. Let me have a look.'

Ben kept his light on the ceiling; some idle attempt at being helpful. The planks that reached across it looked as mouldering as those that had blocked the door. If one of them split, they would have been buried alive. Death seemed to hound them wherever they went.

He didn't know what they were looking for. A miracle, maybe. Chloe was inspecting every individual stone that held the cottage's four walls together, peering into crevices, wiping away filth, guiding her light to places that Ben had only skimmed over. She sifted through the debris bestrewn across the floor, turning over rocks with her boot and dislodging the low mounds of indiscriminate shapes that gathered in its corners. Ben, all the while, did nothing.

When Jess eventually read his messages, she would be none the wiser as to what had happened. He would disappear like Carol Fortune. How long would they look for him before they gave up? The sad reality was that he knew his parents never would.

'What have we got here?' Chloe said, crouched down in the corner.

Ben moved in behind her, to where she was picking apart the rubble with her free hand. He watched her fingers brush aside the dirt, until there was only a thin dust coating something smooth and solid. She took a sharp intake of air. Together they stared down at the human skull and the skeletal remains of the one entombed in the creeper's cottage.

'Jesus,' Ben whispered, leaning in for a closer look.

'Not likely,' Chloe replied.

She raked a hand through the clay, dividing and identifying what bones she could. The deceased was male. In the airless confines of the cottage, the bones' decay had probably decelerated and so she couldn't hazard a guess as to when he had died.

'I reckon he was burnt alive,' Chloe said, 'probably sat in this corner, boarded up in the dark with no windows and no way out. The smoke would have killed him, not the flames, I think. Isn't that what they always say in these situations?'

'You're sure that it wasn't an accident?'

'Someone locked him in here,' she replied, 'and there was no way he was getting out, or maybe he didn't want to.'

'Why do you say that?' Ben asked.

'Well, if *I* were locked in a burning building, I'd be trying to kick down the door or find some loose stone in one of the walls. I sure as hell wouldn't just sit in the corner. I'd say whoever put him in here was waiting outside, watching the place go up in flames, and that's why he didn't try to escape. There was no point. But hey, your guess is good as mine.'

'Who was it?'

'No idea,' Chloe replied, standing up, 'but I think I know who to ask.'

25

They reached the point of the two cottages.

From the outside, both looked as lifeless as last time, like carcasses rotting beneath that greyest of skies. Ben and Chloe took one each for a quick inspection. They couldn't afford to squander any time so late in the day.

Ben's cottage had its half-door open. He took care not to lean his face in too close. The glow of the hearth inhabited the dark without disturbing it. Flames had long fallen, and embers were few. He rapped on the door and caught that familiar scent of cabbage, overboiled and sulphuric, probably the same batch from Wednesday now reduced to a stale broth.

Chloe was across from him – a hood of fur hiding her head – knocking on the other cottage. Its shutter and door were both locked, their wood streaked with a green mould.

Nobody was home.

'Let's keep going,' she said. 'We're nearly there.'

Ben's jeans had tightened and shrunk, shortening his stride. That discomforting, wet sensation had given way to a prosthetic numbness. He was aware of each step – he could hear his socks plunging in his boots – but there was no feeling below the waist. The burning and the throbbing were reserved for his fingers, his ears, his nose, and anything else exposed.

He had saved Chloe another plunge by carrying her over the flood. Ben was aware of how the cold affected her, how it turned her skin a limpid blue. She had looped her arms around his neck like Aoife used to. Somehow they seemed to weigh the same.

'What if they don't talk to us?' he asked. 'I mean, they weren't especially chatty the last time we were here.'

'Once *they* know that *we* know, they'll talk,' she replied.

'How are we for time?'

'Don't think about that,' Chloe said, looking ahead. 'We'll be fine.'

We'll be fine? Ben imagined Alec Sparling ensconced in front of his fireplace, tumbler in hand, sheltered and warm as his housekeeper prepared him his next hot meal. *He* was fine. Their situation was deviating towards the dire.

They were nearing the turn into the village, where the path widened. Whatever awaited them was hidden behind a mass of brambles; seized and conquered by black, bloodless veins of ivy. Ben had expected to hear voices up ahead but there was nothing, only the squelch of their boots and the cheerless creak of trees in the wind.

What a stage for Ben's final act – Tír *fucking* Mallacht, the closest thing to hell this side of life. But if anyone knew some way to ward off the creeper's coming, it was the villagers; the same superstitious fools that Ben had pitied for all the wrong reasons.

They both stopped when they reached the corner.

There was no dishevelled horde waiting to meet them. The village looked deserted.

A few unlocked hatches knocked in the breeze as though trying to warn them away in broken Morse code. Tools rested against walls, slathered in mud. Weak streams of smoke snaked through some of the chimneys. Jugs had been filled. Footprints in the clay were flush with rainwater, deepest outside each cottage and on the worn trail adjoining them. All that was missing were the people.

It reminded Ben of the paintings that adorned the walls of Sparling's study. Life and the colours of its making were absent. It didn't make sense. Had the villagers finally surrendered to the curse? Ben imagined them with their hands held in solidarity, staring at the moon like a stranger in the sky.

'Hello?' Chloe shouted, standing in the centre of the common. 'Tír Mallachts?'

And then they heard it – a groan; plangent and drawn out as though gouged from some wounded beast. A cry for help so agonising that Ben recognised it immediately. How could he ever have forgotten it? Before the interviews, as they introduced themselves, he had heard it. Pained and pitiable, and almost childlike.

'What the fuck was that?' Chloe called over in a shrill whisper.

Ben was already approaching the cottage where the old woman had stood, its door now unguarded and open. Daylight quit at its threshold, and the darkness gathered there like a wall of fog.

Chloe crept up behind him as he removed the torch from his pocket.

'Remember,' he said, 'I told you I heard something.'

'*Something?*' she gasped, her hands gripping onto his shoulders. 'For fuck's sake, Ben. You didn't say you'd heard *that!*'

He twisted on his torch. Its light revealed not a home, but something else.

A bucket on the floor brimmed with scarlet water. Congealed globs of blood could be seen splattered across the walls, constellating around the man atop the table in the room's centre.

Cold wood and naked skin. His head had been rolled in bandages, tightened so many times as to make his skull appear misshapen and deformed in the torchlight. A perforation over his mouth kept him from suffocating. Eyes and ears – sight and sound – were lost to the cloth. Two holes had been carved in the timber board that was his bed, and through this had been looped some wire. It ran over his neck, pinning him in place, garrotting with the slightest press. The lightest film of skin clung to his bones, with every rib and hard part of him protruding. A blanket had been strewn over his legs, guarding his modesty, but offering nothing in the way of warmth. All his fingers looked freshly broken. Lengths of rope trailed on the floor from his wrists where the injuries hadn't been allowed to scab over; lacerations repeated until they graced the bone within.

Ben turned his torchlight over the floor, where the instruments of the man's torture had been thrown like children's toys. Not tidied away but left out so that they may be returned to again. There were stone hammers of different sizes. Some lay flat, whilst the largest one stood erect, its head big as a brick. There were secateurs, too, and a handsaw with brown, blunted teeth. A tangled nest of fishing line had been cast under the table. Beside it, a needle was stabbed into the floor. These tools all had one trait in common – blood.

'My God.' Ben gagged, backing into Chloe.

It was uncertain whether the man was aware of their presence. The only sense not denied to him was that of touch. And judging by his wounds he feared that above all others.

Chloe was by his side immediately, trying to slide her fingers under the wire binding him in place. But even this contact – however well intended – drew from the man a violent hysteria. He forced his neck upward, choking himself, trenching the wire into the cartilage. Bloody spittle oozed from his mouth, clinging sticky to the cloth. His moans were deafening, amplified all the more by the cottage's stone shell.

'It's okay,' Chloe said to him, 'I'm going to get you out of here.'

Ben was hesitant to help. The tortured couldn't stand. And they were in no position to carry him to safety. They couldn't even save themselves.

It was possible that the poor man was another of Sparling's recruits. But what if he wasn't? For all they knew, the bound was deranged. A vile product of a vile bloodline. Kindness would guide their hands to free him and that kindness could be met with malice. Was it for their own safety that the Tír Mallachts had disabled the man?

They were a weak-minded, reticent people, but they had isolated themselves for the sake of others. Could they possibly be capable of *this*?

Chloe dropped to her knees and searched under the table. The man was still frantically writhing above her. His arms, however, remained inert. It was then Ben noticed the iron hoops fixed into the walls and realised their function. It was a torture rack. The ropes attached to his limbs had been fed through the fixtures and pulled hard, stretching and popping bones apart.

'We have to cut this wire,' Chloe shouted over the man's bawling.

The bound couldn't lift a hand to hurt them. His body was broken. Ben passed her the secateurs and trained his light under the table as Chloe went about freeing him. She cut the wire and pulled it through the aperture. The man screamed as it drew across his neck, slicing red through greyed skin.

'It's going to be okay,' Ben said to him. 'I'm sorry that they did this to you. But it's going to be okay. We're going to get you out of here.'

Never had a lie sounded less convincing. Ben felt ashamed to offer the man something so cheap and impractical as *it's going to be okay.*

With his body now released, he tried to raise his shoulders but all strength had forsaken him. The man's frustration was growing and his moaning seemed somehow more desperate than before. He was rocking from side to side, labouring to throw himself from the table, aching to be anywhere else but the scene of his ruin.

'He's going to hurt himself,' Chloe said. 'Help me hold him down.'

Ben did as he was told. The man's bones felt hollow to the touch, with skin so dry as to flake off in their hands as they pinned his shoulders back in place. He weighed nothing. It didn't make sense that he was still alive.

'Check around for some blankets or something,' Ben said, still holding the man down with the slightest pressure. 'He's going to freeze to death.'

If only he'd taken action that day when he'd heard the man's cries. It was easier to ignore him. It's always been easier to do nothing. They could have learned just how fucked up the Tír Mallachts really were. They could have turned and run, taking this poor wreck of a human being with them.

'This is all I could find,' Chloe said, draping over the man's body what looked like one of the women's shawls, only more tattered.

'Jesus Christ.' Ben sighed. 'What do we do? He'd going to die if he's left here like this.'

'At least his eyes are covered,' Chloe whispered, as though she didn't want the man to hear. 'He couldn't have seen the creeper.'

Was their situation really more dire than the tortured? What if that were Ben on the table? Was there any balm for the man's wounds that words could offer?

'Listen to me,' Ben said, loud enough so that the wounded man might hear him. 'Everything that you've gone through, it's over, okay? You don't need to be afraid anymore. We're here to help you.'

He looked to Chloe. She nodded her head as if to say *keep going*.

'We'll be leaving soon,' he continued, 'and we're going to take you with us, no matter what.'

With that said, the man's screams returned. He was too loud. Ben couldn't bear it.

He staggered outside, seeking anywhere but the horror of

that room and the tortured man's shrieking. He could feel the noise like an electrical storm in his skull, tickling the back of his eyeballs.

Sounds travelled far across open land. He imagined every Tír Mallacht – young and old – running stealthily towards them, funnelling through the narrow paths like rats, some carrying reams of rope, others dragging sledgehammers behind them, leaving long gutters in their wake. They must have heard the commotion, wherever they were.

Fortunately, whatever Chloe was doing inside was working. The man's cries had steadily softened to a sad, soulful whimper, like an abused animal that knew only the malignance of mankind, thriving to be quiet so as not to be seen.

They were on the lighter side of twilight now. Ben looked towards where the bleak sky was brightest, where his last sunset had been denied to him. He thought of all those he had ever witnessed and failed to recall a single one. His memories were all borrowed from movies or photographs. So much had been taken for granted.

'You shouldn't be here.'

The shock of the child's voice whipped Ben forward.

Her presence could only mean one thing – the Tír Mallachts had returned.

His nerves surged with an angst that fizzled down to his fingers. He turned to see that same girl standing behind him. She had manifested as she always did, without a sound and seemingly from nowhere. Ben cast an uneasy glance around the village.

She was alone.

The child was unchanged. Same dress, same shock of curly

hair. She stood oblique, with her head bowed, staring at Ben like a security guard who'd found a trespasser during a routine walkabout. He'd never known a kid to emanate such a hostile energy. One that burned strongest around those eyes that he had yet to see blink.

This was the girl responsible for everything. She had known the consequences when she found them that evening, out of earshot of the adults. Knocking off outsiders must have been a hobby of hers.

'Trust me,' Ben said, keeping his anger contained, 'this is the last place I want to be. Chloe,' he called inside, 'can you come out here, please.'

'What's going…' She froze in the doorway.

'Our *friend* is back.'

The child looked to Chloe with the same lifeless expression and then brushed right past her. She skipped through the dark and hoisted herself onto the table, sitting beside the man as though he were a sick relation. *Sick* didn't begin to cover his condition. Her face screwed into a frown when she saw that the wire had been removed from his neck.

'He's not ready,' she said angrily. 'You shouldn't have done that.'

'What do you mean, *he's not ready*?' Chloe asked. 'He's good as dead, you little psycho!'

The child shook her head in annoyance but said nothing. She stroked the man's bandages like he was an injured pet. The weight of their cloth was an anchor to one so weak, and though he moaned from her touch, he struggled to lift his head an inch from the wood. She shifted in closer to his naked bones. His breathing calmed.

'Where is everyone?' Ben asked her, leaning in beside Chloe.

The child ignored him. She hummed some low dirge as she caressed the man's head.

They didn't have time for this.

'Fuck you, kid,' Ben said and turned on his heel.

His legs carried him to the centre of the village, where he rubbed his face in frustration. Ben looked up to the sky like a sailor lost at sea, searching for a star to guide him home. Not long now.

Everywhere he looked the clouds were dull as granite. Everywhere that is, except to the east. In the distance, something bled into the sky, gilding its hem with light, weak and wavering. In the east there was fire.

The hatches should have been locked by now, and the villagers' food and water divvied out. Conversations would have already ebbed like the sun to whispers of departure. Something wasn't right. Ben ran back to find Chloe resting against the cottage's sill, drained, as one who had spent her last drop.

'There's something burning on the other side of the village.'

'What do you mean *something burning*?' she asked, cracking her neck from side to side.

'I don't know. You can see it in the sky, over towards the church.'

Chloe lowered her head. She stared at her boots sunken into the grey sludge, digging the toes in deeper.

'What's wrong?' he asked.

'What's wrong?' she echoed. '*Look* at the sky, Ben. It'll be night soon. We knew when we came here that it was a long shot.'

'Chloe,' he said sternly, waiting until her head lifted to look at him. 'Look around you.'

She glanced at the emptiness on either side and shrugged her shoulders.

'The villagers should be locking this place down by now,' Ben explained. 'I don't know what's going on, but maybe it's over.' Here he reached out to take her hand. 'We can't stop now. We've come too far. Besides, while there's still light, there's still hope. Let's go see what these bastards are up to.'

The kid watched them from the doorway, hands over her mouth so as to hide her smile.

26

Ben didn't know what finish line now awaited them. Whether it were a strip of coloured paper or a serrated wire cut just as convincingly, he would charge right through it. The end was the end regardless.

Streams of sludge wept under their feet as they neared the hilltop. Behind the trees' jagged silhouettes – black against a burning sky – stood Tír Mallacht's church; deconsecrated, defaced, but by no means abandoned. Not on this night.

Through the church's fallen ceiling the misty air was aglow.

There were voices chanting in harmony, and in the lulls between their lament could be heard the one leading the ceremony. The man's words echoed too high and fleeting to make sense of at that distance. But his conviction was without dispute. No volume of voice could ever reach the heights of his faith.

The walls of the churchyard were a mass of briars, alive in the dying light of day when slight, insignificant things masquerade as something more, their wispy arms seeking to snag any who stepped too close.

Ben knew they couldn't afford to delay. But until he knew what was happening, it was safer to remain undetected. The art of secrecy – the villagers' time-worn mantra since their lives were cursed – was now their own safest option.

The path led his eyes within to where firelight flickered and dark bodies stood. The doorway was too narrow and the shadows too enlivened by the many flames that burned there to make sense of anything else. The last of the daylight was dying, like a candle's wick without wax. Ben looked back at Chloe and pointed to the cemetery on the northern side. It was there that a section of masonry had collapsed outward, not far from the altar. He led the way, tugging aside branches and stomping down on clots of weed until eventually he tripped into the open.

The mismatched gravestones each held their own ungainly shadow. They loomed low in the dusk like an army of forgotten oddities. Ben crept by the church's wall. The fallen rubble was lacquered in a thin gloss of firelight. It guided him through the darkness, inch by painful inch. Whatever bones he could still feel were pulsating as though their very marrow was being furiously churned.

The chanting intensified when they reached the fissure. Ben aligned his back against the cold stone and peered inward. There he saw the wasp, standing alone at the altar, his body wrapped in a black cloak or habit with a loose hood pulled over his head.

Ben drew back out of sight, convinced in that terrifying second that their eyes had met.

It was *his* voice they had heard.

The night was too close for the Tír Mallachts to observe

their curfew. If the village in its entirety had turned out for some celebration, then surely the curse had been lifted.

Chloe held a hand to Ben's shoulder, helping him stay upright on his haunches as he angled again towards the opening. This time he looked back into the roofless nave where the flames burned brightest.

There he saw their bodies thronged together; their faces all turned eagerly towards the altar. They were dressed as the one who spoke before them. Some held aloft torches of fire; wooden stakes with a lump of peat stabbed through the spear, their smoke billowing into the sky. Waves of light splashed across the high walls, leaving the church's lower reaches in darkness. Shadows were many, feeding on the firelight and dancing everywhere like devils.

What Ben saw defied any Christian conventions he knew of. The wasp was no makeshift clergyman. And those standing gaunt and wild-eyed in front of him held no spiritual ties to Christianity.

They were, each of them, dressed as the creeper.

Ben watched as the Tír Mallachts removed their cowls. The impression of all those faces – ill-proportioned and malformed – was startling to behold. No single countenance had been born without some defect of the bone or misplacement of feature. Alone such flaws instilled a sense of pity, but together – unified and beaming amidst the shadows with rapturous zeal – they were truly terrifying.

Ben retreated as any one of their many eyes could have seen him.

Chloe's face emerged from the darkness. 'We're out of time.'

Night's awakening was complete. The dim glow by the

wall's debris was all that broke the black. Ben reached for her hand – fingers cold as his own – and held it tight. Squatted together, amidst the lank weeds of Tír Mallacht's cemetery, they would await the end.

Was the creeper out there, watching them, savouring in their last moments? Chloe buried her head in Ben's shoulder. The eerie chants echoed all the louder with his eyes shut.

There was a rustling, back from where they had slipped by the church's corner. Somebody was there. Whoever it was, their step was silent, but branches could be heard to bend and whip.

They were getting closer.

The creeper was upon them.

This is it. This is how it ends.

'Found you!'

It was the girl from the village. She sounded as though she were standing right beside them, but so lightless was the night that Ben couldn't see beyond the glowing crevice.

'They're here!' the child screamed, like a siren to all those inside.

In the merciless dark, Ben listened to the shuffling of their many bodies. They were coming for them. The firelight seeping through the wall's weakness was suddenly blocked. The wasp's long strides had brought him to within an arm's reach of where they hid. There was a phlegmy growl to his every breath, like a hound searching for a scent. Not waiting for his head to crane around the corner, Ben hoisted Chloe to her feet. He could barely stand but his first instinct was to run. She was loath to enter the darkness at first, tentatively dipping her hands into the unknown, peeling aside branches as though each one held a tripwire with an orchestra of bells overhead. They felt their way along the wall, forcing through those invisible snares that toiled to tie them down.

Ben had acquiesced to the end. He had closed his eyes for what he thought was the last time. It was almost dignified. Should the villagers find and capture them, however, he knew what fate would befall him – torture, with the child responsible caressing his wounds with grubby, bloodstained fingers.

'Hurry,' the girl screamed from the darkness, 'they're getting away.'

Ben looked back just as the wasp's head poked out from the breach. He couldn't possibly have seen them.

'Where are we going?' Chloe shrieked, reaching back for Ben in the darkness.

'It doesn't matter,' he replied, fumbling for her hand. 'Just run!'

There was nowhere to hide; no sanctuary from the storm of voices now thundering as one. These people knew every inch of that land. And in the absence of light, they could travel it without second-guessing a step.

Ben and Chloe dashed through the open gate. Neither looked back to see their pursuers, but there was no ignoring the glare of their flames as they crossed by the doorway.

The sudden sense of emptiness outside the churchyard was disorientating. They stepped off the world, into a lightless abyss inhabited by the horrors that called it home. It was too easy to get separated. Ben patted down Chloe's arm and recaptured her hand.

'Leave the torches off,' he whispered.

'How are we supposed to see where we're going?'

'Just hold on to me.'

The pathway rose and fell in ways that defied memory's expectations. There was no knowing how far they would get before their inevitable collapse. It just had to be far enough so that the villagers would never find them.

The torches flared through the archway, merging into a living, breathing blaze of fire, chasing them like hell's private army. The strongest legs amongst them led the stampede, their hooded silhouettes fighting forward, vying to fall upon their quarry.

Negotiating those windy laneways blind was too slow. The thought crossed Ben's mind to divert from what they knew; to take their chances in the untravelled fields beyond. But was there anywhere they could hide that the villagers wouldn't find them? Their tracks in the flooded clay trailed behind them like breadcrumbs.

His arm was suddenly wrenched downward, folding his leg and crashing his shoulder into the ground. In the stupefying seconds that followed, he heard Chloe cry out.

'What's wrong?' he asked.

They should have been moving. Every second counted.

'It's my ankle. I think I've twisted it.'

The voices were getting louder.

Ben imagined the feeling of wire slitting across his neck and the sound of bones popping out of their sockets like champagne corks. He tried to lift Chloe up. But she hobbled in his arms before letting herself fall back down.

'Go,' she shouted, pushing him away, 'get out of here!'

So close were the Tír Mallachts now that their flames illumed the faintest outline of her face. Ben held her head in his hands and looked into her eyes. Only then did he realise that he was crying too.

The chase was over.

'It's going to be okay,' he whispered.

Before she could shake her head, his arms were around her.

27

The villagers swarmed them like ants devouring their next meal. From their number they gleaned an impossible strength. Faces were even more frightening up close, leering and drooling as their many black eyes smouldered like hot coals amidst the flames. They gripped Ben from all angles, hoisting him up and dragging him wherever they pleased. He could hear Chloe's cries but he couldn't see her. All around them the villagers cheered and chanted, screaming at the night like a psychotic circus of horrors. There were children, too, and mindless idiots dancing outside the scrum, adrift in their own sea of madness.

Nobody knew where Ben was. Not his parents, not Jess, not a friend that he had ignored since signing Sparling's contract. Nobody was coming to help them.

He thought of all those blood-spattered tools cast about that cottage. Would the villagers take their pick of them? There was no choice but to submit to the machinations of the inbred and deranged, even if that meant torture.

Night had fallen and, for what it was worth, they were

still alive. But whatever death the creeper held in store for them couldn't have been worse than what the villagers were capable of. In the sunlight they had masqueraded as victims of their own simplicity, eliciting from Ben a feeling close to pity. But the moonlight revealed the truth concealed beneath those elaborate layers of charade and subterfuge, leaving only their cruelty and their madness, and he pitied them no more.

His legs were suddenly kicked from under him. The many hands that held him up were now bent on forcing him down. Mud soaked into his eyes and mouth, blinding and choking. He tried to spit it away, only to let more seep in, gritty between his teeth. As Ben feared, they had been brought back to the village; that spider's web unseen until it was too late.

The chanting ceased in an instant. It didn't fade. It quit like the flick of a switch.

He saw Chloe for the first time since being overrun. She was wincing tearfully to herself, nursing her ankle with both hands. The villagers had formed a circle around them; faces were as skulls beneath their hoods. Ben anticipated the glimmer of tools in the firelight. He looked for a familiar face – for Mary or Nu, anyone who might offer some answer as to what was happening. But their bodies had massed into a single entity, an impenetrable wall of flesh and splintered minds.

He scrambled over to Chloe. 'Are you okay?'

She shook her head, burying it into him as he reached down for her.

'What are they going to do to us?' she asked.

'I don't know,' he whispered, holding her as tightly as his sore arms could bear.

Ben could hear the flames flitting on their torches. A

few villagers were gasping heavily through their mouths. Somewhere unseen, the more mentally disturbed giggled like bold children at the back of a bus. Ugliness and oddity were everywhere, across all ages and genders. The taint was in the blood and they all shared it.

There was no escape. Whatever desperate hope they clung to had died with the sun.

The crowds parted to clear an aisle into the black beyond their flames. There was order to their madness; rules that even the simplest amongst them respected. Ben watched as the wasp's familiar shape grew from the darkness with all the poise of a mantis. The circle closed behind him like bystanders at a bare-knuckle boxing fight. This wasn't the same rough-hewn farmer from their first encounter. He carried with him a foreboding presence like an executioner carried an axe.

The wasp removed his hood in a slow, ceremonial motion and stood, staring down at Ben and Chloe as though he had just scraped them off the sole of his boot.

'She spoke to you about him,' he said as matter-of-fact. 'She can't help herself, that little one.'

Ben didn't reply. He guessed that what happened next might hinge on his response and he had already caused enough damage.

'How many times have you seen him?' the wasp asked.

'Three,' Ben replied, siding with the honest approach.

He'd come to these people looking for help. But the man's face lacked even the softest suggestion of empathy. Ben's optimism seemed like an old joke that just wasn't funny anymore.

'And you thought *what* exactly?' the wasp said, all those

creases frowning as one. 'Did you think that you would be safe *here* of all places?'

'But you...' Ben stuttered, looking at those surrounding him. 'How are you outside after dark? Is it over?'

The wasp stared at him, contemplating the question. There wasn't a whisper from those who only moments ago couldn't hold their sanity together.

'Is it over?' he imitated before cackling to himself.

Such a scurrilous, cruel laugh that Ben shifted in front of Chloe to shield her from whatever the man was planning.

'It will *never* be over,' the wasp said. 'As long as we believe, then he will never die.'

The villagers watched from the shadows of their cowls like a ring of gargoyles. Imprisoned for centuries, with every generation becoming something less as the years chipped away at their minds and bodies, until *this* was what they had become.

'Sparling sent you,' the wasp said, 'always two, every two years. Never was a man so predictable.'

'You know Alec Sparling?' Ben asked him.

'Know him?' the wasp scoffed. 'His family once counted amongst ours. He keeps hoping that one day we'll all forget and that *he'll* go away.'

'Sparling told us everything,' Ben said. 'We know what happened here.'

'It wouldn't be like the man to speak of such things.'

'I know that it was his family who exposed the creeper. He warned everyone who lived here. He didn't know any better. He told them all about him. He doomed your families to this life.'

'*Doomed* us?' the wasp repeated, brandishing his mouth

of maggoty teeth. 'He opened our eyes to the truth. For so long he had led our families astray, reciting the lies of a false prophet, guiding our prayers towards a God that *did not* listen, one that *did not* care. No, he didn't doom us, boy. Tell me, what does Sparling believe happened to his ancestor all those years ago?'

Ben had to brush the dust from his memory. Had Sparling elaborated on the priest's death? He looked to Chloe for an answer but she shook her head.

'How could Sparling know?' the wasp sneered. 'His family fled Tír Mallacht before the man met his fate. Let me tell you, no man of God has any place here.'

'They burned him alive,' Chloe said, staring the man down through her tears.

A sickening smile stretched across the wasp's face. 'Stories say he prayed until the end, even as the flaming thatch fell from above. He pleaded for mercy, to be forgiven, but our families had heeded his lies for long enough.'

'The villagers killed him?' Ben asked in disbelief.

'We had to prove that our faith was true,' the wasp replied. 'And since that—'

'Who did you have to prove it to?' Chloe yelled.

His dark eyes locked upon her. The man was not given to being interrupted.

'To the creeper,' the wasp replied, raising his arms in celebration, to which those around him roared and screamed, baying at the moon like wolves.

Abandoned by the church, the villagers had turned to the creeper, revering it as some kind of deity. Their shepherd couldn't keep them safe, but they could appease the wolf that threatened to tear their families apart.

'Are you going to torture us?' Ben asked. 'Is that why you brought us back here?'

'Why would I want to torture you?' the wasp laughed mockingly.

'We've seen him,' Ben said, 'the man over there, in that cottage. We've seen what you did to him.'

'To be chosen is a gift,' he said, straightening his back, letting his hunch gather around his neck. 'It is the greatest honour amongst us. Bring him!' he shouted.

The wasp studied Ben as though he were watching a child tear the wrapping paper from a present, gleefully anticipating their reaction.

The ring of onlookers parted and the tortured man was carried into sight. His wiry arms hung around the shoulders of the two carrying him, so long that his hands reached past their waists. He was naked, with skin white as the broken bones beneath. The man was – with each movement and in every moment – in indescribable agony. Each one of his wounds had been inflicted with care and precision, and he strained to stand without their help.

One of those supporting the tortured pulled back his bandaged head, manhandling him like an animal. The wasp regarded the poor man with curious admiration. He examined his arms from the shoulder to the wrist and seemed strangely satisfied with their horrific length. Then he brought his eyes closer to the fingers, inspecting them one by one. The wasp pressed his palm into the broken hand and then splayed apart his own, comparing them. He was seen to nod his approval.

'Show me!' he said, taking a step back.

Another villager withdrew nervously from the circle.

He approached the tortured. From what Ben could see, he looked to be cutting staples from the man's bandages. These were slowly unwound around his head as the horde watched on. The more they were released, the bloodier they became, unravelling deeper and deeper towards his injuries. Such a feeling must have bordered on euphoria – to revel in those senses stolen against his will.

The wasp watched on as the man's skull steadily shrank to a size more resembling humankind.

'Now do you understand?' he exclaimed, standing aside, revealing to Ben and Chloe the truth behind the tortured man who they had, only an hour earlier, tried to save.

He was – in horrifying reality, in flesh and blood – the creeper. His skull had been cracked; its bone remodelled. A blade must have been taken to his mouth, dragged through each cheek, where now crude fishing line held it together. The wounds were healing, retaining their ghastly new shape, mutilating the memory of what he once was – a man, and not the monster he had become.

Every tooth had been filed down to a point. Eyes beetled out of their sockets as though the very bone around them had been crushed in, squeezing them outward like balloons set to pop. Scabs glistened with a creamy pus where his ears had been hacked off, and his nose held no cartilage. Broken bits gathered like coral beneath the skin.

It *was* the creeper. But his disfigurement was not the work of some ancient evil.

Nu stepped out from the crowd. Ben hadn't noticed her until then. She wasn't like he remembered her. *I don't like wearing black,* she had told him, and yet there she was. No longer crestfallen. No longer hiding her imperfections. The recesses of her skull were flooded with shadow and her once elfin face was wrought into the most devious illusion.

'Now you know why the creeper would never choose me,' she said. 'I told you, I don't look right. But he's perfect. He's the most perfect one I've ever seen.'

'It was you all along,' Ben said to the wasp. 'All those murders, it was you.'

'The creeper endures through us!' he proclaimed.

The creeper was *a man*. He was many men. Each one chosen to carry out the curse in his name. He couldn't magically appear outside his victims' homes. Sparling had hidden away his entire life for nothing.

Aoife was safe. The Tír Mallachts couldn't have known about her.

But the nature of their faith was deranged with contradiction. If the villagers deified the creeper as some otherworldly power, then why butcher their own into its image? Likewise, why hide away night after night, knowing that the threat was of their own making?

'He's just a man,' Ben said, staring at the creature that couldn't have looked any less human. 'There's no reason for—'

'He is closer now to the almighty than you will ever understand,' the wasp spat, cutting him off. 'He is so much more than *just a man*. He has been *chosen*. It is fate, I know, that you should come here on this night to witness the festival of transcendence, when we stand safe beneath the stars, in the spirit of sacrifice, offering one of our own to the creeper's eternal promise.'

Ben helped Chloe to her feet, crouching low so that she could reach an arm around his neck. Her foot hovered over the earth as she hobbled closer to the wasp, using Ben's shoulder as a crutch.

Her fears were gone, ousted instead by a hatred for those holding them captive.

'You're all fucking psychos,' she screamed. 'It isn't real. Can't you get it through your stupid fucking heads? The creeper *isn't* real! You don't have to do this!'

Chloe had stepped too close. In the swiftest motion, the wasp gripped her by the throat. Ben was immediately wrested away from her. She faltered forward, suspended by the man's hand, choking for air, receiving none. The villagers had seized Ben like wardens in an asylum. An arm locked around his neck from behind, and two other men rushed in to ensnare him from either side. Stronger than any straitjacket. His heels raked through the mud as they dragged him from Chloe's side. The wasp released his grip and she crumbled to the ground. No attempt was made on her part to buffer the fall. The air had been strangled out of her. The weak ankle collapsed first, and the rest of her followed like a bag of bones.

'You'll do,' the wasp said, looking down at Chloe as she gasped for air, pawing where his fingers had embedded their mark on her.

'If you touch her,' Ben shouted, 'I swear I'll—'

'You'll what?' the wasp spat, suddenly staring at him as though he genuinely wanted an answer. 'I'll tell you what you'll to do, boy. You'll watch. You'll watch all of it. Hold him down,' he ordered the men now forcing Ben to his knees.

The wasp returned to the one disfigured into the creeper's likeness, still held aloft, his head slumped lifelessly forward.

With the gentlest touch of his hand, he lifted the man's chin so that their eyes met. Both were human. But Ben could barely bring himself to look upon the tortured one so blessed as to receive this *gift*.

'Can he stand?' the wasp asked the men.

They exchanged a glance. One of them shook his head.

'No matter,' he said. 'He can still kill.'

'What?' Ben screamed. 'No! What are you doing?'

'Silence him,' the wasp requested.

The man holding Ben's left arm swung his fist like a battering ram into his gut. He had never experienced a sensation like it, so beyond his pain threshold that it almost didn't register. Tremors rippled around his body. Through the spots that peppered his vision he tried to breathe, but nothing came. Ben could feel his body deflating. Still, his handlers held him up.

'Hold her down,' the wasp said, beckoning three from the crowd.

Ben recognised one of them from his interviews; the simpleton enamoured by the long summer evenings. He had spoken so softly in the half-light of the stable with a kindness that was now just another lie sold to Ben amongst many others. His hands seized Chloe by her skinny calves, while the other two each pinned down an arm.

'Bring him,' the wasp ordered, moving aside so that the creeper now faced Chloe, his ghastly smile tearing against its stitches.

Ben couldn't speak. He could hardly breathe.

'His first life will be taken on *this* night,' the wasp bellowed, arms held aloft, turning in a slow circle to meet the eyes of all those around him.

Chloe wriggled and squirmed on the ground. 'No,' she shrieked. 'Let fucking go of me. Ben,' she called out, but he couldn't help. He couldn't even call back to her.

The wasp knelt and seized Chloe's jaw with his filthy fingers, muting her cries. 'I'll show you how real he is.'

Their creeper was laid atop her. His head fell beside hers as he snarled through those pointed teeth. Naked bones writhed into her body. The wasp released Chloe's face, but not before slamming her skull back onto the ground. The impact must have all but knocked her out. This *thing* was on top of her and there was nothing she could do to escape.

Ben watched in horror as the creeper's face rose above Chloe's, inches apart, spittle and bile trickling from his mouth like tree sap. She didn't scream. She couldn't. Terror had taken her voice. His arms moved by sheer force of madness, drawing those crooked hands to her throat.

But the creeper's broken fingers wouldn't close around it. They pressed clumsily into Chloe's skin as she blindly jerked her head back and forth to escape them.

His frustration manifested in the most feral of shrieks, like a skulk of foxes being slaughtered. With all his will he yearned to strangle her but his injuries prevented him. He examined his misshapen knuckles more closely like a child seeing their hands for the first time. Those bloated eyes were quaking in their sockets as the rage rose within him.

Another vicious scream startled the one pinning down Chloe's right arm, toppling him backwards. It all happened so quickly. Her free hand grabbed the hammer from the pocket of her parka, raising it, aiming for the vile thing too focused on its lame fingers to notice. The villagers gasped in all that cold air as they anticipated the impact.

But the wasp's gangly leg kicked Chloe's arm mid-swing, sending the hammer flying out of her reach.

'Hold her down, damn you!' he roared.

Ben couldn't believe it. She had come so close.

The creeper stared down at the hammer, recalling perhaps the pain such a tool could inflict; how one so similar had shattered his own bones with ease.

'Please,' Chloe cried, 'just let me go.'

The wasp paced over to the hammer. He was seething over the near miss and his scowl lingered on the one who had relinquished her arm. Only when he held the tool did he take notice of the creeper's fascination with it. He looked to Chloe, held down on all sides, defenceless. And then he returned his attention to the creeper, crouching beside him as though consoling an upset child.

'Do you want this?' he asked, presenting the hammer as a gift.

The wasp closed the creeper's fingers around its handle, securing them in place. The bones cracked like brittle branches. He drew his hands away cautiously, like a father watching his son cycle for the first time. The hammer stayed. Those long, gnarled fingers had clamped around it. The creeper's eyeballs almost popped out of his skull. The tool was seen to quiver as he turned to face Chloe, her arms spread wide, feet held together.

'No,' Chloe screamed. 'Ben! Please.'

The meaty arm around Ben's neck choked even harder. He could feel the blood gathering around his eyes and thought he might pass out. He couldn't get to her. Ben couldn't do anything to stop what was happening.

'Now,' the wasp said, standing back, 'do it!'

The creeper towered over Chloe, raising the hammer high with those monstrous arms. She screamed from fear and for mercy; for the help that wasn't coming. Ben watched it all, as the wasp had wanted him to. With an ear-splitting shriek the creeper brought the hammer down on Chloe's face, again and again, until blood and broken bone were all that remained. The horror of it was so savage, so brutal, so sickening to accept as real that vomit seeped through Ben's words as he called out for her. But she was dead from the first blow. Everything that followed served only to destroy the beauty and life that was now no more.

She was dead, and the night was alive with the screams of those responsible. Adults and children, they had all watched the bloody spectacle. They had done nothing to prevent it. Ben stared in nauseous repudiation at the bloody fur of Chloe's hood. The chorus of their voices was deafening but Ben didn't hear it. If he was still being held aloft or strangled in place, he was oblivious.

Chloe was lathered in that black, slimy mud. She didn't look like herself. Maybe it wasn't her. There were no short, silvered hairs. No bright eyes or big smile. There was only that thing astride her body, flailing those hideous arms in the air to riotous applause.

It was over.

Kill me. Just kill me now.

There was no alternative. Not anymore. Since Alec Sparling's email pinged in the coffee shop, their fate's trajectory was hurtling them towards this horrific finale. They were his sacrificial pawns. And their time on the board was up.

Ben's parents had been right. He had no reason to fear

myths and monsters. It was the people. It had always been the people.

Aoife was all he cared about now. Only one person in the world could lead the Tír Mallachts to her – Sparling. And one of their creepers was outside his home night after night, waiting to be seen. And what happens then? Do they raid his fortress of riches for all its worth? What if amongst Sparling's effects there was a diary or written record of their project?

Benjamin French has a three-year old daughter that he chose to keep secret.

A single sentence was all it took.

Somewhere, far from Ben's thoughts, the celebratory din was dissipating. He hadn't even noticed the change. He saw only Chloe's bloodied, unrecognisable remains and recalled the sight of the creeper raising and dropping that hammer. But now he imagined Aoife's little legs stretched out, lifeless, beneath him.

'And now,' the wasp declared with his beady eyes set on Ben like a hangman paid in advance, 'we have the one with all the questions. I tried telling you to leave, but did you listen? Three nights you've seen him, and I think you know by now that this will be your last.'

Dying didn't worry him. The pain Ben could deal with. His failures, those duties left wanting, were his only concern – Aoife's safety and the loss of the one good thing he stood to leave behind.

Still the men held him down, their limbs coiled around him like hoops of steel.

'Come now,' the wasp said to the creeper, stroking his skull like a pet, 'you aren't finished yet. No hammer this time,' he added to the men who had held him up. 'He needs to do this himself.'

They each took an arm and lifted him tenderly up from Chloe's body. The creeper was giddy now. His eyes were two gross eggs, their pupils a black dilated dot, ogling the next sacrifice. Ben no longer struggled. Any one of those three brutes anchoring him into the mud could have held him without the others.

But he wasn't done. Not yet. In his surrender he saw his only shot at redemption.

'Just let me go,' he said, barely above a whisper. 'I'm not going to stop you.'

The wasp strode over to him. His eyes pinched tight. All those vile etchings on his skin coalesced into that smile Ben had come to detest.

'What did you say?'

'Just fucking kill me, you asshole,' Ben replied.

The wasp's gaze lingered on him, considering his conviction. This was what the bastard wanted – for his creeper to kill without weapon or assistance. His bloody rite of passage.

'You submit to your death?' he asked.

Ben spat in his face. 'Fuck you! Just get it over with.'

The men held the creeper not ten feet away from where Ben was pinned down, looking to the wasp for their signal. That naked monstrosity was salivating at the sight of him; this *man* who Ben had tried to comfort. Chloe had even hoped to somehow save the bastard.

'Release him,' the wasp said, 'but tie back his hands. We don't want him doing anything stupid.'

They did as they were told. Their fleshly shackles were released. Ben gasped for air as one breaking above water. His knees sank into the ground like two pillars. He cracked his neck musically from side to side and stretched his arms as though loosening up for a fight. But the fight was over. All he had to do now was make sure it hadn't been for nothing.

The ring of bodies surrounding him had loosened. Escape obviously wasn't a possibility anymore; even the idiots knew that without being told.

In the mud, Ben finally noticed the ridged tracks, flooded with rainwater, where a tyre had been rolled across the common. Of course, they'd had the means to follow them. Their creeper couldn't *appear*, like Sparling believed. The villagers knew the route that his perfect candidates took every two years.

Ben had known the truth all along. The certainty that such horrors weren't real; the lesson his parents had taught him as a child – the same one that his fears had made him forget.

He dabbed his neck as he always did when he thought of his Aunt Patricia. He finally understood what she had seen all those years ago. And then, voluntarily – as though he had a choice – he brought his hands behind his back. There was no technique to the knot. But it would hold. Not that Ben ever intended to break it.

The wasp knelt in front of him. His long legs would only bring him so low. Ben still had to tilt his head to meet him in the eye; squinted like the slimy innards of an oyster.

'If you try anything, I'll kill you myself. And it won't be quick, do you understand me?'

Ben just stared at him. What exactly did the man think he was capable of? Hands bound and surrounded, only a miracle could save him now. And only a miracle could save his little girl. With all that desperation exhausted, Ben had finally cracked open the hope. Corked or not, he wasn't going to waste a drop.

'Bring him,' the wasp said.

Ben expected to die as Chloe had – on his back, his face like a nail waiting to be hammered into the earth. But he was wrong. The creeper's bones were adjusted to mirror his own. On their knees, facing one another, it would kill him. And not with a hammer or some tool handpicked from the selection box in the nearby cottage. He would die by the creeper's bare hands.

'Stand back!' the wasp shouted. 'Everyone, back. He's doing this alone.'

Ben knew that this was it. His last chance. He focused on those swollen eyes, ignoring every other ungodly feature on the creeper's face. As mutilated as he was, he was still a man underneath his wounds.

'Remember what I told you?' Ben whispered, tears now racing down his cheeks. '*It's going to be okay. I'm sorry that they did this to you.* But I need you to do something for me. Please, promise me this, and then you can kill me. I won't stop you. You can give them what they want.'

The creeper's smile was indifferent to his pleas, his face forever fixed in an expression conceived only to horrify. But the eyes locked with Ben's. Through those pits in his skull that once held ears the creeper was listening.

'Go to Alec Sparling's. Fuck the rules. Kill him and burn his home so that *nothing* is left. Can you do that for me? I would have saved you if I could, but you can still save me.'

Ben may have imagined it, but the creeper seemed to nod his head, so subtly that even the ever-vigilant eyes of the wasp must have missed it.

'What are you waiting for?' he shouted. 'Kill him!'

It was Ben's turn. He took a deep breath and held his head high, exposing his neck. The creeper's long fingers slowly wrapped around it as Ben closed his eyes. In his mind he saw his daughter for the last time, asleep and safe, dreaming of the beautiful life that lay ahead of her.

Epilogue

Alec was sat, elbows on his desk, fingers raised in a steeple, regarding the list of names narrowed down to ten potential candidates. He had spent the month compiling it, beginning initially with twenty-odd students and graduates whom he thought fitting for the role. Two would be chosen, as per usual, contacted first by email and then met in person for the sake of signing contracts and inducing in them the necessary greed to see the project through. Alec had already prepared an updated series of maps, more for his own personal pleasure than the presentation's benefit.

Five months had passed since Mr French and Ms Coogan returned to Tír Mallacht. Not surprisingly, they hadn't been heard from again. Had Mr French succeeded, then Alec knew the man would have come to collect what was owed to him. His absence from the front gate could only mean that the creeper's curse remained and that Alec's strife prevailed.

The conditions were, however, improving as they always did this time of year. The days were harvesting more light and in a few short weeks the clocks would make their jump forward, leaving all those long, dark evenings behind them. Alec's disposition had every reason to scuttle out of the shadows.

Different universities. Same academic disciplines. Alec was well versed in the process. Historians and archaeologists, it had been decided, were best equipped to gather the information he needed. Also, careers in these fields took years to flourish. This made Alec's financial incentive more alluring when it came to buying their confidentiality.

He didn't expect any complications during the recruitment process. It was only afterwards, upon the team's return from Tír Mallacht, did Alec need to depart from his usual procedure. He would acquaint them with how the creeper's curse came to be. Whilst it could also enhance their chances to bring to light a few theories yet to be refuted in the field. Should all go to plan, they would return to the village by their own volition and there seek out a means to save themselves and any undisclosed offspring that they were either too ashamed or too moneygrubbing to mention. Alec was of the belief that everyone was allowed to act a little selfishly when it came to their own survival. He was, of course, no exception to this rule.

Behind the curtains of his study, the shutters had rolled down before sunset. He was glad to have another project to occupy his mind. Alec resolved to approach it patiently, milking it for all the hours it was worth. He would return to his list with a fresh pair of eyes the following morning and whittle the prospective recruits down to five. That would make for an enjoyable distraction. The thought of having something to do always lifted his spirits.

The grandfather clock chimed eight times. Alec had stayed

at his desk later than usual. Without Lara to tend his routine, time had admittedly gotten away from him. She had called that morning to inform him that her mother had fallen ill. The woman's health, to his knowledge, was oft in doubt, and yet this was the first time Lara felt duty-bound to give her employer's wellbeing a miss in lieu of her mother's. She had, however, promised to visit Alec should her mother show signs of improvement. But of this there was no guarantee. As put out as he was by the inconvenience of it all, Alec bade her to pass his wishes on to the woman, though this kindness was spoken through gritted teeth.

Had Lara been on the premises, she would have visited him long before now. It was her habit to inform him of his evening meal by seven o'clock. He liked to pretend that she was only out of sight, in another room, otherwise occupied with her chores about his home.

He poured himself a short brandy and moved to the armchair. The fire had taken promptly to the timber and the man was quietly impressed with his efforts. Alec stretched his old legs out towards its warmth. He closed his eyes and listened, expecting to mark Lara's entry at any moment, only to sigh at the thought of her caring for another. Alec considered calling on the off chance that her mother had since recovered. But he wasn't confident that he could phrase the question without offending the girl's privacy and coming across as pathetic.

Lara had never let him down like this in the past. He emptied his glass, swallowing down these selfish notions. The girl's mother was poorly, and here was Alec condemning her for his empty stomach. He tried not to worry. Tomorrow, everything would return to normal. With this in mind, he vowed to visit the kitchen himself. Maybe Lara, ever organised, had left something out for him in the novel case of this happening. It wouldn't be unlike the dear girl to anticipate his needs.

He rose to his feet, letting himself groan aloud, safe in the knowledge that nobody was around to hear. His legs ached as he padded his way across the study; there was certainly nothing unusual about that. Alec was surprised, however, to find that the door leading into the corridor was locked. He had no recollection of it being so before, even as a child. It must have been a fault within its mechanism. His was an old house after all.

Had Lara returned without him knowing? Surely not. The girl had a quiet step but even she couldn't have passed behind his chair unnoticed.

He rapped on the door and waited. When no response came, he tried again with heavier knocks. The study was starting to feel uncomfortably warm. If Lara was in the corridor or the kitchen, then she must have heard him. Alec pulled the handle hard but it was of no use. Every door in his home was near indestructible by design. A locksmith would be required. In which case he was trapped in the study until daybreak and Lara was shut up, too. He would have to compensate her for the inconvenience of it all.

This problem, like any other, required some thought. And so, Alec replenished his glass and returned to his armchair.

It was highly unusual for a door to lock by its own accord without key or tampering. Lara was not a key-holder for any door bar the main entrance, nor had her mother ever been. Alec slept better knowing that his home's security was in his safe hands alone. The doors throughout the house's ground floor had keys, yes, but they were never locked. To the best of

Alec's knowledge, he had stored whatever keys he had in the top drawer of his desk. There was every chance that the one he now needed counted amongst them. Dinner could still be on the menu.

Alec slid open the drawer and went about rummaging through its various effects. There were envelopes tidied into its corner, a silver letter opener, diaries, and a miscellany of paper. He turned its contents over and over, frustrated by the sudden truancy of order in his life, but the keys were not there.

It was his housekeeper's responsibility to lock the outside door. The key to the inner one always resided in its keyhole. Now, to further his mystification, Alec found that also to be missing. He tested its handle – locked. It would seem his movements were confined to the study, though no longer by choice.

Alec resettled into his chair. The fire needed stoking. But instead of taking due action he simply stared into its flames, too disturbed by the evening's odd turn to notice the needs of another.

Could Lara be responsible? She *was* the only other with access to his home. No, she was dependable, as her sick mother had been. Neither of them had ever flouted his daily rituals or acted out so strangely as to go about his home, locking doors and stashing away their keys. There had to be a reasonable explanation. It would come to him. Alec just had to think awhile. The firelight had retreated from his chair. But there was peace in the crackling of its wood, and an understanding that all would be fine once he and Lara had spoken.

Then, Alec heard it – a sound he knew so well and yet one entirely unexpected in that moment. The grind of the shutters.

They were lifting. Every single panel that guarded the study's windows was furling upwards, leaving only the curtains between Alec and the night, where he knew the creeper had stood since the day he was born.

His fingers scratched into the chair's leather as he stared at the curtains, fearing them to fall from their hooks at any second. He listened to the shutters' slow, metallic roll. And then there was silence. Alec imagined that face described to him by all those now deceased. Did it loom inches from the pane, yearning to be seen?

He jumped to his feet and glanced fearfully around the room, feeling suddenly cold and vulnerable; trapped in a prison of his own making. The windows were many and occupied much of the wall space. The creeper could have been at any one of them. Alec cupped his hands over his mouth, thinking, trying to understand why so many irregularities had assailed him on a single evening. His thoughts raced through a labyrinth of possibilities and no matter which turn they took the conclusion was always the same – this was no malfunction. Somebody had orchestrated this.

Alec returned to the locked door. He hammered on it, alternating between fists, calling for Lara, his voice becoming faster and louder with every passing second of no response. The control panel for the security system was in the corridor, mere feet from where Alec stood, driving his frail shoulder into a door that ten men would fail to budge.

If only Lara would activate the shutters, then all would be forgiven. He would double her salary. She could choose her own reward.

Alec froze at the sound of smashed glass. The curtain was seen to move; its languor disturbed by whatever had broken through the pane and landed with a thud where particles now tinkled on the floor. He watched in horror as the curtain waved gently inward from the night's breeze.

'Who's there?' he cried out.

Another window was heard to shatter, and then another. Every pane of glass in Alec's study – his sanctum from the world – was being deliberately and systematically destroyed. He turned his back on them and clenched his eyes shut.

'What do you want?' he asked. 'I have money. I can give you more than you'll ever need. Just, please, leave me be.'

Feet crunched on broken glass; a succession of slow, measured steps. Someone had entered through the empty frame. A curtain swished open. Alec couldn't contain his shriek when he heard it being wrenched down to the floor. The cold was fast to enter. He felt it like a hand caressing his neck, primed to strangle. The next curtain was torn from the wall. One by one, every broken window was exposed, and Alec stood trembling, visualising the horror behind him – the night in all its moonlit glory, unseen for so many years.

'Please,' Alec repeated. 'I'll give you whatever you want.'

Their step was quieter now. They had passed into the room, treading across its rug, making Alec's home their own. His fortress had been breached, and with such ease. He listened to the scrape of steel as the fire poker was drawn from its holder, like a brass blade unsheathed. Whoever it was, they were scratching at the grate, stirring its embers back to life. A log was heard to tumble onto the floor before the poker was dropped with a padded clamour. Still, Alec refused to turn, to even loosen his eyelids. Something was burning. The fire that he had abandoned had found a means to survive. The Persian rug touched everything that was Alec's; his chair and desk, the tables and fittings, all those treasured things that would burn so easily.

'What do you want?' he called out.

Alec could hear the fragile crick and crack of bone, as though the intruder crossed a frozen lake thawing to fracture. It had to be a man. He was breathing heavily through his mouth, drawing ominously closer; ubiquitous in the blind darkness that Alec clung to.

He couldn't risk opening his eyes. He could have caught a glimpse of the creeper in a framed reflection or in the polished belly of a silver bowl. His father had warned him of the eye. It wants to see. Even the strongest mind cannot quell its curiosity.

The man came to stand in front of Alec. An arm's reach away. Even over the rising smoke his breath was noxious. Few knew of Alec's existence. Even fewer knew where he lived. Was he the victim of an indiscriminate misdeed or was this some vengeful ghost from his past?

'Is that you, Barry?' he asked, unable to steady his voice.

No reply came, only that deep, drawn-out panting and the growl of the hot flames now chewing through his father's rug.

'Mr French,' he whispered, 'is it you? Please, tell me who you are.'

He could feel the fire's warmth feeding greedily on the floor, climbing the legs of his chair, and cooking the contents of each drawer in his desk like an oven. The curtains had caught fire. Alec could smell their ancient mustiness. All those odours hoarded over the years were finally released as one. He imagined the windows barricaded by a wall of the blackest smoke.

It couldn't have been the creeper. Alec hadn't seen him

three times. It was by these rules that the man had survived. Then why was the creeper's face all that he could envisage in the timeless horror of that moment? Every description he had ever known was forced into his mind, ever-changing and yet smiling throughout each terrible guise.

'You can't do this,' he said, every fibre of his being aquiver. 'I haven't seen you!'

His throat was suddenly seized by the coldest fingers, so long that they choked him like a collar. Alec grabbed the man's wrists. They were as bone; fleshless, but extraordinarily strong. He couldn't pry himself free. And this futile fight for air relinquished the rules of a lifetime.

Alec opened his eyes.

It was nothing like he had imagined, not in his most haunting of nightmares. The creeper was more terrifying than he could have ever thought possible.

Flames brushed the grandfather clock as it rang in the ninth hour; fated to burn like everything else in Alec's home – his prison and his tomb.

About the Author

A.M. SHINE writes in the Gothic horror tradition. Born in Galway, Ireland, he received his Master's Degree in History there before sharpening his quill and pursuing all things literary and macabre. His stories have won the Word Hut and Bookers Corner prizes and he is a member of the Irish Writers Centre. His debut novel, *The Watchers*, has been critically acclaimed. *The Creeper* is his second full-length novel.

Follow him on @AMShineWriter and
www.amshinewriter.com